XAVIER'S
SCHOOL OF
DISCIPLINE

XAVIER'S SCHOOL OF DISCIPLINE

S. LEGEND

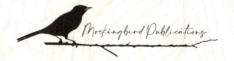

Mockingbird Publications

Mockingbird Publications

www.mockingbirdpublications.com

ISBN 978-0-9920246-9-7 (pbk)

ISBN 978-0-9920246-3-5 (epub)

Edited by: Augusta Mallard

Proofread by: Susan Keillor

Inner Book Art by: Artsy Ape

Cover Art by: Nadia Polyakova

Cover Art Design by: Chiara Monaco

For my beautiful grandmother. May there always be a universe in which we can pick clovers, sing songs and have lots and lots of fun.

DISCLAIMER AND AUTHOR'S NOTE

Beyond lies fiction. This book is not meant to instruct, or depict any kind of lifestyle. This book does not follow any particular set of rules. Although the themes are real, this remains a fantasied version of this lifestyle, written to create a particular feel, one the author loves best. The author does not write "how-to" guides. She writes for kink, for fun and entertainment. Period.

Should you resonate with the themes of this book, it is important to seek guidance that is not this book.

This book contains polyamorous relationships, domestic discipline, and lots and lots of spanking!

Rivers know this: there is no hurry. We shall get there someday.

WINNIE THE POOH ~ A. A. MILNE

CONTENTS

CHAPTER ONE

I t's an odd-looking tree. A lonely alien, verdant in the spring with white flowers that seem only to bloom and die, richly colored in autumn until all its leaves fall away, severe and primeval in winter. Now barren, the serpentine branches snake toward the window of the attic like its begging to be invited in. I run my good hand through my thick blonde hair—the other one's broken—and come up with an idea.

That tree. We could climb it. Brats of old put it here just for us, just for this instance.

"Look, we're not going to get in trouble, okay? Because we're not going to get caught."

Grayson puts a hand to his hip, doing a good impression of Ani when he's fed up. "A brat's famous last words, Finnegan."

It's one am, well past curfew. We should have been home two hours ago, that's if we had permission to be out at all, which we didn't. "What's the alternative? Xavier's going to kill us, Gray. Not just me, you *and* me."

He smirks. "But mostly you."

True. But. "What do you think Will's going to do with you? Throw you a party?"

He winces, and I can just make out his feathery hair waving in the darkness. The moon is out, shining some light on our perilous situation, the twinkling stars mocking us. Ambient light glows from the porch window—someone's watching TV inside. He shivers, rubbing his arms. We both lost our jackets a while back. Grayson is so much smaller than I am, but it's why he fits against me like eggs in a carton. I want to pull him to me; keep him warm. *Later, when you're snug in bed, Finnegan.*

"Fine. Pray tell, what do we do, Brighton?"

I look up to the conspicuous majesty, her sturdy arm outreached. "We climb."

Belonging was a four-letter word. I came to Xavier's school two years ago with no real expectations. I'd never fit in anywhere. Why should here be any different? And yes, I know. You've got to believe in yourself and all that other self-help stuff Ani's always talking about, but without people who are like you, it's harder.

For people like me, it's near impossible.

We live in the shadows of our minds. Without others to pull us into the sunlight, we wilt.

I became Xavier's on a fall day in September. Everyone in the house will tell you I don't have a photographic memory, and they would be right, but I remember everything about that week in detail. Even the first few months are vivid enough. If I close my eyes, I can relive it, like it's happening right now.

Two Years Ago

What am I doing? Am I doing this? Oh God, yeah, I'm doing this.

I lean over to sign the papers, the ones I read through seven times, had my lawyer comb through and then talked over with my brother, who is the same person. Even he thought I should do this, as both my litigator and guardian. I sign with more confidence than I'm feeling, almost angry about it even though this was my idea. Like, we're talking one hundred percent my idea.

"Thank you, Mr. Brighton," he says, in a strong, British accent. He's leaned against the desk with elegance, palms flat, arms extended, slightly hinged at the waist. And even though I'm all the way over here, on the other side, a whole desk span between us, I'm far too close to him. I step back.

Xavier is tall. He towers. His shoulders are massive, spanning at least the length of the bookshelves adjacent to his desk on the left-hand side if you're facing them, which I am—I don't imagine I'll ever be on the other side of his large mahogany desk. No. I'll be standing in front of it, or if I'm invited to, I'll sit in one of two brown, leather chairs positioned in front of said desk at exact angles. Like, he had to have used one of those protractor thingies to get the spacing just so, and it's the sort of man he is.

His eyes are shockingly blue. The first time I sat in his office (me in one chair, my brother Sam in the other) I stared until I gained enough sense not to. They look photoshopped. It's hard to look anywhere else. They pierce you.

If eyes are the windows to the soul like they say, he must have the soul of an archangel—one who smites and then puts you to bed with a kiss to your forehead.

He's tidily dressed in a long-sleeved black shirt, a grey vest overlaid making his chest look that much broader and a silk green tie with a perfect knot. The only thing out of place is his dark hair, fluffed in messy waves atop his crown.

I'm not a tiny guy, I'm five foot nine, with a sturdy build —played hockey most of my life—but standing in front of him, I might as well be an ant. He's got to be well over six feet and I get the same staggering sensation that I do staring up at the thick-barreled trees in Stanley Park, that reach onward to the sky forever.

I run a hand through my blonde hair, pausing to rub at the fuzzy undercut, wishing I had half the composure he has. "Um, you don't have to call me that. I go by Finn." I say the words and then immediately regret them. I don't intimidate easy, but this man does something to me. I can't look him in the eyes and my body won't stop buzzing. The rights he has to me now play over in my head. I want to sit in one of the soft leather chairs, but he hasn't invited me to—I think there's a rule about that—I remain standing.

"*Relax*, Mr. Brighton."

Xavier By Artsy Ape

I guess we're going with Mr. Brighton. I tighten all my muscles and force myself to meet his blue eyes, but my throat is dry, and swallowing feels too thick. "Sorry, I've never done this before."

He smiles. "Lucky for you, I have. Tell me, why do you wrinkle your nose every time I call you Mr. Brighton?" He crosses his arms and that seems to say something.

I feel my nose wrinkle again. *Dammit, Finn.* "Makes me feel like I'm in trouble."

"Isn't that why you're here?"

Everything is hot. Hot, hot, hot. Fuck. *Is he gonna make you say it, Finn?* "Well, I mean, not exactly."

He tilts his head in a pensive way, and I already don't like it. All of it says 'disappointment' and that 'he expected more'. He ruffles his dark hair, the only wild thing about him. Everything else is tidy, but his hair cannot be tamed, or this man would have done it by now. "During your interviews you said otherwise."

"I meant, I'm not in trouble with you." My ears are hot.

"I see. A misunderstanding. You are, as you say, 'in trouble' with me, young man. Sending yourself here means you are in need of swift discipline upon arrival." He moves from behind the mahogany desk, closer to me.

"What, but—"

"—no buts. I always establish my role in the first meeting. I want to make it clear your past behaviors will not be tolerated. A good dose of discipline should do the trick."

My eyes follow his movements as he unbuttons his cuffs and then rolls them to his thick mid-biceps with crisp, snappy motions. Suddenly his black slacks look too pressed and his green tie too green. He pulls a chair out, one I hadn't noticed before, but now it's all I can see. He places it in a spot where the red carpet is slightly worn in the same places the chair legs land, suggesting this is not the first time he's placed the chair in that spot. In fact, I would say he does it often. Even the way the chair spins on his palm suggests how familiar a rhythm the act is.

When the chair is in place, he sits on it. "Come here, Finnegan."

I was wrong. *Now,* I feel like I'm in trouble. The way he says *Finnegan* is so much different than the way he says *Mr. Brighton,* which looking back had a hint of something softer. *Finnegan* is hard and scolding.

The room is large. The back wall is a two-story library with shelves filled with books, connected by a sliding ladder. Adjacent to the library is a stretch of blank wall with nary a painting on it. It's no less odd seeing the wall this time, as it was when I came for my interviews. It's red.

There's crown molding. That's it. Nothing special about it, yet I know it's significant.

But behind his desk, now that's even curiouser. A door. One tall, heavy-looking door. I guess it could be storage, but from what I already know of Xavier, I doubt it. It's gotta be something. I label it as mysterious.

Yeah. Definitely mysterious.

I drag myself over to him. I can guess what's coming, and how awkward? But, ugh, I signed on for this—though now I'm regretting it, oh how I regret.

What did you do, Finn? What. Did. You. Do?

Xavier dwarfs the chair when he sits on it. "Over my lap, quickly. In future there will be consequences for delay."

I look at his lap and back at him and then to his lap again. Am I really going to do this? Go over his lap for a *spanking?* He makes the decision for me, snatching my wrist and pulling me to him, and over his lap I go. Before I know it, my torso meets his muscled thighs and I'm in a much less comfortable position than I'd like to be in. He doesn't bother with an introduction before he's smacking my ass with a hand that feels like a two by four.

Any hope I had of taking this spanking stoically is gone within the first thirty seconds. I have the 'protection' of my jeans and it still hurts. I try to grip the carpet with my hands, then the chair leg, something, anything, but nothing helps my position. All I can do is take the spanking, smack after sharp smack. Finally, he lets me breathe. That's when he starts lecturing. "To clarify. This is what I do to naughty boys."

We both know I'm not a 'boy'. I'll be twenty-eight this spring, but that's part of this. Humiliation is an aspect of spanking. "Yeah, okay."

He lets go a wallop on my ass that fucking *hurts*. "Yes, sir, not 'yeah okay.' Show me you understand."

"Y-Yes, sir," I say, hoping we're done, but no such luck.

He spanks until I'm sure my ass is reddening beneath my clothes and then at long last, he stands me up. With the way he's looking at me, I know I'm not done, but I want to be, so I try my best at charming him. "You're in charge, sir. I understand. I get the lesson. It's all good behavior from here."

"I'm glad things are beginning to sink in intuitively, but we're far from done, Mr. Brighton." Okay, *that* Mr. Brighton might have had a bit of a smirk attached to it. Fucker is onto me. "You know what we discussed, it's even in the contract. All discipline at this school is applied to a *bare* bottom. No exceptions. Undo your jeans. I want those and your boxers pulled down to under your balls. I'll do the rest."

Fuck. Did he just say *balls*? Unfortunately for me, even though the spanking does nothing to turn me on, the humiliating way in which this is being done, does and my cock starts to harden. I really don't want to pull my pants down and show him my hardening cock, but I also know the punishment for refusing punishment and I'd like to get through my first day with just the one spanking thanks. I do as instructed, my face red from both the pre-spanking I've just received and anticipatory embarrassment over showing him my cock.

Though admit it Finn, you'd like to show him your cock in another scenario, one where he's also showing you his.

Oh my God. Shut up. Shut up brain. But for the record, okay, yeah, I totally would. Xavier Harkness is hot, so fucking hot and totally my type. More than my type.

He doesn't pay it any attention, even when it's pressed against his thighs. Oh God, I'm going to leak on him, aren't

I? I try not to think about that. I can't be the first dude that's leaked on his thighs during a spanking, can I? I probably won't even be the last dude today. He pushes my white t-shirt up my back and rubs my tender flesh. "This is a naughty, red bottom I have here, don't I?"

"Xavier!" I say, attempting to stand up.

He presses me down easily; I don't fight him. He laughs, and it's pleasant. My heart squeezes. "There you are, Finn. I thought I'd lost you for a moment. Why are you so tense? Did I not answer all of your questions during our meetings?"

"You did, but you're terrifying, sir." I give up all bravado, because what's the point? My pants and boxers are pulled down and I'm over this guy's lap.

He chuckles, patting me on the bum. All of it makes him more human, and the lines of authority blur just enough I can settle back into me, but not nearly enough for me to think he's not the one in charge here. "Not much I can do about that, I'm afraid," he says. "I will be getting on with it though. I have other appointments, and you have work to get done."

I do?

"As much as this will feel like a punishment, it's not. This is discipline, which you will receive from me every Friday. No exceptions. We'll go over that in more detail the first time, which is *this* Friday—it's all in your schedule."

I hold back my groan at the sound of all that, reminding myself I wanted this, all the while very aware my ass is still out and vulnerable for him. I also remind myself why I chose him. Of all the schools I could have sent myself to, I picked this one *because* of Xavier. Not only are his methods more personal—which I liked—there was a feeling I got from the first meeting, one of safety and warmth despite his cool exterior.

My brother and I scraped up enough money so that I could be assigned to Xavier personally, which was hard enough. To be *one of his* required extensive interviews and then, a spot had to become available. When we got the call that there was an opening, it was a happy day. Sam and I celebrated with beer and wings even though there was still the rigid interview process to go, but it was the next milestone after having the money in the first place.

We're not rich, but we're not poor either. It's just that to come here, to Xavier's school, it's fucking expensive. After Dad died, we inherited his estate, which consisted of a modest, four-bedroom house and several thousand dollars, which evaporated quickly with funeral and living costs. I was still in high school, Sammy was barely an adult, but now he had teenage me to contend with, which I don't wish on anyone. I was an asshole who missed his dad. I *needed* Dad. Dad was a strict, firm bastard, but it worked for me and I knew it even then.

There was never Mom, not for me. She died in a car accident not long after I was born. Sam was nine. I wish I knew her, sure, but it was harder for Sam who did. It was losing Dad that sent me over the edge.

"Finnegan? You still down there? I require a response."

"Oh, uh. Yes, sir."

"Do you know what you're saying yes sir to?"

I groan. Lying is probably not a good idea at this juncture. "No, sir."

"Then you're not ready to chat yet. I'm going to continue. We'll see in a minute or so, shall we?"

He doesn't wait for an answer, since he's not really asking for my opinion, and when the first strike lands, I know he was going easy at the beginning. This is not my first spanking by far, it's just the first one from him and *wow*, he can give a good one with just his hand. It stings, and my eyes pop open a little wider with every smack. It's normal to try to get away from the thing that is hurting you, and instinctively I move to avoid the spanks when they get extra fire-y. He lets me resist some, but his strong arm across my back holds me in place.

It's nice you can't run away from him, isn't it, Finnegan?

Yeah, it kinda is. I seldom agree with my inner voice, but on that, we are totally on board.

Then he stops and I melt over his lap. The pain is still there, but inside I feel better. A chunk of me has broken open, my guard comes down; I'm more connected to myself. I'm floaty, like I get when Sam makes me meditate. I've been on a fucking journey, yet I haven't gone anywhere. How can a simple spanking do so much?

"Let's try again. This is not a punishment, this is discipline; soon you will know the difference. You will be disciplined every Friday regardless as to whether you have done something to earn a punishment. For maintenance; it's extremely helpful and effective. This session is noted in your schedule, it's non-negotiable and I wouldn't miss it if I was you. Understood?"

"Yes, sir." I pant and catch my breath. If this is only discipline and not a punishment I can only imagine, though I'd be lying if I said I wasn't curious. Yeah, yeah, curiosity killed the cat, but welcome to Finnegan Brighton. I'm complicated.

"You are here because you want someone to hold you accountable, otherwise what do you do?"

"Procrastinate any way I can, including drink the weekends away."

"Yes. What is that costing you, Finnegan?"

That's when the tears come. Not during the one hell of a spanking I was getting, but now and because I've been opened, it all floods out, releasing a knot I never knew existed as tears stream up my face—I'm still upside down—and the spanks start again. I feel the pain of it, but at the same time, thoughts stream across my mind. I want to do something with my life, but I don't know what. Sam managed to half-raise me and put himself through law school. He'd be far more successful as a lawyer if he didn't have me to support. And he shouldn't have to, I'm a grown adult.

I have a hard time holding a job. Turns out, employers don't like it when you miss shifts and show up late, but I hated every minute of my existence at any job I managed to get. Sam would be pissed at first, but even I can admit he's got too much of a soft spot for me. Then it was looking past the fact I'd spent the week playing Fortnite rather than job-hunting instead of kicking me out of the house, which he probably should have done. He'll never make me leave the house we grew up in though and yeah, technically it's *ours*, but I haven't paid anything into it like he has. I didn't fork out the ten grand required when it needed a new roof, and I certainly don't pay the ever-increasing annual property taxes. If anyone should leave, it should be me, so at least Sam can start a family of his own. I'm too much of a mess to have one.

Sam's more concerned about the good life I'll have, and I know it's because he feels responsible, like if I don't succeed, it's because he did a bad job raising me and maybe I should have gone to live with our uncle when Dad passed. I could feel his guilt like it was another person living with us, and it exacerbated the shame I was already feeling. It would build to a point where I couldn't look at my brother. I wasn't showing up and we both knew it. I wanted to though, and sometimes I even did. Soon after, I'd have a new job and both of us would get excited, filled with hope that this time, *this time* I would make it.

But it was only the beginning of a new cycle.

"I hate my life. I'm miserable. I don't want to be this," I say, through tears to a man I barely know. I don't even know what *this* is, just that something unnamable and deficient is there and I want it removed so I can be me. I have a good life, people would kill for the life I have, yet I squander it.

The bareness of such vulnerability rises in my chest. Yeah, I know that's rich when I am bare, bare-bottomed, and over his lap getting a spanking like a child, but these are things I don't say to anyone. Sometimes they've leaked out of my mouth to Sam, but that's a rarity. I know it burdens kind people like my brother who will take that shit on. I don't want to be a fucking burden to anyone yet doing things on my own never turns out; I don't know how to get out. I'm stuck in a hole I can't climb out of—there are no ladders in my hole.

He stops spanking and rubs my tender ass. I get the sense that he wants to say something but thinks better of it. He carries on with his 'orientation day speech.' "You procrastinate because you get overwhelmed, and this leads to you not finishing anything. You won't have time to procrastinate here, but somehow, I think *you* might manage. This time there will be firm and consistent consequences for you."

I shouldn't want or need that. I'm a grown adult, yet I'm comforted by it all the same. The comfort doesn't make the embarrassment go away, though. Yeah, I'm already over his lap like a child, my ass bare and now red in the air, my cock

13

pressed against his thick thighs, and crying, but *that*, the reminder of consequences, somehow manages to make my body heat further.

"Yes, sir."

I sniffle and at the same time, my pants are being pulled down further, and the butterflies in my stomach become active again.

"I am strict with my boys and you are one of mine now, Finnegan. I won't allow you to waste your life away. I knew immediately how smart you were and when I'm done with you, you'll know it too."

A warm new sensation breathes through me; his praise instantly becomes an addiction. I want more of that.

"You can obey me or have a sore arse. Either is fine for me. I wonder what you'd prefer?"

I sniffle some more. "I don't plan on disobeying you, sir."

"No one ever does. All right, we're going to finish up and then we're going to have a chat."

With my pants pulled down further, he's got more surface area, which he takes advantage of, focusing on my sensitive sit spots and thighs—the thighs are the worst. He didn't say to keep quiet, but I feel like I should. Isn't that how an adult takes a spanking? Only it's getting harder, because it really hurts, especially when he works over the backs of my thighs. My jaw tightens, I grit my teeth and attempt to minutely move my legs to lessen the impact. It does little.

When we've reached a crescendo of pain, he stops and I'm grateful, boy am I grateful. I'm panting hard again, and this time the pain lingers even after he's stopped. I try to maneuver some, to get comfortable, but there is no comfort. I guess there's not supposed to be. "Did you read over what I sent to you, hopefully multiple times?"

He sent me a tome on the rules of the school, plus a second document with his expectations for me, specifically. I wasn't going to read it. I mean, skim it to satisfy my curiosity, yeah, but not read it. Sam made me. Sam might be a pushover with some things, but with other things, he channels Dad, I swear to Christ. I'm going to have to thank him for that one. "I did, sir."

"Thank you. Then I assume you know the rules, expectations and consequences?"

"I don't have them memorized, sir, but I've read them over a few times."

"I don't offer leniency. I suggest you keep them on hand your first few weeks and consult with them until you have them memorized. I believe the best way to learn is by having the experience. If you earn a spanking for something you forgot, all the better. Spankings are teaching opportunities and I think you'll find a lot of benefit from them."

That remains to be seen, though I knew what I was signing on for when I approached this school, so it's not that I don't have some inkling that I *need* this—loathe as I am to admit that out loud—but like he said, I need the experience to confirm.

So, we'll see.

"Got it, sir."

"Let's make sure."

The next round of spanking is shocking. There's no keeping quiet as my sore ass gets sorer and I'm kicking hard enough my jeans slip down to my feet. He has to lift one of his strong legs over mine and clamp them shut over top, so I can't move them anymore. *Fuck, he's strong, Finn.*

"What do you imagine the difference between discipline and punishment is?" he asks.

He stops spanking and while I'm glad for the respite,

I'm already anticipating the rest of the spanking. The flesh of my ass quivers. He must notice too, reaching down to rub some for me. It feels nice and I relax again. "Well, you said I was in trouble, which is throwing me a bit, but I'd say, keeping that in mind, discipline is more than one thing. It's a touch off of trouble, maybe a step before trouble. Pushing it and toeing the line, maybe. But it's also a form of training to assist habit forming."

"Very good." That bubble of pride rises again. "And punishment?"

"I imagine that's more to do with straight up disobedience, rule breaking, that sort of thing." I know I've got that one right, so I anticipate the praise this time, with a little apprehension it won't come.

"Correct again." I let go of a breath, happy to be praised again. "To clarify with the being in trouble, I can't in good conscience punish you for things you did while you weren't here, under my care, but that doesn't mean I'm pleased." Hearing he isn't pleased, my heart sinks and the tears fall again. He rubs my back. "I give discipline as a reminder, but sometimes as a warning and that's what this is. I'm not pleased with your previous behavior and I am showing you how I feel about that in the language I speak, one I wager, you'll understand subconsciously."

That throws me. Spanking a language? I'm not sure about that.

"You've done well so far, Finn. I'm pleased. Just a bit more now."

I'm going to be a fucking sucker for pleasing him, aren't I?

Yes, yes you are Finn.

I can't hold back this time; my ass is on fire. I know it's got some to do with my ass's endurance waning, but he's totally going harder. I learn how fucking sensitive my thighs are. I learn that I don't want to find out what a punishment spanking is all about if this is just discipline. When he's done, I know it somehow. He stops and rubs my back some more; there's quiet for a few heartbeats, and my cheeks are tight where the tears are drying. I stopped crying some time ago. "All right, up you go."

I stand and immediately wipe my face. It must be fucking red and splotchy. Perfect.

"You may pull your clothes up; no corner time today and then sit."

Did he say *sit*? I do what I'm told though, really fucking grateful for the no corner time thing. I am not looking forward to that and my plan is to avoid it at all cost. I hiss and bite my lip when I pull my boxers over my ass, which is hot and thick. I dread pulling up my jeans, but I do it quickly—rip the Band-Aid off—and carefully sit in the brown leather chair. Least it's soft.

He hands me a Kleenex and then returns behind his desk. "I want you to see William for some care after you've settled into your room in the House."

"William?"

"He's your Head of the House, in the House you'll be staying in. He might have some of his own rules, and you'll follow them. Am I understood?"

"Yes, sir."

"I thought you would be best suited to that House. William is one of mine too, as well as Grayson, they've been instructed to help you. Let them help you."

"I will, sir."

I do my best not to let it show on my face how much I'm not about their help. I'll go to William for *care* or whatever, since Xavier told me to, but other than that, I'm keeping to myself. As if he knows—how could he know?—Xavier's eyes darken. "I won't like to learn you haven't followed my instructions, Finnegan."

"I said I would let them, didn't I?"

He taps his fingers on the desk, studying me like I'm an amoeba. Maybe I am to him. "You're being awfully cheeky for someone who's just had a decent spanking. Tell William I'll be by the house tonight. I'm going to check on you personally."

I keep my disdain over that to myself. I want to cross my arms at him, but I force them to remain at my sides. "Yes, sir."

"Very well. You have your instructions. Everything I want you to complete tonight is in this outline here," he says, pushing it across the desk to me. "There's only one thing left and then you are dismissed." He stands and walks around to the front of his desk. "Come here, my churlish boy."

I stand, confused. Come here? Come here for what? When I get close enough, I find out as I'm pulled into strong arms. Is he *hugging* me? I spend half of the hug unsure it's a hug, and when I finally am sure that yes, yes it is a fucking hug, it's over. He's got a sly smile on his face. Bastard. "You may leave now, Mr. Brighton."

CHAPTER TWO

I use the Kleenex I was given as I leave the office, the document Xavier gave me clutched tightly in my hand. I notice right away, I'm lighter. The sting in my ass seems to bolster the lightness. Huh, maybe I'm cured? Maybe I don't need to stay here five years? Even though I've signed the contract, I get seven days to exit, no questions asked, but I can never come back.

The school is massive, one of the largest ones in Canada. There are other, smaller discipline schools, but Xavier's is the size of any prestigious university campus. It's split into a collection of school buildings on the east side of campus, where classes are taught, and housing on the west and northeast sides.

On the west side are apartments and small houses for the professors and men in relationships with one or more partners. To the northeast are the Houses. If you're in a House, you live with six or more men of varying designations from Top to brat.

Separating the Houses from the other housing is a large expanse of well-manicured forest, making it lean more toward 'woodsy park,' with benches and trails, but still densely packed with trees and other flora and fauna.

The classroom buildings extend from the east side of campus, all the way to the southeast side, close to where the front gate stands firmly keeping non-students and staff out and keeping students—without necessary permissions—in. There is an on-campus hospital and a clinic known colloquially as the infirmary. There are other on-campus health care facilities as well, like physios and chiropractors.

Sammy teased that I'd spend a lot of my time in these places with how often I manage to injure myself.

There's a bookstore and other shops and food joints, plus a Student Union Building (the SUB), where clubs meet. The SUB also has food places within and serves as a general hangout space. If you want to play sports, you sign up at the SUB rather than online and if you want to watch a movie, there's a small theatre. If you don't want to study at home, no problem; there are four libraries. Need groceries? There's a marketplace with farm fresh produce and other goods.

Basically, there's enough on campus, you don't need to leave. It's able to cater to over ten thousand students.

It's easy to get around. The entire place has a network of roads and a plethora of golf carts available for use, since it's a good twenty-minute walk from the Houses—here the majority of the students stay—to classes.

Despite the colossal size of this place, I find my House. It's called Alpha House—there's a sign and everything out front. I know my stuff was already brought here. Someone took it so I could have my orientation meeting with Xavier. *Some orientation, Finn.* I heat from head to toe thinking about the way he pulled me over his knee, with my pants down, spanking away as normal as you please. I can only imagine what he must have seen, my round ass, the skin jiggling just a bit as his hand made contact, slowly turning pink and then red. At least that's what it felt like and with the buzz humming across my tender flesh, that's what I imagine, though I haven't seen it.

What does it look like, Finnegan?

I don't know, but I kind of want to find out. That's weird though. Right? Yeah, that has to be weird. Who wants to see their own spanked ass?

I can't believe I'm here, walking through the grand landscape of this campus. I pull in an awed breath and admire the trees, donning their fall reds, oranges and yellows. *It's just like the pamphlet I saw for this place.* It was after one of my job losses. I was down and instead of the usual 'hide in my room' thing I do, I got out of the house.

Thinking about that, remembering it was a pamphlet I came across, rather than something I'd found on the internet seems outlandish—who uses pamphlets anymore? —but that's what I was handed. A man in a school uniform like the one I'll be wearing while I go here; navy blue shorts and blazer, with white button-up undershirt, complete with blue tie and white socks that hugged tightly to his calves.

He didn't say a word, but something of his smile hinted to knowing, and like he knew I should be one of the people to receive a pamphlet. I'm not even the kind of guy who accepts pamphlets, but I did this one and I couldn't let it go.

Xavier's School of Discipline, it said on the front. Heat burned across my skin.

The word *discipline* conjured a whole host of scenes in my head, including, but not limited to times I was in trouble when I was a kid, any sort of discipline I'd seen in movies, TV shows and cartoons—from spanking to a kid being sent to his room. Even those times I played 'house' with my friends at ten, when our parents weren't paying close enough attention to us and the things we'd do. I knew from a young age that any sort of anything to do with discipline makes me blush, but at the same time, I'm hopelessly fascinated.

That's how it began for me, as a fascination I didn't understand. As I got older, it was all fantasy, novels and poor-quality videos on the internet. The novels lacked for me in that most of them focused on the sexual kind of spanking and discipline, which, while I'm all for that kind of thing now and then, it's not really what I'm after. It didn't take me long to figure out that spanking is largely non-sexual for me. There's still arousal, but its own kind. It's similar to sexual arousal in some ways—the tingling in special places, the racing heart—but it also isn't.

This makes it harder to find what I'm looking for in the world at large.

I received that pamphlet a lot of years ago; I read it so many times it was destroyed before I finally took the plunge to tell my brother what I wanted, which was a disciplinarian. It was humiliating to say. What kind of grown man wants another man to keep him accountable in such a personal way? I had visions of Sam telling me how stupid I was, but I should have known better. Sam was as supportive as he is about anything else. Maybe more than.

He wanted me to have what I felt I needed, even offered to help me look, because no way we could afford Xavier's school back then. My search began online, joining sites made for this kind of thing, but unfortunately, these sites weren't just for my specific brand of spankee, but for the other kinds of things like BDSM, a category spanking gets thrown into, because it's used in those scenarios.

But spanking is a category all its own. A true blue spankee, and spanker, in my experience, seems to be born with this need and it's very spanking specific, complete with particular things associated with spanking like scolding and the embarrassment factor.

Through these websites, I met some good people, and I met some bad people, but none of them were right. I didn't belong with any of them. This resulted in me giving up on the idea, and things got worse.

The anxiety I'd always experienced to some degree heightened. I barely left the house anymore, which meant I wasn't finding a job anytime soon. Sam supported me, like a parent would have, because he is part parent to me, but I began to feel like a leech. Instead of the guilt of the situation inspiring me to find a job, I procrastinated. I'd do it tomorrow, or on Monday, or next week.

That wasn't the only thing I would do later. Everything became later to the point Sam did everything, because he got fed up with piles of dishes and laundry. The more Sam did, the more guilt I felt, but did I do anything about it? No.

By the time I finally approached Sam with the old, tattered pamphlet I'd kept for years, Sam was quickly becoming a hot-shot lawyer. I said I'd be willing to use the money Dad left me. I'd been saving for something special, something big. It wasn't enough, but it was a good chunk. "No," Sam said. "I'll find a way to pay for it. I want you to have this, you need this. But let's check out all the schools like this one, just to make sure it's the right one."

After a lot of research, Sam agreed Xavier's school was the best one, we proceeded finding a way to get the funds, get accepted, and now I'm *here*. Even though I know a great deal about what goes on here, I don't know exactly what to expect and nervous excitement bubbles through me.

Welcome to the rest of your life, Finnegan.

When I get to the door, I almost knock, but it's my house too, right? I take a breath and enter. Inside is absolute chaos. The music is loud, someone's throwing a ball against a wall, there's stuff everywhere—the fan above me spins with several items hanging, some occasionally flying off. Ugh. This is way too much for me. Even more reason to head straight to my room, if I knew where it was. I see stairs to my left and upstairs seems like a good guess.

I'm almost to the stairs, and home free when someone comes out the door from a room toward the back, a towel slung over his shoulder, his long dark hair flying everywhere. The ball being thrown at the wall abruptly stops. "Grayson! Clean this up. Will is gonna *kill* you and I'll let him."

Someone pops up from the couch, a light brown head, buried in baggy clothes, wearing headphones. "Sorry, Ani, can't hear you," he says, then resumes his position, molding into the pale green couch like he's part of it and continues throwing his ball. There's something to his voice, not quite an accent, but something posh in the way he uses words.

Only, both 'Ani' and I devise that Grayson actually can hear him, he's just making a scene and unfortunately, I'm spotted.

"Stop it with the ball, or I won't wait for Will to deal with you. Oh, hello. You the new guy?" Ani says. His demeanor changes instantly from fond rage, to pure sunshine.

"Uh, yeah. Finn. I was just going to find my room."

Grayson stops with the ball and pops up again, removing his headphones to sit around his neck this time. "Xavier said that's my job. I'll show you where you go."

"And then straight back here, you're cleaning this up, mister," Ani says.

"Will needs to stop being a tyrannical ass. C'mon dude. I'll show you," Grayson says to me.

Interesting. He won't leave the job he's been given by Xavier, but he's done this whole 'fuck you' to Will. What could that mean? With the way I know things work around here, it seems pretty fucking brazen. I watch, mesmerized, as he walks past me and up the stairs. "You come back down here too," Ani says to me before I can escape.

The look I get has me sputtering. "I, uh. Yeah. Yes." *Eventually*, I don't say. I still have plans of sitting in my room a good long while before I ever come down here to 'hang out.' He disappears whence he came, and I follow after Grayson, up the long, dark stairway that creaks too loudly as he storms up it. I try softer steps, but the wood still groans—not going to be any sneaking out of this place.

Grayson's shorter than me, and skinny under all those clothes. His longer tuft of feathery hair on the very top of his head bounces as he walks, and he carries himself with relaxed purpose. This guy is a conundrum.

He leads me down a hall and to a room he barges into like he owns the place. It's a simple room with a bed against one wall, a desk against another, with a window in between, a flowy blue curtain swaying with the light breeze.

My stuff is there in piles ready to be unpacked. I didn't bring a ton. Just clothes, my own bed linen (Sammy insisted even though I could have just used what the school provided) and some schoolwork kinds of things, like my laptop and notebooks. Sam wanted to come at the weekend, even though it's a four-hour drive here and then four hours back home again, to bring me some of my books and a few other knick-knacks he insists will make this feel like my home away from home.

There is nothing about this place that says home to me.

I expect Grayson to *show* me my room and then promptly leave. That's not what happens. He flings himself down on my unmade bed and pulls out a Nintendo Switch from the giant pocket in the front of his baggy shirt. He starts playing like we're buds who've known each other for ages. The kind of buds you don't need words with, the kind you can spend time with in silence and feel their friendship like it's a living thing in the room with you.

Only, Grayson and I are not that kind of friends. We're not even friends. Right now, he's just an interloper taking up space on my bed. I tense, irritated, and think about telling him all about what I think of him being here like this, but I'm new. I don't want to be *that* guy in the house.

He looks up. "You don't mind, do you?" he says.

Mind? Of course, I mind. I don't know you dude. Not to mention, if it's alone time he's seeking, I'm sure he has his own room. Or maybe he's avoiding cleaning up downstairs. I'm sure I could have him removed if I wanted. That Ani guy seems like the kind to drag you by your ear.

But, sigh. There's something there in his eyes. Something I instantly connect with. A sadness, a pain, an indeterminable longing and I can't fucking do it. "I don't mind."

"Cool."

He pops his headphones on, and I'm relieved I don't have to dream up conversation. It's not that I can't; I'm just not in the mood for it. I set to work unpacking my things and am only slightly exasperated by his presence since I can't rub my sore ass like I want to. For the most part, him being here turns out to be a comfort I didn't know I needed. First days are hard anywhere, this kind of first day is on another level.

I hang my clothes and arrange my desk adding the picture of Sam and I with Dad. It was one of the last times we went fishing together before he died. The only thing I can't do is make my bed, but I do pull out the freshly washed linens. They're laden with the smell of home and Sam was right, bringing my own bedsheets was a good idea. He even insisted on a new, Canadian goose-down duvet, so he'd know I was 'cozy' at night.

My brother. Such a fucking sap sometimes.

Grayson notices I want to make my bed and without me having to ask him, he sets his Nintendo console aside and grabs a sheet. "I'll help."

"Thanks, man."

We make the bed together and there's an ease between us I didn't expect. Like we've got some kind of energy connecting us; an energy that's similar. "No problem. Us brats gotta stick together."

"What did you call me?"

"A brat. That's what you are." And then he goes about smoothing out the first sheet like he'd said something totally normal.

I'm offended. "I am *not* a brat."

"Ah, one of those kinds of brats then," he says.

My brow frowns. "One of what?"

He grabs a pillow, stuffing it into the blue pillowcase. "A brat in denial," he says, but then he studies me. "Or maybe just a brat who doesn't know what he is yet. It's one or the other, definitely one or the other."

I'm about to ask him if he's even talking to me, or to himself, but I don't get the chance. From down below a deep voice bellows, "Grayson!"

Grayson's eyes widen. "Shit! Fuck. I gotta go." He looks around and spies the open window, heading for it. "You never saw me. Know what? You don't even know I exist."

I don't get time to figure out what all of that means. He's

lifting himself up the ledge as the door to my room bursts open—no knocking in this house apparently. A tall, burly man storms in dressed in pants that are more holes than jeans, showing off his thick thighs. Wow his jaw. It's strong, a firm and unmovable thing that gives his frame a sense of steadiness. Wavy blond hair brushes the edge of that jaw; the sun seems to glint off it. And is that a cowboy hat? Yep, yep. He's wearing an *actual* cowboy hat in the house.

Not that I mind.

"Grayson Bartholomew, you stop right there, or the spanking you'll get will be worse than the one you have coming."

From what I've seen, my guess is that Grayson will hop out the window anyway, but he doesn't. He turns around. "Now, William. There's no need for all this. You'll scare the new guy."

William looks to me as if he can suddenly see me now that Grayson's pointed me out. "Hello Finn. Welcome. I'll be having a chat with you shortly. Sorry about this," he says, making his way into the room.

"Will. No. *No.*" Will easily lifts Grayson over his shoulder with a crisp smack to his ass.

Grayson and Will By Artsy Ape

"Let me go, you brute!"

"You wanted my attention, darlin', you got it. See you in a moment, Finn," he says to me, and then carts Grayson off.

It's not long before I hear smacks ring out from down the hall. I know the sound, I just listened to it for what felt like forever when Xavier spanked the life out of me. Holy shit, it sounds like one helluva spanking. And it dawns on me as I continue to listen, what Xavier meant when he said, 'Head of House.' Will is in charge here and he can spank me too.

Of course, I knew this. It all returns to my brain—the rules, regulations and protocols—but I'd put it out of my mind focused on the prospect of having to answer to Xavier. Wow, yeah. It will be hard procrastinating around here.

By the time I'm done with my bed, the spanking has stopped, but I'm so invested in what's going to happen next, like I'm watching a movie play out, I've got my senses tuned. Even with all the reading and all the questions, I didn't expect the House to be so involved.

And now I've got to know what happens. Will Grayson be upset over being spanked? Mad about it? Fearful? How does it all work? I dunno, but I have to *see*.

Only, that means not sulking in here over the spanking I got—the one I literally paid for—which let's face it, that was my plan. To prolong making the decision to go downstairs or stay in my room, I change my clothes. My ass is still on fire. I take time to rub it, before I slip into grey sweats and a white t-shirt. White t-shirts are my go-to, they match my blond hair and people always tell me they make my green eyes pop.

This time I get a knock on my door. "Finn? Can I come in? It's William."

"Yeah."

He opens the door and even though he's not fiery anymore, *wow* the energy that comes off of him naturally. He's powerful. He's more the in-charge-kinda-guy versus the needs-someone-in-charge-of-them-kinda-guy. He extends his hand. "Time for a proper introduction. Pleasure to meet you, Finn. I'm William, but you can call me Will, or sir when the time calls for it." He winks. "Welcome."

It's not often I don't know what to say back, but I don't, and my throat closes up. I do shake his hand though.

He smiles. "Looks good in here," he says, peering around and then cutting to the chase. "Well, I wager you'll have something for me to tend to, sweetheart."

Oh right. The 'care' Xavier mentioned. "You know, I think I'm good," I tell him. The words just slip out.

"Don't think so, darlin'. Pants down and over the bed. Now." He turns expecting his will to be done. "There should be some ... oh here it is," he says, taking something from a cupboard I haven't been into yet. "Aloe for your tender cheeks."

He's so *normal* about everything. "Couldn't I put that on myself?"

"I suppose technically you could, but that ain't happening. Lose the pants, kid. Not asking a third time."

Kid? I'm no kid. But I do drop my pants—less concerned with people seeing stuff than I was earlier today, I've devised no one here thinks too long over stuff like this—and throw myself over the bed, making my displeasure known. I jump a little when I feel his hand. The skin is tender, and that aloe is cold. He's gentle though and when he's done, some of the sting is relieved—not gone—and yeah, there is something nice to the ritual. I could fall asleep.

"All right, stand up."

Jeez this guy. He's oddly militant for someone who also uses the terms 'darling' and 'sweetheart.' I do though, pulling up my pants and *wham!* I'm pulled in for my second hug of the day.

What's with all the damn hugging around here, Finn?

I do not know.

"You okay now, sweetheart?"

"I was okay before, promise." I should worm my way out of this hug but, well, it's a *really* good hug. He's hard and soft at the same time and he smells good, fresh like after a heavy rain. It's not quite as solid as the hug Xavier gave me, but then again, I'm not sure anything's going to be. Oh God, what am I thinking? I'm analyzing hugs. What are these people doing to me?

He kisses the top of my head and then pulls away. "There now, you're properly inducted. Dinner's in an hour, but Ani wants to talk to you. You should go down there if you're done here."

"Yeah, that's the thing, I was planning on chilling here for a bit."

"Sorry, kid. Not on your first night. Downstairs in ten minutes. That bum looks too sore for another spanking. Xavy must really like you by the way."

I'm not sure I agree that a harder spanking means more 'like,' but that's not my issue. "But, I don't want to come downstairs." *Dude. Finnegan.* Why do I sound so juvenile? It's this house. This house is doing something to me.

"Too bad. Ten minutes, Finnegan. The response you'll be looking for to that one is, yes sir."

Heat blooms across my face. "Yes, sir."

He winks and dammit, it's hard to be mad at him. Still throw my pillow at the door when he shuts it behind him. Since I've only been given ten *lousy* minutes, I use them to check my phone. There's a message from Sam. Maybe I should call him tonight, tell him about all this craziness...? If he agrees I should come home, I'm going straight home. But when I see the text, I change my mind.

Hey little brother, hope it's a good first day. So excited for you! This is the start of something new and your own—I can feel it.

Included are the heart and unicorn emoji. It's a bit him making fun in a fond way—a joke between us about special unicorns—but he's also serious. He believes as much as I do, that this is my chance to find out who I am.

I return the text.

First day great. Can't wait to tell you! I include the smiley face emoji.

There are many schools like this one, designed years ago for the ever-growing emergence of people like me. They were so successful at improving the population on a large scale, they're now supported by law, and you can even get sent to one for breaking laws as part of your reform.

Because they are supported, the chances of you getting out of your contract once signed are low, so you'd better think long and hard about entering one if you're a crazy person like me, choosing to do so. It's also why the vetting process is so thorough. They're not letting just anyone into these places. They've got to deem you a proper fit, that you really do have that *thing* inside you, making you right for this kind of lifestyle.

And it *is* a lifestyle. The idea is to experience what's healthy and functional, to familiarize yourself to the various kinds of domestic discipline relationships, understand what's most beneficial for you and define what you need. Then you leave and find a mate to continue the lifestyle with. Often, you find someone while you go to school here, which is ideal. They'll already be aligned in the same ways.

I check the time. Has it been ten minutes? Can't believe he only gave me ten.

I take a quick survey of my room, my eyes landing on the crisp papers Xavier gave me. I should look them over, so I don't miss anything I'm meant to know—Xavier made it clear he wasn't giving quarter for ignorance. Besides, could give me something to do if I run out of things to talk about. I snatch them up and head downstairs.

I get to see the result of what happened between Grayson and Will. I'm greeted to the sight of an only slightly contrite Grayson who is cleaning up, but probably slower than I've ever seen anyone clean. I remember him helping me with my bed and bend over to start helping him. "Ah. I don't think so, Finn. He's doing that on his own," Will says, from his spot on the couch. I guess he's overseeing the task. *Man, that hat, a white Stetson*—his easygoing demeanor complements it, makes him all the more attractive.

"That's not fair," Grayson says. "I finally get a brat to pair with. We should get to stick together."

"I'm all for that, Graysie, but not in this case. You made the mess; you clean it up on your own. Besides, Finn is wanted in the kitchen."

"I hate this house. I'm running away," he says, but I get the sense he doesn't mean it. That it's just histrionics.

Will looks skyward. "Sorry about all the chaos today, Finn. We're not usually quite this insane."

I brighten from the inside out. I'm more entertained by all of it then I thought I'd be. "It's okay. Uh, I meant to tell you, Xavier's coming by tonight."

Will's eyes perk up; Grayson's head swivels. "*Finn.* That's need to know shit," Grayson says, picking up the pace five times. He somehow manages to make even the word 'shit' sound posh.

"Language, Grayson. Lordy be, you'd think that spanking you got would inspire good behavior."

I expect more snark from Grayson, but that's not what happens. His lip trembles and his eyes glass over. "Okay, Will. I fucked up, okay? Please can I have some help? I don't want Xavier to see this."

Will sighs, but he remains firm. "I'm sorry darlin'. This is just the thing Xavier needs to see. Besides, I've got to tell him anyway, you know this."

Grayson doesn't answer. He wipes more tears as he cleans faster.

"Don't worry, I've got him," Will says to me. I must look as distraught as I feel. "Go'on to the kitchen."

I nod and force myself to ignore the tug to stay. *Can you*

relate to him, Finnegan? Yeah, yeah. I know well the sensation that comes after you've done something self-righteous, only to realize there were far less childish ways of dealing. After, regret drowns you. There's lots of, "Why can't I go back in time and just *not* do the thing?"

Fuck would time travel help my life a lot.

I step through to the kitchen, and I'm hit with instant nostalgia. The open books, the watchful eyes on the two men pouring over them, and commotion all around as two help Ani, ducking over and under to miss colliding into people and things and carry on their respective jobs. It's how Dad would have run things—me at the table doing my homework, while he and Sam made dinner, though this kitchen is a tad more chaotic.

I run a hand through my hair. It's a bit overwhelming. I don't know where to go or what to do with myself. *Where do you fit in, Finnegan?* "Uh, Ani? You want me to come back when you're less busy?"

"I'm never less busy, baby. Park your ass in that chair," he says, looking toward the kitchen door. "I'll be with you in a moment."

"Ani, the buns," another guy says trying to squeeze his way past Ani and make his way to the oven.

The other dark-haired guy has to dodge the one going after the buns, so he can continue putting together his tray of vegetables. "Christ, Christopher," he shouts.

There are a lot of people in this house.

I sit where I'm told, gingerly on my tender butt, glad I brought my document from Xavier. I try to bury my head in it.

"Hey, you must be Finnegan. We heard all about you. I'm Bellamy," one says.

"And I'm Stephen Bray," the other says. "But everyone calls me Bray."

"Except for when he's in trouble," Bellamy adds.

"Hey!"

"You two better be doing homework," Ani says, somehow able to juggle all the balls over where he is and keep an eye on them too.

"Jeez, Ani. We are. We're just introducin' ourselves," Bellamy says.

"Problem is, I know you two better than you know yourselves. Keep working."

They both mutter 'yes, sirs,' and that effectively ends our conversation. I should read, but I'm too distracted by the exciting kitchen. Ani's giving orders, managing calm and frantic at the same time, while the other two are just frantic. I consider offering to help, but I see why there are only three over there—the kitchen area can only handle three without too many collisions.

The eating area is large, and against the wall closest to the double swinging door that leads out to the living room. The table is solid wood with a bench seat on one side, and a row of chairs on the other. All of it looks too hard for sitting on with my ass throbbing like it is. Haven't these people ever heard of chair cushions?

There's a door leading out to an expansive deck. I can see the porch swing through the window, I can see the backyard space—plenty of room for barbeques and laying out in a chair on the lawn with a good book.

Once again, there's a portion of wall with space for days and nothing to look at, just like I saw in Xavier's office. At least his wall was a shade of red, this one is a boring white.

Somehow, Ani manages to get away from all the mess, and deal with me. *Wow.* Ani. His muscles are leaner than

Will's, so he looks deceptively smaller from a distance. He's not. I get a better idea of how large he is this close. He's got the most beautiful copper skin with long black hair cascading down to the middle of his back and ancient eyes. There's a feminine quality to him, but it doesn't detract from his abrupt male form. I like him immediately without knowing anything about him. He's got that sort of energy, the kind that calms you without asking anything in return.

"Mmmhmm," he says. "Oh boy, you're going to be trouble for Xavier. I wonder if he knows what he's gotten himself into?"

Did I say I liked him? I take it back. "You don't even know me." Yes, I'm glaring.

"I know you fine. You're trouble, but that's why we'll love you to pieces. Stand up, I've been dying to welcome you," he says, with all the pure sunshine.

"Why do I need to stand up for—"

God dammit. I should have known. Before I can stop him, I'm pulled out of my seat and into yet another hug, which I will not analyze. Except that I can't stop the thought that his hug is the softest I've gotten today. I can sink into it and I don't want to let go. It soothes the overwhelm stirring in me, and it seems like a good place to camp out for a bit.

"Oh, I know honey," he says, like he knows how I'm feeling, kissing the top of my head. "But you'll feel much better down here than upstairs. We don't bite."

"Not true," Bray says. "You have a hairbrush and it definitely bites."

"It only bites those who give me too much sass." Ani releases me. "What'cha got there?"

"Directions from Xavier."

Ani takes them. "Looks like you have homework too." *I*

do? "There's no time before dinner though, you'll have to do it after. It's not much, he would prefer for you to get to know everyone tonight as first priority."

"What's with the homework thing? I thought classes didn't start till Wednesday?" I ask.

"But you've got your books, don't you?" Ani says. I nod. "He wants you to read up before your classes. This document also contains each syllabus to your classes, he's specified how much he wants you to read."

Homework before there's real homework? These people are crazy.

"Don't let Xavy see you scowling like that," Ani says, handing back my stupid documents.

"Well, what about them? Don't they have homework?" I say referring to the two in the kitchen.

"They don't. Different Tops, different assignments. Don't worry about it for now. I'll make sure you get it done after. You can set the table for me. We'll need eight. Christopher will tell you where to find everything. I've got to have a chat with these two now."

Christopher doesn't look to be in the best of moods. "Can't Johnny Rae help him? I'm busy, Ani." But one look from Ani has him moving toward the drawers to show me. "Sorry, Finn was it?"

"Yeah."

"Sorry, Finn. It's extra hectic today, because school starts this week. It is good to meet you though." Christopher is cowed in on himself, he's talking, but he's not really here.

"Don't mind him," the other guy, Johnny says. "He's pouting because Professor Lancaster—his Top—isn't pleased with him. He'll be in a better mood after a good spanking."

"Johnny!"

"Well, it's true. Plates are up there, Finn." Johnny has hair as black as Ani's, but it slants across his brow long, short at the back. He's slimmer, like Grayson and by the sparkle in his eyes, he's his own kind of trouble.

"Knife, fork, spoon, for tonight," Christopher says, his face a little red from the talk of spanking, which I get. I'd be just as flushed if someone said that to me, in fact I am some right now on his behalf. Yet, my body takes a sigh at the idea of spanking, for reasons I can't explain. "You good?"

"Yeah, I think I am," I say.

I'm finishing setting the table when Will and Grayson return. Will's sporting a dopey, sunny smile after Grayson, as he twirls him into the room, spinning him with an arm in the air, Grayson's eyes dancing in time with Will's motions. *Well. That's a one eighty.* "I need to borrow Finn, Ani. Xavier boys' meeting," Will says.

"We're about to eat, Will," Ani says. It sounds suspiciously like a complaint.

Will pulls Ani into him. "I know, darlin'. I promise we won't be gone long, okay? Ten minutes max." He seals the deal with a kiss that has Ani swooning a bit.

"Ten minutes, William." Ani points a wooden spoon at him, dripping with tomato sauce.

"C'mon onto the deck, Finn."

I follow them out and Will leans against the sturdy deck rail that sits at the level of his mid-back and pulls Grayson to him with his back to Will's chest, and Grayson manages to sink into the harder man. I think about sitting on the porch swing—it looks comfortable—but opt for leaning against a deck rail too, facing them. There's a breezy chill, it's fall and I'm not wearing a jacket, but shoving my hands into pockets is enough for a little warmth, since we're not meant to be out here long. Ten minutes if Will doesn't want to piss Ani off.

"We're the only three in the house who belong to Xavier," Will says. "You'll meet the others eventually, but the three of us will have to have our own meetings separate from the house, as well as with the house, and with the others from Xavier's group of us."

"That sounds like a lot of meetings," I say.

"House meetings are more frequent. I only do these 'Xavier's Boys' ones when necessary and the ones Xavier holds with the others are once a week during Friday night discipline, though many of us usually stay after and it can turn into an unofficial meeting of sorts."

"Yeah, meanwhile, house meetings are like, every five minutes," Grayson says.

"They are not," Will argues.

"Feels like it."

"Anyway, this ain't formal. Just five minutes to tell you about some of the structure. We have a few different rules than some of the others, and you end up forming a bit of a nuclear family feel."

"How many others are there?" I knew Xavier had other boys, not how many.

"Three more, they live at Sigma Phi house."

"Which rules of ours differ?" I can't help asking, I'm fucking curious.

"We have regular bedtimes and curfews. The others don't so long as they regularly get to bed at decent hours. Also, Xavier's a stickler for presentation. What you're wearing is fine for the house, but do not let him catch you *going* places like that."

Shit, right. I forgot about that. "Any others?"

"We don't automatically get to go to socials, or parties.

No one else in the house has to gain permission from their Tops, but we do. Xavier is not just the headmaster of this school, he owns it. We represent him; he has to know what we're up to and approve of it."

"Not to mention he's super anal retentive," Grayson says.

"*Gray*," Will warns, squeezing him.

"Well, it's true. Try to deny it."

"He's just particular is all," Will defends.

"See? I'm right. Anyway, I'm glad you're here, Finn," he says, far more animated than earlier.

"He's already decided you're brat brothers," Will explains, entertained by Grayson. It's clear he adores him.

There's that word again though. "Even if I was a 'brat,'" I say, with air quotes, "it seems like there is no shortage in the kitchen."

"Oh sure, there are brats in the house, but you're the only other one of Xavier's brats in *this* house and Emmery is no brat even if he's also not a Top."

I did not expect so many dynamics. They're sprouting up everywhere. I struggle to keep up.

"I have a couple of my own rules, but they're simple," Will says. "I'm big on respect, which includes watching your language, and I like to know everyone's comings and goings in which I reserve the right to cancel even if they may otherwise have been approved. Understand?"

"I do, sir."

"Good. That's all I have to say. We'd better get back inside before Ani has all of our heads. You have any quick questions before we go in?"

Do I? Not really, I'm enjoying watching the house unfold a lot more than I thought I would. But then I think of something. "What's with all the hugging?"

Will bursts with laughter. "Of all the things you coulda asked. You're gonna fit in fine here kid. C'mon." He heads toward the door, dragging Grayson with him like they're stuck together by some invisible magnet.

"But wait, I was serious. I want to know. It's ridiculous!"

"Yeesh, he'd better not let Ani hear him say that," Grayson says to Will as if I'm not right behind them.

"I'm still here, Grayson."

Grayson leaves Will to return and latch onto me, his feathery hair flopping all over the place. *His hugs are like a cushion.* I have a flash of us cuddling on the couch. No. *No.* I do not cuddle. "I know you're here Finnegan. I'm keeping you."

I scowl down at him, but he's too charming to send away. My arms encircle him as if guided by some other force and there's a *click*. The shock of it has me squeezing him. We are *found* together.

I have never belonged more.

CHAPTER THREE

I pick up on some of the subtle dynamics of the house. Like that, while Will may be Head of House, Ani also has an authoritative role. But the rest of us are, well, they keep using the term brat, which is a boat I'm not sure I want to throw myself into just yet, but to use their term, the rest of us are brats.

I detect a spectrum. Christopher doesn't rank anywhere near a Grayson level brat, but Johnny is close, he just toes the line better than Grayson does. Stephen, or Bray as he likes to be called, is a silent troublemaker, gaining allies via whispered schemes and animated facial language. Bellamy though? That guy is a *fucking* brat. He got himself spanked at the dinner table by Ani, the rumored hairbrush made an appearance, and after still being a 'sasspot' (Ani's word), got sent to the wall to think about behaving. So yeah, found out what that expanse of wall was for and noticed others through the house: long stretches of plain wall, nothing on them. Grayson pointed out to me, *whispered* to me, that they were intentionally kept boring since they were for thinking, not entertaining.

Wasn't hard to devise that Xavier's red wall must be for the same purpose.

When Bellamy was released, Will told him he was going to be having an early night, because clearly all that sass meant he was a tired boy.

So fucking intriguing, all of it.

Yet somehow, even after all that, I thought my attempt to escape after clean-up from dinner was done, (and after Ani made me do all my homework) was gonna go oh, so smoothly. I claimed I wanted an early night, but Will was onto me. "You tired, sweetheart?"

I could have lied, but I *couldn't* lie, not with Will looking at me like he was, so fucking earnestly. "No."

"Then you're staying down here with us."

Part of me wanted to storm up the stairs anyway to see what would happen, but with the way my tummy plummeted, butterflies knocking around in there at the same time, I slumped onto the couch instead. Plus, there was the memory of Bellamy staring at a wall to deter any outright defiance.

"Ugh!" Yeah. A complaint came out, and no one cared. Apparently complaining about things like that is as common as the cold around here—everyone took it as a sign I was settling in.

Once it was established that Finn would not be leaving the living room, Grayson plunked down beside me, making himself too cozy, his thin form pressing against me. Will had tender eyes for us, while he got comfortable in the large armchair beside the couch.

Ani pulled Bellamy into his lap.

"Ani, lay off," he said, but even I could detect the minor loosening of his muscles and the way he sunk into Ani, like it's just what he needed. Chris put a movie on and then laid between Johnny and Bray on the other sofa. With his feet in Johnny's lap and his head in Bray's, he looked like a lounging bunny, letting Bray card his fingers through his hair, smoothing away the edges of his day.

I catch on quickly that the living room is a sacred place. One couch in particular stands out, a pale green one, with cherry blossoms in various phases of life, blooming over the surface. Unlike the other furniture of this house, which is newer and in excellent condition, it's seen better days. But it's likely those days it's seen imprinted into the worn, tattered material, making it irreplaceable.

It belongs here.

Adjacent to the area where the couches and TV are, is a long table with chairs, which I'm going to assume is also for homework, perhaps when less supervision is required. From what I've seen so far, I doubt that less supervision is a thing that happens often. Across the room from the long wooden table is an air hockey table, and a board on the wall with the names of everyone in the house listed up top, and scores underneath.

Now, we're halfway through the movie. It's one I've seen before, and I like it, but I'm too fascinated with spying on everyone to pay close attention to it. Grayson's wound himself around me like an octopus does, twisting both his arms around mine and a leg hooked over and snaking around my mid-thigh. The discomfort of such intimacy should have stiffened me, but I've softened into it, gone so far as to lean my head to rest against his feathery mop.

What's weird to me is I don't feel weird.

Other people have changed and shifted as well. Ani got up to make us popcorn and when he returned, Bray was spooned behind Bellamy since he'd whined at Bray to keep him warm, leaving Johnny and Christopher to rearrange themselves. Ani sat between Will's legs on a cushion, on the floor, so Will could play with his hair. It's dark in the room, except for the flicker of the TV. Everyone's got someone and there seems to be an unspoken dance as to who goes where and who needs what throughout the evening.

The doorbell rings, and we all jump, except for Will. "That's probably Xavier," he says.

"That's the trouble living in this house, too many visits from the headmaster. What the fuck did one of you do?" Bellamy says.

"Thanks for reminding me of your presence, Bell. You need sleep. Go," Will says, firm as a mountain.

"It was a perfectly, valid question," he says, but he springs off the couch like a cat, glaring at the whole world as he strides by and up the stairs.

"That boy needs a lesson on manners," Will mutters as he makes his way over to the door and undoes the lock.

Xavier is there in a long, black coat with shiny black buttons. A blue scarf covers his neck, nestled under his chin, framing it, making the rest of his features categorical. His dark hair loops and curls in a messy sort of way, a sharp contrast to how tidy the rest of him is, down to his polished shoes. The cold breezes in, but Xavier stands firm in spite of it, withdrawing his permission for it to enter beyond the woolen barriers. "William. May I come in?" his deep voice says.

And it runs through me.

Warmth spreads through my belly, *I know you*, even though I don't. How could I? I want to go to him, but that would be weird. The House might have its dynamic, one they've pulled me into without prerequisite, but Xavier is different.

He's not yours, Finn. Yeah, I know that.

46

Grayson leaps off the couch, pulling his warmth from me, the cold bites into where he was, and I watch transfixed as he leaps into Xavier's arms like he isn't the headmaster of the whole school, or a strict-ass Top. After Grayson's performance over what Xavier would see and hear about his behavior, I thought Grayson would avoid Xavier. That's what I would have done, but not Grayson. Xavier can't even get his jacket off because he has an armful of Grayson, who's trying to mold himself to his body.

"What's all this?" Xavier says, in his thick English accent, which is just that much softer for Grayson, running fingers through his feathery hair, hugging him tight.

"Some big-ass fit," Bray says. Will glares at him—I guess 'ass' is on Will's list of 'no' words—but Bray doesn't let up. "Well, it was. I'm sorry for my language, but we've had to put up with it all day, it's getting ridiculous."

Xavier looks to Will. "Bray's not wrong. It was a fit, and it was taken care of sir, at least I thought so," Will explains.

"Mmmhmm," Xavier says, figuring something out. "It sounds like you and I need to have a chat, Mr. Worthington." Grayson nods into Xavier. "William, I want to see you and Finnegan in the study. I'll just be a moment or two with this one."

Will takes my hand and leads me to the study, which is upstairs and down the hall to the right, at the end. All I can think about is how glad I am that Will told me to go change before Xavier got here. Grayson might have a particular level of comfort with him, but I'm not ready to test him yet; I want to show my personal best. The jeans aren't fun against my ass, but it's little discomfort compared to Xavier's disappointed stare.

The study is a good size. Much smaller than Xavier's office, but large enough for a sturdy desk and walls of books.

Despite there being only one leather chair, I know that this place is for formal meetings. I spy a leather strap hanging on the wall beside the door and there's a suspicious cupboard that doesn't really need to be here—I'm gonna guess it's got other implements of doom within, much like the ones outlined in the student manual.

A lone, armless chair sits beside the desk and I know *exactly* what that's for. I shiver.

"Grayson'll be okay you know. Sometimes we just need Xavier, that's what he's for."

"Even you?"

He nods. "Even me, sweetheart."

"You seem like an Xavier though."

He laughs. "I guess in a lot of ways, I am, but even with all my experience, I don't feel ready to fly without him yet."

That's surprising. "You seem so strong, though."

"And I am. It's okay to need people, Finn."

Maybe for some people. I don't *need* anyone. "What about relationships? Is anyone in the house, dating?"

He smiles wide. "Not really... Okay, maybe, sorta? We're fairly incestuous I guess you could say with no official statuses between anyone. No bets are off, but I kinda have a favorite, even if I'm not always his favorite."

I remember him kissing Ani, but that's not who he means. "Grayson?"

His eyes turn to adoration, like he's been hit by cupid's arrow all over again. "Yeah. He just gets me in the heart, and I adore his brat even if it's no end of trouble for me. Xavier has a rule for me; when anyone in my House is in trouble, I pay in some way too. I'm responsible for y'all. I catch it a lot for Graysie, but don't seem to matter. I'm such a fool for him."

"That doesn't seem fair. You can't surveil every move we make."

"True, but it's more about the things I missed leading up to it; there are usually a ton of signs when a brat's about to brat. It's not a straightforward thing, and it's not automatic —because it's true, I can't prevent everything—so if Xavier feels I did all I could, I'm off the hook. Y'all are still responsible for your own behaviors at the end of the day. And before you feel too bad for me, I want the responsibility. I like it. Gives me the best feels."

Huh. I think he's nuts, but whatever floats his boat.

Xavier enters like a cool breeze. The warmheartedness I saw with Grayson is gone, he's the ice swan again. Only, things are already different than they were this morning. It's only been a day, but this house has affected me. A wave of tingles washes through me at the sight of Xavier, but the awkwardness has receded. He takes his place in front of us both, leaning against the desk with folded arms, his polished boots still on and glistening. Will guides me to sit in the chair and stands behind me, his hand rested on my shoulders. "I came to check on one boy, but it looks like he's not the one who needed me."

"I'm fine, sir." I puff my chest and harden the lines of my face. I don't need checking up on.

He raises a brow high. "I know you are *fine*, but you left me with the impression you would disobey me."

That has me backtracking, biting my lip. "I uh, yeah okay. I might have had the dastardly plan to hide in my room all day. But I did learn something," I add, as though that might get me off the list I'm sure he has me on.

Why did you just rat yourself out, Brighton? I don't know, there's something about him, okay?

Will laughs hard, slapping his knee, while Xavier's

amused. "I take it your plan did not come to fruition?" Xavier asks. I shake my head. "Who stopped you?"

"Everyone. You can't get a moment of peace around here."

"Which was *my* dastardly plan," he says. "Thank you for your honesty. Homework's done?"

My cheeks light with hot embarrassment at being asked about my homework like that. I only just stop myself rolling my eyes at him. "Ani wouldn't let me not do it, or I couldn't watch the movie."

"Hmmm. One would think that you would have finally found the freedom you were looking for and prolonged your homework, so that you didn't have to watch the movie."

I ... oh. That's totally a move I would have used in the past, but yeah, didn't even cross my mind. He turns to Will. "Grayson told me what happened," he begins, and I perk up. I didn't actually find out what happened. I saw the mess and assumed he was in trouble for making it.

"He was upset with me for telling him he couldn't go to the Gamma social. I believe he used the word 'tyrannical.' But you know how he gets at those parties, and I couldn't be here to take him, I've got obligations with my little brother that night. I told him I'd take him to the Sigma Phi one the following weekend, but that wasn't good enough."

Xavier nods. "Your logic is sound, William. You did what you could, and I have spoken to him. He wasn't upset about the party anymore. He was more upset about my reaction to his tantrum. I made it clear what I thought." Why do I get the impression that means spanking? A lot of things in this house seem to mean spanking. "But you didn't tell me, Finn. What did you learn today?"

Dammit. I was hoping he wouldn't follow that. "I never knew there were so many different kinds of hugs, and uh, that it's not so bad." I run a hand through my hair, my nervous twitch.

Xavier nods coolly. Will's having a hard time preventing himself laughing some more. "There are also many different kinds of spanking, Mr. Brighton." I think he might be teasing me, just a little bit, but he also means it.

"Hey! I've been super good."

He looks me over. "For now. There's a strong brat in you, dying to come out. I've got both my eyes on you."

"I am not a brat." Why does everyone think that? No way I'm anything like Bellamy or Grayson.

"If you say so," he says, but I can tell he's not convinced. "Regardless of what you are, you're under my care now. I want exemplary behavior. I knew you had no intentions of obeying me, as instructed."

I blush and look to the ground. No, I hadn't. In my own way, sure, but not as he specified. Will puts his arm around me, and I surprise myself by leaning back. "I got this one, sir. He's one of my favorite kinds of brat."

I smile up at Will. He's good at what he does too, he seems to pick up on emotions, like they're a tactile thing in the room.

"I trust that you do, William. You've done a good job, but I want Mr. Brighton to understand there are consequences for his actions and his intentions." His eyes flicker to the strap on the wall. "Early night for you, ten instead of eleven. Next time, I want you to obey my instructions of your own accord, thank you."

I burn everywhere over correction like that, but I'm not going to argue. Not with him looking at me like that. I force my eyes to meet his. "Yes, sir."

"Good. Thank you. All right you two, I must go, but I will see you both at some point tomorrow."

He leaves, turning sharply on the polished shoes he never took off—I already know Ani will complain about that —and strides out leaving a feeling in his wake. It's pervasive and consuming but also remarkably secure. "C'mon, troublemaker. Grayson could use an early night too. Another hour downstairs and then it's bedtime."

Later, when Will sends me and Grayson off to bed, it feels weird. Pretty sure I haven't been 'sent to bed' since I was a teenager, but I go with it in the spirit of trying new things. Eleven o'clock is early for an adult bedtime as it is, ten is beyond early. Once again, I expect Grayson and I will part ways, but he follows me to my room and shuts the door behind us.

"What now, Grayson?" because I've learned he's the kind of guy you say that to.

"Don't you wanna see it?"

"See what?"

"My ass after Xavier's spanked it. He doesn't like tantrums, let me tell you Finnegan, does not like them at all." Even the way Grayson holds himself is a bit posh, which contradicts the ways he's dressed, still in his oversized clothes, despite knowing he would have to see Xavier at some point.

"Why on Earth would I want to see it?" I say. I'm curious, but he doesn't have to know I'm curious.

"It's a thing we do around here. I saved it for you, thought we could bond over it."

"Bond over me seeing your red ass?"

"Yeah, and then you show me yours. Trust me, it's awesome."

I was all for looking at my own ass in the privacy of my bedroom, but letting him see...? "That makes no sense, Grayson." But he won't leave. He makes himself at home on my bed again as I pull out pajama bottoms—man am I gonna feel relief getting out of these jeans.

"It makes all the sense. C'mon. Try it. If you don't like it, I'll never bother you about it again."

Somehow, I know there's no chance of him not bothering me about it again, and I'm about to tell him no, but he's got that look again, the one that's the thread of something the same in me. "Fine."

Fucking giddy, he stands on the bed and pulls his too large jeans down to reveal pale-white legs—he needs some sun—and an ass, which no longer matches the color of his legs. "Holy shit." Actually, this is kinda interesting, why didn't I think to look at mine?

Grayson's ass is a deep shade of red with a couple of berry-like splotches. "That's two spankings worth back there," he says, full of pride.

"Wow this is, beautiful." I'm almost jealous which is a weird reaction to a red ass, but that is how I feel. "Well, what about mine?"

I yank my jeans off and pull down my boxers trying to look. "Amazing, this is good. Really good. He went hard on you for your first time, he must expect you can take a lot."

Unexpected pride blooms in my chest, knowing he's impressed and at the idea that Xavier might think I'm strong. "Do you mind doing my aloe? I was gonna ask Will to do it, but he always gets to," Grayson says.

Even though he *asked*, he assumes position on the bed like I've said yes before I have. I roll my eyes and grab the aloe from where I saw Will get it out of the cupboard. "Will told me you're his favorite," I say, as I rub aloe into his ass, which is still hot.

"He did not."

"He did. I already picked up on how crazy he is about you."

He's quiet as I finish up and I regret saying anything, but I thought this was supposed to be some sort of (strange) bonding ritual...? Now I feel like an idiot. But then Grayson rolls over smiling, his large shirt covering his cock. He slides off the bed pulling his pants up. "I love him too, Finn."

I sense a 'but'; one that never comes. "All right, I'd better go before William comes up here, unless you're gonna let me sleep with you?"

I don't know what to say to that, because I'm not sure he's joking. "Um, yeah. Maybe another time...?"

He laughs. "You'll see. Night, Brighton." He hauls off and whacks my ass, hard.

"Why you little—!" But he's gone before I can strangle him.

In the morning, I note more than Will wandering out of Will's room. Bellamy's stretching and yawning as he walks out scratching his belly in a red-striped pair of pajama bottoms and a white t-shirt, followed by Grayson. Ani, Christopher and Johnny come from another room. "Does anyone sleep in their own beds here?" I ask.

"I did," Bray says, joining the group that's gathering at the top of the stairs.

"Not from lack of invitation," Christopher says.

"Can't a guy sleep in his own bed for once?" Bray says.

"A guy can, Stephen Bray," Ani says, pulling Bray to him. "But we missed you."

Breakfast is every bit as chaotic as dinner, only this time I'm given a cooking task. "I need one and a half dozen eggs cracked into this bowl and whisked," Ani orders.

I take a moment to appreciate his almond eyes and the way he's tied his hair back into a long ponytail. He's shirt-less this morning and I get the full effect of his biceps; they're a lot bigger with his shirt off, plus the view of his well-shaped shoulders, like giant caps on top of his arms. "See something you like, baby?" he says.

Dammit, Finn. I'm sure I'm blushing seventy-two shades of red and look at the ground.

"Aww, it's okay. If it helps, I have a huge crush on you. Those eyes are so green."

I have to bite my lip to keep from smiling too big. He gives my ass a firm smack and I get a taste of his bite, before he heads off to bark more tasks at people. I sit on one of the tall chairs at the counter, actually en-fucking-joying the discomfort zinging through my backside, leftover from that spanking yesterday, and get to my task. I'm eight eggs in, when my phone buzzes in my pocket. I think it's going to be Sam, but it's not, it's Xavier.

I'd like you to drop by my office today. I'll be in from three to six pm.

I don't expect the thrill that runs through me. It's a different kind of thrill than I've experienced before. Attached is that classic tummy-drop mixed with a bit of, *am I in trouble?* which feels good and I have no idea why. I genuinely don't want to be in trouble, my ass is still getting over the first spanking, yet there's something tantalizing about trouble, and me in it with him.

Him specifically, Finn. Don't forget that part.

Yeah, yeah.

There's a new tug from within me, one that wants to play. I want to say something snarky, like that I'm busy between three and six, and could he please take into consideration *my* schedule, only, he knows my schedule. Hmmmm. I go for subtle snark instead.

Not like I can say no.

I press send and shove my phone back into my pocket, returning to my eggs before Ani sees I'm not cracking. I'm done whisking the eggs when my phone *rings*. Shit. I scramble for my phone and yep it's Xavier. Oh God. *Oh God*, why do I do things? "Hello," I say and try to sound really fucking innocent.

"Finnegan."

"That's me, sir." Fuck, what's with me? Stop. Stop!

"You know, Mr. Brighton, if you're going to insist on being cheeky this morning, I have a paddle with your name on it for when you get here."

Too far, Finn. Time to smarten up. "I'll be there, sir."

"*Behave* yourself."

Fuck is he chilling.

I get off the phone, my heart beating wildly from the interaction. Grayson's staring straight at me. He worms his way into my lap and I'm too stunned to do anything about it. "See? Told you, you're a brat. I know my own kind."

I get brave and put my arms around him, pulling him to me. We fit together nicely, like a puzzle finding its last piece. "I'm torn," Will says from where he's drinking his coffee at the kitchen table. "You two sure make a pretty picture, but I think you're gonna spell trouble for me."

Ani snatches the bowl of whisked eggs away. "You might have a sore ass," he says to Will.

"Ani," Will warns.

Ani bites his lip, lowering his eyes just a bit. "Sorry, sir." Will nods.

"Was that for the language?" I whisper in Grayson's ear. He nods. "Ani can get in trouble for that too?"

"Of course. No one's safe from Will in this house."

"See, they're already co-conspiring. Stop whispering you two. Matter of fact, gimme him," Will says confiscating Grayson from me. "You should be with me anyway, darlin'."

Grayson can't help his smile from widening. I haven't forgotten the way he answered my question last night, but that changes nothing, Grayson's as into Will as Will is him.

"And you have another job. Chop," Ani says to me.

Ani sets a cutting board in front of me with onions and tomatoes on it and a knife. I could complain, seeing as I usually would complain about being given task after task, but right now I'm too relieved at being accepted into the House so readily. Even though this whole thing had been my idea, the list of reasons I shouldn't come here was long and this whole in-house living situation was at the top of that list. "I don't like the whole living with several other guy thing, Sammy," I said. "I'm not easy to live with, it's going to be a disaster." I've never lived with anyone, but Sam and he only put up with my habits because he had too.

"You don't give yourself enough credit," he said. "They'll love you."

So, I chop onions and tomatoes without complaint. If anything, my good behavior can prove I'm not a brat.

At breakfast, Will interrupts us halfway through. "Now that we're all here and Finn's had a night to get used to us, I'm calling our first house meeting." Everyone groans. "I see cell phones have creeped their way back to the table. I'm gonna be real strict on that this year. If I keep seeing 'em show up, I'll bring the bucket back."

"Bucket?" I ask.

"The cell phone bucket," Bellamy answers. "We would have to submit our phones at the beginning of the meal. No one likes it."

"I don't care if you like it. It works. Keep your phones off and away from the table and we won't have an issue. House meetings will be held on Sunday nights," he says.

Everyone groans again. "Will, why can't we stick to Mondays?" Grayson says.

"Because I have an obligation on Monday evenings across campus, this year."

"Us three already have a weekend meeting, Friday nights, and now another weekend night is hijacked?" Grayson complains.

"I'm sorry, darlin', but that's jus' the way it has to be for this year."

Grayson crosses his arms and tries to burn a hole through the table with his eyes.

Will ignores him. "Anything else?"

"Yes. The chore chart. I'll post it on Sundays," Ani says. "It's each person's responsibility to check it and ask me if they're not sure what to do, Finn. This lot knows that."

"Got it," I say, not looking forward to chores. Sammy did most of that stuff. I've been spoiled.

"I would also like to give a friendly reminder that I need to know where everyone's going to be. I don't have time to chase everyone down. You go out, you can use the board, a text, tell someone—I'm flexible—I won't be flexible if I have to worry about you for hours. Send a message if you'll be late. Understood?"

There's a round of reluctant 'yes sirs.'

It's not something I'm used to anymore, Sam did all that with me when I was a teen, but we haven't done mandatory check-in-type stuff since. "I have to grab one more book from the on-campus bookstore and then Xavier wants to see me," I volunteer first.

Will nods. "Anyone else?"

"We're going over to Gamma house," Bray announces, on behalf of himself and Bellamy.

"For what?" Will says, raising one brow—how does he do that? But I'm getting the impression that this Gamma House is the naughty house.

"I want to see Anthony," Bray says.

"And I want out of here. Everyone's so tense this week," Bellamy says, reaching for another slice of toast.

"That house doesn't have a Top this year. I still haven't figured out if it's some kind of bizarre-o Xavier joke, or a mistake, but I don't like you boys going to a place with no Top home. Especially you two," Will says, his eyes on Bray and Bellamy.

Bellamy rolls his eyes. "We are grown adults, we can be left 'home alone,' Will. Jesus."

Will likes his attitude even less. "I have half a mind to tell you to stay home, but yeah, so long as Logan doesn't mind Bell."

"He doesn't," Bellamy says.

Will's lips draw into a line watching Bellamy butter his toast, Bellamy not paying any mind to Will watching even though I'm sure he knows. Something moves between them; an unnamed thing and I can almost see the cogs of Will's brain turning. With a heavy exhale, he lets whatever's on his mind go. Will turns to Bray. "You know Arthur doesn't have a problem with it," Bray says.

"Yeah, and that's the problem," Will says, under his breath. "All right be home for dinner. You, Johnny Rae, we need to chat after breakfast."

59

"About what? What did I do?"

"Nothing yet, I want to keep it that way."

"Chat means spanking in this house," Grayson points out for my benefit.

"Grayson!" Johnny says.

"Well, it's true."

"Enough you two. Christopher?" Will says.

Chris blooms with pink from his neck to his cheeks. "Uh, yeah so I have to meet with Scott today."

"Good, maybe he'll spank you and you'll be in a better mood," Johnny says.

"What'd I ever do to you?" Chris says.

"You were in a snit all night, to start," Johnny answers.

"That's not what you said after I—" Chris begins, but Will cuts him off.

"I'm gonna hand out spankings for everyone in a minute." Everyone gets quiet. "I'll be across campus for most of the day in a Top meeting and workshop, but we'll be allowed to check our phones to take care of our Houses, so text me if you need me. Ani?"

"I've got a lot to bake around here to prepare for the school year, I want to fill the freezer with muffins."

"Did Tom okay that?" Will asks.

Huh. I did not expect that. It's easy to forget with how authoritative Ani is that he's not a Top.

"Yes, sir. That and the loaves of bread I want to make tomorrow."

"Okay, but I want you to commandeer someone at some point for house meals, y'hear?"

"Yes, sir."

What was that all about?

"All right men, you're dismissed except two of you to help Ani, I don't care which two. I have to get ready to leave." Will slides out taking his coffee and plate with him, leaving his plate at the sink.

"Not it!" Bellamy and Bray shout, running from the kitchen and almost into Will on the other side.

"You'd better give your heart to Jesus, because your butts are mine!" Will shouts, just before the door swings shut.

Gray, Johnny and I can't help laughing.

"I would Ani, but I have to get over to Scott's," Chris says.

"Yes you do, sweetheart, you go ahead."

"We did it last night," Grayson complains, the 'we' referring to me; we're quickly becoming a house pair of some kind. "That should exempt us from breakfast dishes."

"True," Ani agrees. "But unfortunately for this morning it's down to you three, which means I need one of you or Finn and I'm gonna bet you don't want to be separated from him just yet."

Ani runs loving fingers through Grayson's feathery hair. "Ugh, no. But this is unfair for the record."

Johnny takes that as his cue to run off, "Thanks guys!" and it's just us three left.

"I'll make sure you're both exempt from dinner dishes," Ani says. "How's that?"

"Yeah, I guess that's fine," Grayson says, slinging himself off the chair, while I wonder how I got nominated. I was totally fine with it being Grayson and Johnny doing the dishes.

I get up too though, I'm too new to complain. "So where's everyone from?" I ask as we wash and dry and put away.

"Will grew up in the south, but it doesn't take a genius to figure that out. His mom's Canadian though, so he's got dual citizenship," Grayson explains. "I'm from here too, but both my parents are from the UK. We still have a home there."

"Ah, I detected a small bit of accent," I say.

"Yeah but his poshness is all—"

"—quiet Ani, jeez."

"You're going to have to tell him at some point, honey," Ani says. "But I'm sorry, I'll leave you to doing that."

Grayson's scowling though and won't talk anymore. "What about you, Ani?" I ask.

"Born and raised in Canada. My father was a strong, Plains-Cree and my mother is Métis, her First Nations' heritage also happens to be Plains-Cree."

That explains his amazing hair.

"Bellamy and Christopher flew here from Eastern Canada. Johnny Rae grew up here in Vancouver, but both of his parents are from Japan."

"And Bray?"

"His dad is a tall Scott if you can believe it, who moved straight from the UK to Canada where he met Bray's mama, who's African-American," Ani says.

"No, I can believe it. I detected an accent there too." A really cool one. I love accents. "I'm boring, born and raised here too, though my mom was an American."

"I'm sorry, Finny. Did you lose your mama?" Ani says drying a plate and returning it to the cupboard.

It's a question I get often, one I'm never sure how to answer, because I know when people hear the next part, they get all weird, no matter what I say. Best to get it over with though. "She died shortly after I was born. I never knew her. Dad's gone too," I add to get that out of the way and hope they'll tell others for me. I have a harder time with that one.

"I'm sorry, baby. I know what it's like to lose a parent," Ani says and thankfully leaves it at that, indicating he does know. "Overall, we're a bunch of crazy Canucks. Will's totally outnumbered."

"It's true," Grayson says. "But I do have a thing for burly, Texan cowboys, so sometimes I go easy on him."

Huh, those two. I don't know how to process them. My brain wants to label them, but maybe they don't need one?

"Good to know." I twirl my dishtowel and snap his ass with it. He turns around his mouth gaping, whatever words he's gonna say stalled on his tongue. I'm just as shocked at my own behavior, but I blame the House. They're infectious.

Grayson's shock changes to smug and his eyes flash a playful sheen. He begins winding up his towel. Ani sets his wooden spoon down on the counter between us, sending a clear warning. "I don't think so you two. No horseplay in the kitchen."

He doesn't even stay to make sure we'll cool it, but I guess he doesn't have to with an admonishment like that. He heads into the pantry, Grayson leans over. "There's a ton of horseplay in the kitchen. All about timing, Brighton."

I nod and then sink my hands into the soapy water. A frothy lightness consumes me and then pours out, like water spilling from a full cup. It's too much, yet not enough. I'm giddy. I'm nervous. I'm excited. *What's going to happen next?* becomes its own kind of emotion. One I barely remember, even though I've missed it.

I want to be part of the action.

"Can we hide that thing?" I whisper.

"We *can*. We can do whatever we want. The real question is, are we willing to suffer the consequence?"

Grayson checks toward the pantry, before plucking up

the spoon, going through the act of 'drying' it and putting it away in the drawer. "Don't say I never do anything for you, Brighton."

My body jitters delighted, waiting for Ani to return and notice as we do up the rest of the dishes. "By the way, what's wrong with the dishwasher? S'it broken?" We're doing the dishes the manual way.

"Don't even start on that one. A lost cause around here. Both Ani and Will agree dishes are some sort of bonding experience we need." He takes a pan from me to dry.

"Gotcha."

Too soon, Ani returns. "All right, where is it?"

"Hmmmm?" Grayson says.

"My spoon, Grayson. Where did you put it?"

"Oh. You didn't want us to dry and put it away?"

Ani knows which drawer to fish it out of. "You want to be a wise guy? Put your hands on the counter, Grayson."

"What? Ask Finn. He watched me dry it with his eyes." Ani crosses his arms, not moving. "Oh, c'mon, Ani. It was a joke." But he does place his hands flat on the countertop and stick his bottom out.

Ani slides Grayson's oversized shirt up his back, pulling down his pants and boxers. I'm not the one being spanked, but man does it feel like it. The hotness of *that feeling,* the unnamable one I can never quite describe or articulate, rockets through me. I shouldn't watch, but I *have* to, biting my lip all the while.

"This bum needs a break. You'd think you'd behave yourself this morning after yesterday."

Ani lands five successive smacks to each cheek. Grayson winces and hisses contracting his body. "Jesus, Animki!"

Ani rubs and pulls up his pants for him. "Be a good boy, Graysie."

Ani brings him in for a hug, and Grayson takes the opportunity to wink at me. Ah, I get it: consequences. We can goof off all we want, but there are real and immediate ramifications around here if we do. Not all of them serious. Many of them fun.

"I will, Ani."

Ani laughs. "We'll see. *Finn.*"

I jump. I was not expecting to be called on. "Uh, yeah?"

"Don't think I don't know you were part of that. The only reason you're not bent over with your bare bum out, is because I have a soft spot for the pretty, green-eyed, new guy. But that's the only warning you're getting. Work you two."

Whoa. That takes the breath out of me. I want ... I want more of that, no matter how humiliating.

He's walking off again, my eyes follow him awestruck. "How did he know?" I whisper to Grayson.

"They always know, Brighton. They always bloody know. It's irksome and oddly comforting. Half the time you want them to know, even when you don't want them to know."

"What?" That doesn't make a lick of sense.

"Don't worry about it. I have so much to teach you. There's time."

And I want to learn. I get back to my task, the buzz of *that feeling* kindling yet more excitement for whatever's to come, and if I need more of it, I just look to the spoon Ani left for us on the counter.

***

We finish and I'm dismissed to head up to do things like shower and call Sam who'll be freaking out about now. "Finn, I was going to call you if you didn't call me soon. How was the orientation with Xavier?"

How much do I tell him about that? How much does he want to know? He knows what this school is all about, but does he want to know the gory details? In any case, I'm not ready to share them. "Things are good. They went well with Xavier and I think I've made some friends."

I tell him my take on everyone in the House so far and touch a little on the rules since I know he'll be curious. He listens to every word, only a few 'uh-huhs' and 'yeahs' interspersed until I'm done gushing. "I'm so glad, Finn. We still on for the weekend?"

"Yep, looking forward to it."

I make sure I'm dressed decently, since I'll be seeing Xavier, and I head out to get my book. I don't see anyone on my way out, and I don't go looking either.

When I get to his office, the butterflies are there, ramming around like heavy ball-bearings with wings. *Calm down, Finn.* I can't help it though, he's my disciplinarian now *and* I think I might have a crush on him.

Is that okay? Can you crush on your disciplinarian? Fuck. Is that normal?

In any case, the swirl of sensations does a lot of things to me inside and I'm not sure I'll ever be near him without my heart knocking against my ribcage, like I'm about to jump off a cliff. I'm admitted by his receptionist, and when I enter, I start at seeing the bright-red bottom standing in the corner. *Am I supposed to be seeing this?* But I was told to enter.

The boy—as we're called, even if none of us are boys at all, you have to be twenty-five at minimum to be eligible for Xavier's school—is standing with his nose in the corner of the red wall, his pants pulled down below an ass that's got to fucking throb, clearly on display. His hands are laced atop his head, his legs are spread wide as they can go.

God, I could stare at his thickly muscled ass for days. Can't help it. Not only is it gorgeous, it's well-spanked. I'm not at this school by accident, I'm aware of my spanking thing, even if I'm new to other aspects. Spanking, everything to do with it, has always caught my attention, maybe most especially when it's in an embarrassing fashion, like this.

I can't stop the thought: that's going to be me someday whether I like it or not. I'll be in trouble, it's inevitable, and then I'll be in the corner like this guy, red ass out for anyone Xavier allows in, to see.

Although all of this was outlined in detail, the words alone are enough to have me flush with hot embarrassment, *seeing* brings it to a new level.

If you're going to do something worthy of punishment, don't expect to be given privacy over it. That someone else might walk in to see you, in such a depraved position, is an excellent additional deterrent.

It works—knowing punishments aren't required to be private—I'm well and truly deterred. Yet, I'm so fucking curious as to what it will feel like to be in that position. It's only a matter of time.

Xavier clears his throat from where he is behind the desk. "Mr. Brighton."

Oh my god you were staring, Finnegan. I turn to see his smirking face, amused. "Sir. Hi."

"You're not in trouble, though the day is young. Sit."

I'm quick to do so in one of the brown, soft leather chairs, with the all too real threat of what's on the table for disobedience looking at the wall. Feeling sorry for buddy in the corner but fucking glad I'm not him, I sit and run a hand through my hair, make sure my posture's a little taller, and second guess my choice of dress. I love white t-shirts and a nice pair of jeans, but maybe I'm underdressed?

"That's Emmery. Emmery, Finn's here," he says.

Emmery doesn't dare turn around. "Hey, Finn. Tell Grayson he was wrong."

"Mr. Thompson. I gave you leave to greet Mr. Brighton, not to chat."

"Sorry, sir."

Xavier is smiling though; he lives for this. He takes his place before me, leaning against his desk, crossing his ankle over the shin of his other leg, spreading his arms to either side of him, palms on the desk. His wild hair manages to be cheeky, defiant of the rest of his tidy attire. If a ruler were a person, it would be named Xavier and no line would ever be crooked again. I suppose that's why his hair continues to fascinate me, it's juxtaposition to the rest of him, an unsolved mystery.

Jesus. I'm staring again, this time at him, working to keep my mouth closed so I don't gape at him. Feeling it inside is one thing, but I can't let on about this stupid, burning attraction I have for him. I look away but fuck, there's no denying it, I have the hugest school-boy crush on Xavier. He's more than my type, he's my type on steroids. I've got to squash that shit fast. I can't fall for my disciplinarian, I just can't. Not to mention, there's no chance someone like him would ever have interest in someone like me. There are so many other men here more suited for him.

And how do you know what suits him, Finnegan?

Shut up, brain.

"How was your first night? Grayson didn't scare you off, did he?"

I'm surprised he'd say Grayson. "Grayson? I'm pretty sure I'm about to become his second teddy bear for when Will's not around, sir."

"Really? That's unexpected. Ask Christopher what Grayson did to him on his first night. I suppose that means I'm not the only one enchanted with you," he says, winking.

I shiver in the best way, and fiddle with my t-shirt, tempted to shove my hands into my pockets. "I didn't realize I was so magical, sir."

Stifled giggles come from the corner. "All right Mr. Thompson, pants up and c'mere," Xavier says.

Emmery races over, colliding with Xavier's torso. "I'm sorry, sir."

Xavier presses him close. "Come now, it's over. You're going to be a good boy, yes?"

Emmery nods, his tumble-y mane of dark hair nodding with him. He's about my size and fits well in Xavier's arms.

Watching them, a feeling grows and it's not a good one. It's one that bubbles, and churns sickly in my gut: jealousy. I don't like the feeling. There's no need for it, yet it's there, which is illogical. Xavier isn't mine. I'm 'one of his,' but I am not *his*.

I try to relax my balled fists, even when Xavier kisses Emmery's head, but I can't, needing the tactile distraction. I squeeze them harder.

"Off you go brat," Xavier says and for the first time, I *want* to be a brat.

A smile sweeps across Emmery's face just for him before they part, then he looks to me. "See ya around, Prince Finn," he says, laughing.

Wha...? Oh, the 'enchanted' comment. "Funny," I say pursing my lips. "See you Friday?"

I'm making an assumption. Any man at the school can be sent to Xavier for discipline—and truly, any man can be disciplined by any Top he crosses—but there's something in the way they interact, it's the same thing making the jealousy show its ugly head.

Which I fucking hate, because I think I'm going to like Emmery and I don't want to have to say I have these jealous feelings about him. "See you Friday," he says, his eyes twinkling with mischief.

When he's gone, I fiddle with my shirt more, shove a hand in my pocket and then let go of my shirt to run the hand through the long part of my hair on top. Can Xavier tell what I'm feeling? It might as well be plastered all over me in neon. Maybe if I run away, he'll never see it. I make myself stare straight ahead, willing my feelings away, but Xavier smiles after Emmery and scorching jealousy smolders through me all over again. *Pull it to-fucking-gether, Brighton.*

"It sounds like your first night went well. I'd hate to lose you, Finnegan. I pick my boys carefully, especially the ones I take on personally."

That soothes a bit of the ache in my chest. "I was overwhelmed at first, sir, but everyone made me feel like I already belong."

He nods. "Very well. I'll trust that to continue. I still have six days to concern myself with, though." Is he worried I'll leave? "Until tomorrow then."

"Tomorrow, sir?"

His face cracks into a smile; I've played into his hand. "I've elected to check up on you daily, Mr. Brighton."

"Daily?" I don't bother to hide my whine.

70

"Yes. Problem?"

"No, sir." It seems excessive to be honest, but this is about what he thinks is best; that's why I came here. "I just can't help feeling like I'm in trouble."

"You're not. You'll know when you are, which if I get any more cheekiness when I ask you to do something, you will be." His voice is firm, carrying notes of caution.

I look down and bite my lip at his scolding. God that voice does things to me. "Yes, sir," I mumble.

"Eyes up here, Finnegan." I snap my head up. "So, tempted as I am to spank you again, I'd better work you in slowly."

My jaw drops. "But sir, I've been good."

"You have. Good boys deserve spankings too."

"How many different kinds of spankings are there, sir?"

"You'll find out in due time. Now, carry on before I change my mind."

I'm warm all over, how can all this spanking *activity* liven me so? My already pleasant mood lifts. "Yes, sir. Getting out of here, sir."

I half-expect a hug at this point. I may even be disappointed when I don't get one.

CHAPTER FOUR

I look up to the conspicuous majesty, her sturdy arm outreached. "We climb."

He's giddy at the prospect. "I like the way you think Brighton. Attic?"

"Yes. We'll slip in through the attic and no one will know we weren't in bed. Will's not home yet and Ani doesn't usually check unless we don't make it down for breakfast."

"Genius. Just one thing, what if Ani did check?"

"We're screwed, obviously. It's worth a shot though, don't you think?" I *can't* get sent to Xavier's office. Not with the warning I got and not with how concerned he's been. I'll have to admit he was right, which he annoyingly always is, and then he'll be the watchdog from hell.

"Totally worth a shot. Let's do it," Grayson says.

I start up the tree, which isn't easy with my broken hand, another problem for later. This tree has always been a source of wonderment for me. When I first moved to the House two years ago, I noticed everyone and everything had a place it fit, no matter how odd. Even each of the random assortment of magnets on the fridge mean something to somebody.

They belong.

This tree though. It's tall as the house with an expansive network of branches. Mostly, it's just there. Growing. Overlooking, perhaps? but I'm still sure it's an outsider wanting to get in. No one sits under it—even though we could—and no one talks about it, even though we look at it every day.

But now, it's the tree Gray and I used to sneak into the house that one time—I'm surprised more of us don't—and it's come into our sphere. Once you're in our sphere, you're in and we'll love you forever, even on your worst days.

"Why don't we talk about this tree?" I ask as we begin the climb in darkness. Him first, so he can help me up, compensating for my injured hand. The tree shakes, moving, almost as if it's adjusting to fit us.

Gray understands me, the thing I like best about him: he knows how my brain thinks with all its odd inner workings. He shrugs. "We will now."

Yes. We will.

It's Wednesday, the first day of classes. The house is chaotic as everyone rushes around looking for things that have suddenly gone missing, bickering, and being ordered around by Will and Ani.

Being as it's Xavier's school, we're all required to dress in uniform, which keeping in tone with the school, is a tad on the embarrassing side. For the *Taken in Hand*, it's shorts that go to just above mid-thigh instead of pants, and tall socks that stop at the swell of the calve. We'll be permitted pants for the winter months, which will be announced with the changing weather, but for now, it's shorts with tall socks giving us a younger look. Another one of those little details, which delineates us from the Tops. The top half of the uniform is a white, long-sleeved button-up shirt, with a navy blazer over top, embossed with the school's crest on the right side.

When I saw myself in the mirror, fully dressed for the first time, I flushed with a hint of the kind of embarrassment that gives me the good tingles. I remember the guy I saw, all those years ago, wearing a similar outfit—there have been minor changes to it since—he had a playful twinkle in his eyes. I'd say he was proud to wear the uniform and I am too, even with the hint of embarrassment that's not likely to go away anytime soon.

It's odd to see Grayson dressed so crisply. He has a nice shape to him, which I could feel was there, but it's the first time it's been revealed to me. His hair bounces away on top of his head, refusing to participate in any of this 'proper' nonsense, even if in some ways Grayson's kinda proper.

"You look good, Finnegan Charles," he says, newly fascinated with my middle name, which he learned last night. He leans in and we come together in a kiss. It's a chaste one, one of friendship, with the foreshadow of something more.

I want to chase that more.

"Gray! *Grayson.* You were fiddlin' 'round with my tie last night," Will says. "Where did you put it?"

Grayson pulls away from me. "I gave it right back to you, you hung it over the bed frame, remember?"

"Right, thanks darlin'. Whoa! Finny. You look sharp," Will says.

"Thanks." I've never been good at compliments. "You too."

Will isn't a professor, but he is a Top. He gets to wear pants. Another reminder for us taken in hand, of his status which is equal, but not the same. Taken in Hand is the official, legal jargon used, but the Taken in Hand around here seem to prefer the term, 'brat.' Take immense pride in it, even.

I have no idea why.

Ani is wearing shorts, and it furthers the mystery I've been attempting to solve on my own before I finally ask, since that's the only way I seem to understand the things I'm feeling at gut level. Ani is an authority in the house— there's no question about that—but he's more to the Taken in Hand side of things from what I've observed. I haven't been able to articulate it in full.

I start to devise a poll bar in my mind with 'brat' on one end, 'Bellamy' in brackets beside, and 'Ani' at the other. It's some kind of spectrum from a Bellamy to an Ani. Where do I live on this spectrum?

The uniform is stunning on Ani, the socks fit snug over his massive calves and I'm reminded of the physique I know is there, the one I admired forever at breakfast this morning when he was shirtless again. His long hair is braided, hanging heavily down his wide back. "Oh honey, you're gorgeous," he says to me, but I should be saying it to him.

"Thank you. I clean up all right, I guess."

"Remember when you're out there on your own today, we're around, never far away and we're still yours no matter where you are." Then he kisses me too, and it's different from Grayson's kiss, with some similar notes of *more for later*.

"Bellamy! Give me that back right now!" someone (Chris I think) shouts, from the top of the stairs followed by heavy footfalls barreling downward.

Bellamy zips through the living room and runs smack into Will.

"What in the name of Pete is going on, Bellamy Francis?" Ani says as Will crosses his arms and does a good impression of a brick wall.

"He took my lucky boxers," Christopher says, entering the living room, his dong flopping around everywhere, since he didn't bother to put other bottoms on.

Will spins Bellamy around giving a loud smack to his thinly clad ass. "Give them back."

"*Ow*. We used to have fun around here," Bellamy says, but he does give them back to Christopher.

"Not first thing in the morning," Will says, not done with him, laying a crisp set of smacks to the seat of his pants.

"Ow! Ow! Ow!" Bellamy rubs his ass, glaring at Will like he didn't deserve it, but we all know he did—even him, if he cared to admit it.

No one feels sorry for him, especially not Will. "Finish getting ready without the antics, or there's a lot more where that came from."

Bellamy heads off grumbling about places of no fun, while Christopher yanks the boxers over his ass, which is still a healthy shade of red from the spanking he got from his Top, Professor Lancaster; he's been in a better mood ever since.

"Why isn't that hair tied back, Christopher?" Ani asks. "You want me to come up and do it for you, honey?"

"Would you? Always looks nicer when you do it."

"Glad to, sweetheart. Don't you go anywhere without saying bye to me like you did the last time, Finnegan."

Boy did I hear from him about that one. "Wouldn't dream of it, Ani. Besides, Will told us he wants us all to meet at the front door this morning before he's letting us leave." I sit myself down on the pale green couch, placing my book bag down beside it.

It's not long after they've gone off in one direction, Bray comes in with a crisis for Ani from another. "Where's Ani? My jacket's ripped; needs fixin'." Bray's thick braids move with him in an organized way from where they sit on top of his head. He's shirtless, his dark brown skin smooth and toned, a gorgeous set of abs trailing into his school shorts.

"Well, this is a fine time to ask for a repair," Will says.

"Just happened."

"Wear another one," Will says.

"They're all in a state of similar repair."

"Stephen Bray. This is something you sort before the start of school, not the day of."

"I thought I had this one." He shrugs.

"We'll be talking later. Go pick one of mine for today."

He gets spun around for several smacks to his bum, which have him scowling, but it's clear he's appreciative of the blazer and maybe even the correction if the way his body relaxes, is anything to go by. It's on a subconscious level; I relax too as the chaos in everyone is sorted.

"Good Lord, this house. If we get out on time, that'll be the miracle. Where's Johnny?"

"We haven't seen him since breakfast," Grayson says, answering for the both of us, like we're one unit now. He's been my shadow. He collected his clothes and brought them to my room to get ready with me this morning. Yes, he appeared in nothing but his boxers. No there wasn't anything I could do about it.

"I better make sure he's not doing something that'll make us all late. Although maybe I should let the people of this house be late and suffer the consequences. I'd catch it too, but it'd be worth it," he grumbles as he heads off, his blond, chin-length hair, down and wavy, flowing behind him. He's still got the gait of a cowboy, all dressed up like that. He calls behind to us, "You two stay there."

"You gonna tell us what the meeting at the door nonsense is about, William?" Grayson says, but he doesn't get an answer; he's gone.

Grayson climbs into my lap, leaning his head against my shoulder, like we've done it a million times, his body slackening as he gets comfortable. Maybe I should feel weird about how close we are after only a few days, but I don't.

When he's settled, I take the spare moments to look over my schedule, my *new* schedule, which I'm still fucking sore about. During my last meeting with Xavier, he sprang it on me.

"Oh, by the way, here. Your new schedule," he said, knowing full well I was going to have a reaction.

"New? What was wrong with the old one?" I took the new one from him appre-fucking-hensively, already not liking it, even though I had no idea what it said.

"You are here to accept my guidance, are you not?"

"Well yeah, but—"

"It was wrong for you."

Sam and I picked that schedule together. We decided on general studies, since I had no idea what I wanted to do and Sam and I both agreed on ample down time. I chose the three-course option; an art class with two others.

"There are five classes on this one, sir."

"I know. I wrote it up personally," he said. Yes he was being facetious.

I thought I had an easy out. "I can't afford the extra books, sir. Sorry." I pushed the schedule back toward him. It's the same tuition cost whether you take three courses or seven, but you're expected to pay for textbooks on your own dime.

"They're included," he said. "They'll be dropped off tonight."

Dammit. "But sir, I've done homework for two of the classes that are no longer on here."

"You have, which was a smart move on your part. It wasn't time wasted, some of the point of it was forming the habit. You'll have a bit of catch up with the new classes, but plenty of time to do it, not to worry."

I wasn't worried about it, I just didn't want more classes, but I didn't have another acceptable excuse. "I don't want to take five courses, sir. Can't we talk about this?"

"I understand, but if I were you, I would get used to the fact that you are." That was the first time Xavier had shown any kind of annoyance with me. I didn't like it.

I responded with snark. "Why? No one else had their schedule changed." I crossed my arms and slumped in his large brown, leather chair, which I swear felt colder that day than usual. Yeah, it was a full-on pout session.

"First, I will remind you that you are not the others— you are you and I will make decisions for *you* accordingly. Second, you came here to be challenged did you not?"

"Well yeah, but—"

"—and you agreed to submit to my authority, yes?"

"Yes, sir, but—"

"—no buts. You will do it and you will lose the attitude, or I shall help you lose the attitude."

'Help' means spanking around this place as Grayson often points out. I took up the sheet again to read the schedule over a second time. My brow pressed together. "I'm not, I'm not …" I had to take a breath; it still came out as barely a whisper. "I'm not smart enough to take these courses, Xavier."

He set his pen down to meet my eyes. "You will need to work at some of them, yes, but not because you're not smart enough. I've booked you time with Osh. He's going to tutor you when you need it and it will give you the opportunity to spend time with my other boys at Sigma Phi. Either way, you'll meet him at the specified times to do homework."

I got the memo: the schedule change was non-negotiable, and it did cross my mind that I still had three days to exit the contract. "Yes, sir. May I go now?"

"You may. Be here tomorrow at four pm."

It was hard not to stomp out of there and I surprised myself going to Grayson rather than calling my brother. I knew Grayson would commiserate, and boy did he. "How dare he change your schedule like that! It's just the sort of dictatorial thing a Top does."

But while we each knocked back a beer and complained about Top antics, we both knew inside that the decision Xavier made had been the right one. That didn't take away my fear, or the mean-boy in my head who really believes I can't do it, bombarding me with negative thoughts at every turn. The same guy was responsible for my near meltdown in Xavier's office, staved off only by Xavier's firm direction and the knowledge that I didn't have a choice.

That brought comfort. So odd.

When Will found us, we were six sheets to the wind. He sobered us up, spanked us both and sent us to bed early. When Will came in to say goodnight, he found me crying. "What if I can't do it, Will?"

"Oh darlin'," he said, climbing on the bed, cuddling me close. "Xavier never gives us anything that's too much to handle. Hard maybe, but never more than. Besides, everyone's gonna help you. That's what we're here for. You just gotta let us."

Will soothed me enough before he left. I woke up the next morning refreshed, but now, it seems more logical to tear the paper up, pretend I never saw it and move ahead as per my original plan. Or maybe there's some angle I missed, maybe there's still time to change his mind.

"You feeling better about that now?" Grayson asks, inspecting it too from where he is on my lap.

I'm not excited, but I'm not as freaked about it as I was. It's digesting. I do feel something about it though, which I haven't been able to put into words but it's galvanizing like butter melting within me, near ready to sizzle. I set my jaw firm. "I'll be fine."

"Fucksake, Finn," Grayson says, looking over his shoulder, making sure Will didn't hear him say that. "My head still hurts from the beer last night, and if you need to do it again, I'm here for you, but don't let it drive you crazy. *Talk* to someone."

"I talked to Will about it last night. Was helpful."

"Ahh. You need more than talking then. This is a job for Xavier, and I'm not touching it," he says, climbing off my lap as I bend over to slip my new schedule into my day planner, which I tuck into my book bag.

"What's that supposed to mean?"

I don't get to find out. Will returns, wrangling Johnny who's pissed. "I keep telling you, I would have been down right when we had to go."

"Not how it works. Sit there. One, two three ... why am I so many short?" Ani returns with Chris. "Okay, six includin' me. Where are Bells and Bray?"

"We're here," Bray says, Will's blazer a little big on him.

"Wonders never cease, we're making it out of here on time," Will says.

"What's with this togetherness bullcrap?" Grayson asks. "We never have to leave together like this."

"It's not a thing yet, but it was brought up during the Head of House meeting. Xavier might roll out a new rule that we all leave together. It's to help cultivate family, being responsible to each other, that kind of stuff."

"That's stupid," Bellamy says.

"I agree," Grayson says.

"I kinda do too," Christopher says. "I know exactly who's going to make us all late."

Bickering breaks out over Chris's comment, everyone thinking everyone else is blaming them.

"Y'all, hush," Will says, and waits till we do. "That's why I didn't want to say anything. It's not mandated yet. We were all told to give it a try and report back."

"Good, tell them we don't like it," Bray says.

"Unfortunately, not the kind of feedback Xavier's looking for. In any case, never mind about it for now. All right Star Crew, let's roll out."

CHAPTER FIVE

I tumble into the attic, because I only have one fucking good hand. *Why, oh why, do you do these things Finnegan?* I have no answer for myself. But my brain has one for its own question. *You want to get caught.* I would argue, but it might be true. It's been two years of living this lifestyle and while I've learned a thing or two about myself in that time, there are some things I have to work out in the worst way possible.

It sounds easy enough to have a problem and to work out said problem by approaching another who might have helpful advice, or even serve as a great sounding board, but that's all cerebral stuff. Feelings live in the body. There are a few ways to work these feelings out, methods employed by many like yoga, weightlifting, going for a run, just to name a few. But for me it's spanking. Spanking is—for reasons I still don't know—the fastest way for me to work out feelings, especially the hard ones.

But can I simply walk up to any of the people who will gladly give me a spanking and ask? *NoooOoooh.* Life would be so much easier if I could. Ani's good at that for the most part; I need to take a page from his book.

Grayson climbs in behind me, while I pray our tumbling didn't wake anyone and rejoice that we've made it into the house. Ha! We're home free. I spring up and move to open the door, but it's locked. Of course, it is. I scrub a hand over my face. I'm running out of ideas.

"Won't open, eh? Hmmm, maybe we can find something to pick the lock with in all of this junk?"

The attic is filled with old boxes of junk. We don't come up here much. Sometimes to find that odd or end Ani needs, or to grab extra blankets and dish ware stored here. It's got a vaulted ceiling, and creaky floorboards, which means we have to step lightly.

"Yes. Yes! That's genius. You good at lock picking?" I move boxes, searching, coughing at the plumes of dust. A dull throb in my hand grows, letting me know I might need to take more painkillers.

"No, but that's what the internet is for, I'm sure we'll find a video online that'll show us the way."

I take a breath, we're close. So close. At least we're in the house. This house is my home now, and that's no insult to Sam, it's just, my home with him hasn't been home in a long while—I was just the leech who lived there. Here? I know I'm supposed to be here. Being home is the safest place there is, even with the imminent threat of spanking around every corner. It might even be what makes this place safe—not that I'll ever say that out loud; that's not how it's done.

I close my eyes, taking a moment to inhale the scent of our house, the unique one that's ours, the one I can't smell anymore unless I really take the time to notice. I can't possibly smell it, because I'm part of it now, and you can't smell your own scent, but I have faith it's there.

Fresh rain.

I inhale it in gulps.

My first class is with a heavy-set African man, his hair cut to marine precision, with unforgiving eyes, yet somehow I know he'll fucking hug me the moment a spanking is done. It's just the kind of place this is. "Take your seats everyone," he says, with the hint of an accent. "We have a lot to cover. Every minute lost after the bell rings in taking your seats, is a lick with my strap for the whole class, which will make you late to your next class, which I'm sure your next professor will appreciate just as much as I do."

The men scramble after that to take their seats; no one is standing by the time the bell rings. Each class has a strict professor and a good portion of the first class in each is spent going over protocol and consequences. I follow suit writing down notes on each when I see that everyone else is.

No one from my House is in any of my classes today and there isn't time for friend-making. I'm considered a first year and am the only first year in my House. I get a lot of time to ruminate on things. The rules are the least of my worries, it's the syllabus of each class, especially the new ones Xavier wants me to take that have me tied up in knots. I don't think I'll be able to do them.

Although, I wish I could. They sound interesting, they're skills I'd like to have, but I've never been good at school. Unfortunately, school is a requirement to come here and the thought of going to classes seemed like a happy little idea at the time.

I'm spent by the end of the day, after all the classes, irritated after winding myself up about how I won't be able to pass any of these classes and the last thing I want to do is meet with Xavier. What I want to do is to pass out in my room. I head to Xavier's though, since I don't want to find out what the consequence for pulling a no show would be and hope the meeting's a short one.

When I arrive, he's with another first year I recognize from one of my classes today, Eric I think, and that combined with my level of tired ratchets my irritation up a couple levels. A more rational me knows he's running a whole school, and this is normal, but I don't care right now. Why not tell me to come back later? Or at least allow me to wait outside so I can be on my phone or something?

He pauses to take stock of me, and I get tired of waiting for him to say something. "I can come back later, sir."

See? Polite. I'm so fucking polite.

"I see, Mr. Brighton. Allow me to save you from yourself. Over there, facing that corner will work just fine for me."

But it doesn't work fine for me! I want to shout it at him, but I don't want to throw a tantrum in front of Eric. I also know Tops think corner time, which includes time facing walls, is helpful to ones like me, 'saving' us from the spankings we're on our way to earning, but it's also time for thinking after a spanking, or even before you're about to receive a spanking. I head to the corner, unable to stop the tears of frustration from falling. "Finnegan, do I need to show you proper corner position?"

I know him well enough in just the few days I've been

here to know that's Xavier for: *if I have to show you something you should know by now, there will be consequences.* "No, sir," I answer, lacing my hands on top of my head, spreading my legs. I glare at the red wall grateful he can't see my face.

"Thank you, brat."

A wave of something goes through me with *brat*. It's still not a term I've called myself, I'm still not sure I am, but I'm less opposed to it than I was. I am soothed by his praise. *So fucking typical, Finnegan.*

I should be enraged, but I can't find it in me. I am distracted knowing someone's in the room, while I stand in the corner, in position. At the same time, it's already happened so much in the house, I'm not as shocked to find myself in this position as I might have been only four days ago. When you're staring at a wall, you can't help but put focus on things that are gnawing at you. Things you could normally distract yourself from.

It's my upset over the scheduling changes making me weepy and frustrated; I'm overwhelmed. I'd rather go home to sulk about it in a ball on my bed where I can pretend this problem doesn't exist.

"Okay, my Finnegan," Xavier says, once he's finished with Eric and when he's gone. *My Finnegan.* Don't read too much into that shit Finn. "You may come out now."

When I turn, all I see are his open arms and I run for them, colliding with his torso, just like Emmery did. Then I cry. "You knew I'd be like this," I say, making his vest wet.

"Yes. Changing your schedule was big. I also knew you needed the night to digest it and apparently, get drunk with Grayson on a school night."

"Ugh. Does Will tell you everything?"

"Everything. Blame me, it's a rule."

I nod into his chest, liking it here very much. I don't want to leave. Xavier is solid, and I forever want something this solid beneath me. But too soon, I'm taken by the hand to a chair I'm familiar with. He grips it, spinning it on his palm with practiced precision, it lands in the spot that belongs to it. "What? Why?" Some of the, 'this is so unfair' feelings return.

"Because you need it, love. C'mon, you'll feel better."

"How on Earth did you come to that horribly wild conclusion?" I say.

But he's already unbuttoning my school shorts. "You'll see. Blazer off."

Wiping at my wet face, I remove my blazer as he pulls down my shorts and boxers in one motion, my ass bare to the room. I hold my blazer out to him, and he hangs it off the chair. He guides me over his lap and soon I'm in the same position as last night when I was over Will's lap. "Wow, William was not pleased about the drinking on a school night."

"He was not, sir." He borrowed Ani's wooden spoon, since we were in the kitchen when he found out about our ill-conceived way of dealing with our problems on a school night. I faced a wall while Grayson was spanked. Johnny, who was there, muttered about idiots, but I could tell he felt sorry for us.

"This is going to hurt I'm afraid."

"I doubt you're afraid, sir."

"You've got me. There's little I like more than spanking a firm, round bottom; especially when it's already pink like this."

I roll my eyes at his glee, glad he can't see me do it. He

rubs my tender flesh. "Sometimes I call this a thinking spanking, but I think today it's more for letting go, don't you agree?"

That's ... yeah. That's what all this—the *this* being the mess wrapped around my heart—feels like, something I need to get rid of. I chose a school schedule that was easy and Sammy, well-intended, didn't give a word of opposition. Not that Sam's responsible, he's not, I'm a grown adult, but he's a 'yes-person' in my life. I came here to have 'no-people' who will kick my ass when I'm not living up to my potential. I'll never push myself beyond the barrier where fear's holding me.

But Xavier will.

I need that to be able to let go.

It's hard and I'll hate him for it sometimes, but it is what I want. "I didn't think I could pull off five classes. I'm still not sure I can," I admit. "But I want to let go of thinking I'm too stupid to try."

"Good. That's my boy. It's a process, Finn, remember that. You're bound to feel this way again, but each time, you can let go just a little bit more. We're all going to help you. You don't have to do it by yourself, and you don't have to feel like you're a burden."

Like he does, he cuts right to the quick. That's exactly how I always feel with Sammy. He's more than willing to help, but I feel like a burden he got stuck with, so I keep it all to myself. Only, it ends up making me more of a burden.

He starts in hard. Why so fucking hard? I was spanked less than twenty-four hours ago. But already, the heightened sensation has the edges of reality blurring, and somehow that floaty place eases my grip on ... what was I here for? Right, courses I didn't want. I don't need. Things become crisp again and as if Xavier can tell, his hand lands stronger and sharper. Then he pauses to rub for me, as I collapse over his thighs, my heart dashing like it does when I'm gliding down the ice on a breakaway.

"Sir. That hurts." I wipe at the wetness coming from my eyes, teetering off balance until my fingertips are tented, pressing against the floor to steady me.

"I know. It's supposed to." He continues to rub. "How are you doing, Mr. Brighton?"

I'm—oh wow, I'm good. My ass is on fire, but I'm good. "Mmmmmhmmm."

He chuckles. "Oh really? I knew you were made for this."

"Sir? I'm ready to get up now."

"Oh no you don't. I decide that. Besides, you need to answer my questions." Dammit. "Tell me about trying."

Ugh, talking. This is a spanking, shouldn't that automatically let me off the hook of talking? "It's not gonna kill me to try, okay? Happy?"

I can't see him from this position, but I swear I can feel his eyes like lasers, burning through the back of me—but like soft lasers, the kind that also care about you. "I see. No, I'm not happy."

He spanks again, his hand connecting sharply with my bare ass, and I have to kick to relieve the sting, releasing muffled grunts and cries. He only spanks on. I don't give in; I refuse to let up. I tighten my jaw to hold back other noises I want to release, I contract all my muscles, which only makes it hurt more.

As the pain grows, something snaps inside me, or maybe it's more like a knot untying, giving slack to the rope I'm tethered to.

And I let go.

He hasn't stopped spanking, it doesn't hurt less, but I stop fighting.

I shift when the smacks get to be too much on one cheek —Jesus Xavier, spread it out, man—but now that I've let go inside, the pain of it's an odd comfort, wrapping around me, draping me in bliss. In this place, trying doesn't seem so hard. It doesn't anger me.

"Finn? You still there?" His voice is deep, cutting through the layers I've travelled while he spanked away.

"I'm here, sir." My voice is groggy, cracking in places.

He rubs my back and the tender flesh of my ass. "Shall we try that again?"

"Mmmmhmmm. I mean, sir? Trying doesn't seem so bad anymore."

"Oh?"

"Yeah. I don't know why, it's just melted away. And well, you got me, right? If I fail, you got me?"

"Of course, my Finnegan." But he said it again. My Finnegan. *Still no, Finn.* "Let's finish up and then we'll chat."

I stifle a groan but prepare myself. He tilts me further forward, so that my thighs are more available and when his hand comes down there, I cry out, tears pricking my eyes. This fucking sucks, but I'm already looking forward to the relief it will bring. It clicks for me how this—getting a spanking—brought me to a place where I could surrender at warp speed. Struggle to win freedom.

Are there other ways to get here? Yeah. But for me this is Zen. I will never admit that out loud so long as I live.

When it's over, my face is hot and wet, but I'm a million times better, the world is a calmer place. "Why does that work?" I say. It's an infuriating conundrum.

"Isn't it enough that it does?"

When my boxers and shorts are back in place, and I'm encapsulated in one of Xavier's solid hugs, I let go some more, letting him carry all the heavy energy I pack with me, for just a moment. Though I think - I think a chunk of it really is gone. Floated away like a dandelion puff to wherever it is spanking takes things.

Xavier hands me his personal handkerchief. "Sit," he says. "I want to thank you for not throwing the fit you wanted to yesterday."

Sitting is unpleasant, but it's better in Xavier's soft leather chair than it will be on the hard, wooden chairs at the kitchen table later. "My drunken rebellion doesn't count?"

"It counts, and we'll discuss it during discipline on Friday, but I am pleased with William's care of the pair of you on that matter."

I smile. Maybe I should be worried about Friday, but I'm not.

"How was your first day of classes?" he says, leaning against his desk

I could be imagining what I want to see, but something new is in Xavier's eyes: softness and it's just for me. I lap it up. "Exhausting. All I wanted to do after was go home and die on my bed, but someone wouldn't let me."

"What a horrible sounding someone," he says. He walks over to me and smoothens an errant lock of hair, the one that won't stay put, behind my ear as I shift on my aching ass cheeks, enjoying the tingle his fingers leave behind. The two sensations marry together; backside ache, tenderness and I'm gone for him. I don't know how other people fall for people, but apparently this is what it is for me.

"All right. I suppose I have no more excuses to keep you, even if I'm not quite ready to have you gone. Enjoy the rest of your evening, Finnegan, and for your arse's sake, behave yourself."

I smirk. Behave has become our goodbye. "Yes, sir."

I try to hand his handkerchief back; he shakes his head. "Keep it. I've got more."

I head home, clutching my Xavier-kerchief, still floating on whatever cloud that spanking set me on. Once again, the after-spanking effects are lightness and airy joy. I don't get how it does this to me.

'Isn't it enough that it does?' Xavier'd said. Jury's still out on that one for me.

"Well, someone got a good spanking," Grayson says, when I walk in the door, and I duck my head, unable to look at anyone.

"Lordy be, Graysie, leave him alone. You do look good though, cowboy," Will says.

The pair are tangled together on the pale green couch; clearly, they missed each other today, which is sweet—it's not like they were apart for long. Will's blazer is off and shirt open, it looks like Grayson was working on Will's pants. "How was school, dearest Finnegan?" Grayson asks.

"Good, but exhausting. I'm going to lay down before I begin the mountain of homework I have."

"We should take this upstairs anyway, Graysie. We'll come with you to your room, so we can take care of your poor tushie."

"Will!" I say. Jeez.

"What's all the noise about?" Ani says, coming from the kitchen. His long hair is loose, a dish towel slung over his shoulder—Ani's work is never done around here.

"Finn needs his tushie taken care of," Grayson says, smirking at me.

Ass. We both know what he's doing.

"I have time. I'll do it," Ani says.

"Can't I just do it myself? I'm highly capable."

"We know all about how capable you are," Ani says. "He's mine. You two go finish whatever it is you were starting."

They head off to Will's room, and Ani takes me to mine. "On the bed, honey," Ani says, moving to the cupboard.

I know the drill by this point, but instead of pulling my shorts down, I pull them off, setting the handkerchief Xavier gave me on my desk. I lie on the bed.

Ani takes the time to warm the aloe between his palms, before spreading it onto my thankful cheeks. "Mmmmm, feels good Ani. Thank you."

"My pleasure, sweetie. You've got a cute bum."

On impulse, I reach out to grab a lock of his hair that's hanging over the top of me. His loose hair is wavy from being in the braid all day. "This has got to be the softest hair I've ever felt," I say, still enjoying the ass massage, kinda hoping he'll go further. I spread my legs in an attempt to look more enticing.

"It's like that is it, Finnegan B?"

I peer my head back at him and nod.

"We'll spend some time together, don't you worry. But for now, you'll have to settle for cuddling. Blazer and shirt off," he says, getting bossy.

I groan. "What is it with this house and all the hugging and the cuddling?" I say, but I do respond to his orders. You respond to Ani's orders in this house too.

There's a glint in his dark eyes as he fishes pajama pants from my drawers for me, holding the waistband and unfolding them in a quick snap. "You'll get used to us."

He proceeds to *dress* me like I'm a little kid, instructing me through putting one foot into the pants and then the other, with me holding onto him for support. "Coulda done that myself," I complain, but I haven't let go of him. He's shirtless, in a pair of soft jeans and his skin is warm against mine and I smell it again. *Fresh rain.*

Most people in this house do. *Is that our scent?* Every house has a scent. When I walk into my aunt Alice's house, it smells like lilacs and lilies with a hint of whatever incense she's burning. When I walk into my buddy Jeri's place, there's the overwhelming stench of pot. In your own home, you can't smell its scent, unless you leave it for long enough. When Sam and I came home from camping trips after Dad died—Sam trying to do the things we always did, trying to keep as much 'normal' as he could—it still smelled of whiskey and his cologne.

But then one day both were gone, and it was replaced by a new scent, a cleaner one that spoke more of Sam: organic laundry detergent and the lemon essential oils he liked to burn around the place. I hated that Dad had been cleaned out. I knew it wasn't on purpose, but it pissed me off all the same. I didn't mention it to Sam, because how crazy? 'It smells different in here, Sammy. Get the Dad smell back...?' No.

Besides, I'm probably the only one that notices stupid shit like that, like the way houses smell. But it is a universal truth and I know that's the scent I'll begin to carry with me. Soon I won't smell like organic laundry detergent and lemon essential oils, I'll smell like fresh rain.

"I know all about how you coulda. Get in the bed," he says, pulling back the sheets.

I give a withering look to his continued bossiness. At least I try to, but I'm not sure how 'withering' I look, getting put to bed. At least Ani climbs in with me, wrapping his strong arms around my torso. I nestle back toward his chest, reconsidering this cuddling thing. Maybe it's not so bad. "So what's your deal? Who's your Top?"

I can feel him smiling behind me. "I'll tell you all about it if you close your eyes. You need a nap and I need to get back to bossing people around enough so dinner gets made."

I would complain about the nap thing, but I'm too fucking tired. "Deal."

"My Top is Professor Ingalls, or Tom. This is my fifth year here, although I don't really plan on going away. I like going to school and I like taking care of a full house. Tom's happy for me to do it."

"Does that mean you and Tom are more than a contract?"

"Yes, as much as that means around here. You won't find too many monogamous sorts at this school. Xavier's as close as it comes, and he's not monogamous by definition."

That's surprising. "But, Xavier spanks everyone."

"For starters, spanking doesn't mean the same as sex to *everyone* even if it might to some. Xavier's his own brand of poly. I've seen him with someone, and he was okay with them being with other someones, but Trenton was his only someone."

"Was?"

"They broke up over a year ago. It was bad. Xavier won't admit it, but his heart was broken. He adored Trenton."

"I thought it'd be the other way around, to be honest. That man's made of stone."

Ani laughs. "He is, but all Tops have a soft spot a crater deep for their brats. It's a universal rule."

He's got no soft spot for me. If anyone doubts it, they just need to ask my ass. "That mean Tom has a soft spot for you?"

Just the thought of Tom makes Ani more pliable. "Uh-huh. Doesn't mean he's not really strict with me too. He's hard on me, but I like it. I'm at the low end of the brat spectrum; though he does bring it out of me. Wait till you see us together. You'll get what I mean."

Aha! I knew there was a spectrum.

"Not you though," he continues. "You rank somewhere up there with Grayson, maybe not quite so much a Bellamy, but I can feel the brat sizzling through you."

"People keep saying that, but I haven't done a bratty thing, not even a bratty word."

"You're settling, that's all. And it's fine when it happens. It's you. The right Top will pull it out of you."

"Doesn't the right Top also spank you for said brat behavior?"

He laughs. "Yeah, but in a way it's an unravelling of your energy, which they take apart and guide you to putting back together." I nod and yawn. "Now sleep, baby. You're tired. Xavier might not be my Top, but he'll still have words for me if I don't make sure you're getting proper care around here."

I nod and I eventually drift off to sleep.

Friday comes too soon, and I have to count on my hands the days I've been here. "Holy shit, day seven and I haven't even thought of leaving for at least three of those days," I say out loud to myself, but of course there's always lots of someones nearby to hear me. I look around the kitchen to make sure Will's not one of those someones who will spank for 'language,' even though I know he's not here at the moment. It's just a thing all of us in the house do, used to trying not to let him hear us say such things.

"You might change your mind after tonight," Gray says.

"Grayson!" That's Ani.

"What? He might. Xavier owes us for the other night." He climbs into my lap. "You're not really thinking about leaving, are you?"

I look around to everyone in the kitchen, all of whom are now focused on me, waiting on my answer. Ani and Chris are making pierogies at the counter, the one Johnny's sitting on, *not helping*, chewing on a whip of licorice. Bray's pretending to do his homework, but really, he's texting with Anthony from another House—Ani's not onto him yet, but I know he will be—and Bellamy's been sent upstairs to take a nap before dinner, which he did not like, let me tell you.

Will's the only one missing. He's in a meeting across campus with the other Head of Houses, but his presence is felt in the way each of us still looks over our shoulder before we dare utter a curse word and that each of us has been ordered to get done what we need to before dinner, or else, since most of us have another place to be afterward. I like the feeling of all of it, being wrapped in it. I'm not trading it; I can't imagine losing it. "I'm not leaving," I say. The room collectively relaxes. "Not that you'd let me anyway—yeah I'm onto you, Grayson."

He smirks. "I wasn't going to let you. I already hid your suitcase." He hops off my lap satisfied.

I get a phone call and I'm supposed to be doing homework, but it's Sammy. "It's Sammy, Ani," I say. "I won't be long, all right?"

"Sure, sweetheart."

I head into the living room. "'Lo? Sammy?"

"Hey, brother. How's things?"

"You know, they're pretty damn good. I like it here, Sam. Definitely staying," I tell him.

"That's good, Finn. Look, the reason I'm phoning is, an opportunity came up for me this weekend. I don't have to go, I was supposed to come help you get set up—I want to help you get set up—but if I work this weekend, I get to work on a case that could help me make partner eventually. I could come next weekend for sure."

I can hear how fucking excited my brother is at the possibility, but I know him, and I know he'll be feeling a whole pile of guilt about even asking to skip our plans. And really, he doesn't have to ask me anything. Isn't this part of why I did this? So Sammy could finally have his own life? "Sammy, I'm fine. I'm set up anyway and I'm always surrounded by seven others who won't leave me alone. You go get that partnership, brother."

"Really?"

"Really."

"Okay, I'll come the next weekend for sure, Finn. I have to bring your stuff anyway."

We chat for a bit and I fill him in best I can, but it's hard to explain the House, it's something you experience. When we get off the phone it hits me, we've reached the end of an era; Sammy and I are on two separate paths now for the first time, and I'm not sure how much I like that part of it. Sure, we're supposed to be doing our own things, but we've never been apart like this.

We've been inseparable since I was born. I've looked up to him, still do, and following my own thing without him feels wrong-footed. We were supposed to make it together, but we've ended up in different worlds. I sink onto the pale green couch, unable to go back to the kitchen. I stare at the ceiling. Eventually, Grayson comes looking for me. "Ani sent me to check and see if you'd been abducted by aliens. I told him to leave you alone for five minutes."

My eyes widen. "How'd that go over?"

"Not well, let me tell you. My ass still smarts. You all right?"

"Fine."

He looks me over. "I know I'm not one to talk, but they always make you say it and take it from me, it's better now than later when you brat it out and get yourself into all kinds of trouble over it."

I shake my head. I don't want to talk about it and I'm not going to 'brat it out' or whatever he thinks I'll do.

"Fine. I'm not that person in your life, but you'd better come into the kitchen before Ani sees you in here like this."

I return to the kitchen. Thankfully Ani's busy, which means if I am displaying outward signs of whatever Grayson thinks he saw, he doesn't notice. "I hope you're taking out your books over there, Finnegan B," Ani says without having to turn to look at me. The handle of his bite-y little hairbrush pokes out of the pocket of his apron—is it really necessary for him to carry that with him?

"Yep. Planned on it." I pull out books and set them up at the long kitchen table. None of the homework I have is stuff I wanna work on. It's all hard, it's all a struggle. But the ache in my backside as I shift against the hard wooden chair reminds me Xavier's got me. They all 'got me,' and I slide into my books willing to give it my best shot.

I'm still feeling weird about the whole Sammy thing as I get ready to go to discipline night. I shouldn't though. Sam needs his own life. Hell, I'm the reason he never married or had the kids he wanted. I *want* him to have this. I just miss what we had. I regret not enjoying what we had more, all my tantrums over nonsense tarnishing my memories of us.

Will gets real fussy over me and Grayson. "How many times have I told you Grayson? Not that shirt. Change."

"I don't see the big deal. It's tucked in."

"*Now*." He points to the stairs. "And you, you can't go with your hair like that. Ani! *Ani!*"

"Right here, for Pete's sake Will—" but he stops cold when he sees the look on Will's face. Ani and Will run the house together more of the time than not, but then there are times like now when we're all reminded it's Will who's Head of House.

Will has a more easy-going canter than the Tops I've met so far, but the tall cowboy was assigned Alpha House all by himself—the House with the most 'brats'—for a reason. "What do you need, sir?"

"Please do something with his hair." Will scrubs a hand over his face. "I'm going to make sure everyone else is where they're supposed to be, if you two aren't up to my standards by the time I'm back, you're both grounded tonight."

He storms off, Grayson gets the look from Ani no one wants to get. Grayson ducks his head. "You know better," Ani says. "C'mon you two. Let's get you fixed up."

Ani leads the way, pulling me by the hand, Grayson follows fuming. "I maintain, there's nothing wrong with this shirt, so long as it's tucked in."

"I want you in your nice baby blue polo by the time you come out. It brings out your pretty eyes, understand?" Ani says, ignoring his complaints.

"Yes, sir."

"And you ..." He drags me off to his room, plunking me down on the soft lavender comforter. Ani's bed has pillows, so many pillows—he likes fancy pillows. Then, he fishes items from his dresser drawer.

"It's not like it's long enough to put in a ponytail," I complain. "Xavier's never complained before."

"I know, but we can put product in it to tame it some, and he's never complained because it wasn't discipline night. You're expected to make extra effort. Don't you read outlines?" he says, combing my hair out and pulling styling mousse through.

"I can't be expected to memorize every little detail."

"Ah cheeky, cheeky boy tonight, I see. I'd lose that attitude before Xavier gets hold of you. And yes, you are expected to know what's in the outline. Not have it memorized yet, but what's stopping you from reading it over on an important night, huh?"

"Nothing, I guess."

"There, you look sharp now, brat. It's a good thing you're on your way for a spanking, you need it."

I scowl at him. "I don't need a spanking—no one needs a spanking!" Why do I feel like that needs to be carved into the walls around here so certain people will understand that fact?

"We'll see about that, but for the love of all that is sacred, don't make tonight the night you unleash the wrath of your inner brat."

"I'm not a brat."

"And my name isn't Animki. C'mon, let's make sure Grayson is doing what he's supposed to be."

Downstairs, yet more people have run-ins with Will. "Ani, you've got to do something," Bellamy says, when we enter the living room. "Will's saying Bray and I don't get to go out tonight. We had plans."

"Were those plans you ran by him like you were supposed to?" he says, sweet as pie.

"Well, no. But I don't get why he's being so strict on that this year."

"It got him into a lot of trouble because of you lot last year."

"Okay. Message received, but can't you talk to him? He relaxes when you talk to him."

"'Fraid not. Wouldn't be right in this case. Tell you what, you can help me do some baking, that'll be fun."

He scowls. "I hate this house!" That's the last we hear from him as he storms off.

Will returns and I have to say, he looks fucking amazing, especially when he's on a Top-brand warpath. Lightning sizzles through him. He's also dressed as fancy as I see him when he's not in his school uniform. Normally it's relaxed, hole-y jeans, plaid, sleeveless vests, and his white Stetson, but tonight he's in black slacks and a blue, long-sleeved, button-up shirt, hugging the lines of his physique. His chin-length hair is tame and looks blonder against the blue. "Wow, now there are two well-put-together boys. Thanks for your help, Ani. Sorry I'm hard tonight," he says, pulling Ani in for a kiss.

Ani's eyes sparkle. "You know your hardness is never an issue for me."

It really isn't. Not to any of us. Even Bellamy, despite

his protests. Experiencing a Top get firm is one of life's greatest joys, so long as you can keep your ass out of target range. We do straighten up some.

"I want everythin' to be right. Xavier's going to be on me this year." His eyes flick to me briefly and then back to Ani again, but I catch it. *What did that mean?* "All right, best behavior you two, I mean it. One toe out of line and my earlier consequence stands."

"Yes, sir," we both say. There's no room for fucking around tonight. Even Grayson's quiet.

Together we head to Xavier's office and I finally learn what's behind that curious door. It's a large room filled with walls of implements and other odd-looking benches. There's even a large, four poster bed. Xavier's eyes are on me, watching me even with the other boys here. It's my first night, it's also a few hours away from the end of my grace period for exiting the contract. A feeling surges in my belly, one that says I should tell him my decision personally, but that would be stupid. There are so many men who attend this school, Xavier only needs to know if you plan on leaving, not have his time wasted with something he'll see in the coming days. I smile over at him when our eyes meet, he looks away without smiling back.

Fine. No big deal. He's busy. There are six of us tonight; I can't expect his attention just for me like it is when I'm here on my own. I'm stupid for thinking it would be. *But you did think it would be, Finn.* I turn my focus to trying not to focus on him, but every cell in my body is aware of him and only him. *Jeez, Finn. You had to crush on Xavier of all people, didn't you?* And sure, yeah I like Ani, and Grayson, hell, I wouldn't kick a single one of my housemates out of bed, but that kind of thing is not the same as the way I'm crushing on Xavier.

I watch him pull a strap out of a cupboard and I want to die. Being strapped in front of people for a misdemeanor is probably one of my top fantasies and I don't even mean sexual fantasies—us spankees are like that, it's what sets us apart from the BDSM crowd. Is he going to use that on all of us? He lays it on a tall, backless cushioned chair, undoes two of his dress shirt buttons and then, fuck, his cuffs, proceeding to roll up the sleeves to mid-biceps. *Stop staring, Finn. Stop fucking staring.*

"We have a newbie in our midst tonight, boys. Emmery, you met Finnegan the other day. Trevor, Osh, this is our dear, Finnegan Brighton."

Trevor and Osh do not look like brats. I might be stereotyping, but they look more like Top types than brat types. Oh god, now I'm saying it—I've already split the room into Tops and brats without thinking about it. "Nice to meet you, Finnegan," Trevor says with an accent I can't place, but it's rough; the man's got to be tough as nails.

"Very nice to meet you, Finnegan," Osh says with no accent, but the Canadian one like I have. He's Japanese like Johnny, with jet black hair, tied up to show off his undercut. Both Trevor and Osh are handsome, and both have something dark in their eyes; it's that above all that gives me the 'Top sense.' They carry themselves with the confidence of lions.

"Finn will go last. All of you have reason to receive more than the standard, so I will be using my strap tonight. Mr. Brighton?"

I jump, I wasn't expecting him to call on me. "Yes, sir?"

"Watch closely what they do. I will expect you to replicate their posture and protocol, understood?"

"Yes, sir."

"William, you're up first."

I can't help myself. Spanking and everything to do with it fascinates, me and watching a guy like Will get a strapping is my jam. Unfortunately, I know I'm red with all kinds of embarrassment, the heat creeping up my neck, even if I'm not the one on the chopping block, *yet*. Grayson grabs my hand. "He's magnificent to watch take a spanking," he leans in to whisper in my ear. "He can take a lot, and he turns the best colors."

I nod. He's telling me it's okay to want to watch, that he enjoys it too. Right. We all do. We all have the same wiring inside. I bite my lip, but I do watch. Besides, didn't Xavier want me taking notes? I stop feeling bad about it.

Will removes his nice black slacks and his boxers, both are folded neatly and placed over a chair that's to the side. He then pulls his shirt up, so that his round, muscled ass is fully visible and he lays over the cushioned stool that's got thick, sturdy legs. It's a wide stool, wider-than-most hips, longer than them too. He goes straight over until his hands touch the floor. It's a tall stool, which means going all the way to the floor, has even a tall guy like Will's legs *well* off the ground. The tops of his thighs are now supported some by the stool and his legs stick straight out into the air.

Will is now the shape of an 'L.'

It's a vulnerable position, and an embarrassing one, ass up high like that. I can see the most private parts of him, but they are still well out of target range. "It occurs to me, William, that two in your care managed to get absolutely pickled on a school night, is that true?"

Oh my God. I'm one of the someones. That's me and Grayson he's in trouble for.

"It's true, sir."

"I'm not one hundred percent convinced you could have avoided that one; however, you do need a reminder to tighten ship if things like that are happening. That's what this is for. Any questions about it?"

Xavier wants people to talk in that position? It doesn't look like a comfortable talking position. "No questions, sir. It's clear. You'll be happy to know I have been tightening ship since, but this is a good reminder to continue to, which I appreciate. We have a meeting Sunday. I'm going to introduce new rules."

Dammit. No one's gonna like that, which means they're gonna be pissed at me and Grayson. We look at each other, wincing with the same thought, but also on the verge of laughter. We got our asses handed to us, but it was kinda fun getting in trouble together.

"Very well. Let these help you focus this week."

"Yes, sir."

Now that both of Xavier's arms are visible, with the sleeves rolled up and all, I can see when his biceps flex, as the strap is pulled into the air and then extended to *crack* down onto Will's upturned ass. Grayson and I flinch more than Will does. *Wow.* He can take a strapping.

And it's a thick strap: firm leather folded in half secured into a solid leather grip. It makes a sharp, *thwack!* sound when it strikes flesh.

Xavier swings over and over as Will's ass gets redder and redder. The flesh of Will's cheeks waver in anticipation of the strike he knows his coming, all the while remaining solid. But as the strapping progresses, Will struggles some. He hisses, and the muscles of his arms get tighter. Xavier stops for a moment when the strapping becomes intense and rubs his back. I feel really fucking sorry I got him into this, and Grayson is too. We cling to each other, squeezing with every crack of the strap. "Final six, William."

Will nods. "Ready, sir."

How can he remain so steady?

The final six look *painful*. Holy fuck. Will's not quiet for these, no one could be. They're hard and the welts that rise up look sore. "Ah! Ow, thank you, sir." His jaw is set firm and he's clinging into the carpet with his fingers best he can.

I look to Grayson with 'we fucked up' eyes and he wordlessly agrees. I remind myself that this isn't punishment, but discipline. What does he hand out to ones like Will for a real punishment...? "You're all done, William. You took that well, as usual. You may come up now and take your position."

I expect Will to look distraught, at least some tears, but he's smiling. Not just any smile, the smile of a man walking on air. "Thank you, sir. I will carry this with me throughout my week, and I appreciate you taking the time to correct me."

He does?

Will leaves his clothes where they are, and heads over to a plain wall to stand in front of it. He spreads his legs wide and makes sure his shirt doesn't cover his very red ass so it's on display, then, he laces his fingers together on top of his head. The large muscles of his lats have to press against his shirt with his arms so wide. "You're next, Osh," Xavier says.

After the Tops have had their turn, I devise the pattern; remove your pants and underwear, neatly fold them over the couch next to the most recent set, assume position over the stool, then when strapping is over, thank Xavier and then take position at the wall.

But when he gets to Emmery, the first 'brat' of us to receive his discipline, I notice subtle changes in Xavier's demeanor. He's softer with Emmery and I recall what Ani said about Tops having a soft spot for their brat. *That's what your jealousy with Emmery was about, Finn. Xavier has a thing for Emmery, when what you want is for him to have a thing for you.*

Yeah, I can admit that. No, I don't like it.

The protocol is the same, but he's not nearly as hard on Emmery, even though he's had several misdemeanors this week, compared to all of the Tops who each had one. Still, Emmery fidgets and squirms twice as hard. From there I go down a road I should not go down. My head plays over and over the soft touches from Xavier to Emmery's face and the gentle, if firm way he instructs him to get over the stool.

Has he done anything like that with me? I play over each time we've met, scanning through the touches, the hugs, even the words but nope. I can't come up with anything like what I just saw for me, remembering what Ani said about Xavier being softer with *his* brat. Unfairly, I get angry at Emmery, but the rational part of me knows it's not Emmery's fault. It's not even Xavier's for that matter. You like who you like, it's just my dumb luck I ended up wanting someone like Xavier who isn't going to like me back.

Ugh. Why am I such a teenager inside?

"Mr. Brighton."

I jump at my name and I'm surprised to see Grayson walking over to the wall where the others are standing. I spent so much time going over this dilemma in my head, I've missed his strapping altogether. *Pull it together, Brighton.*

I try to, but I can't help the 'what's Emmery got, I haven't got' thinking that runs through my head. I'm sure something shows—I tend to wear my heart on my sleeve—by the way he's analyzing my posture. His arms cross at me while I remove my pants and boxers, which I know is Xavier for, he's trying to devise what my problem might be.

I don't chance looking at him again as I get into position. The whole thing is ridiculous; I've been here seven days, and he's been perfectly clear in each meeting. We have a Top, Taken in Hand relationship. It's true something like that is not without its own intimacies, but no one else seems to have a problem keeping it to the discipline kinds; of course, I had to make it more in my head.

Ugh. Maybe I shouldn't have done this? The 'this' being come to Xavier's school. No. For that much, it's clear I should have, probably sooner, but maybe it's not too late to be assigned to another Top?

These are all the things I'm thinking as I make my way over to the stool. The position is even less comfortable than it looked, and even more undignified. My ass feels very exposed, and I didn't think about how my weight would be on my hands with my legs so high off the ground. I'm almost in a handstand. I'm reasonably tall, but not as tall as Will, which means my ass has to go further forward for me to touch the ground, which means it's higher than his was, showing more of my special places.

I know that's the point. Humiliation is a key component in disciplinary spankings. Still. Ugh!

"Ah Finnegan. Not the end of your first week yet and already earning punishment for consuming to excess on a school night?" He's amused.

I can't help the smile that cracks thinking about it. At the time, yeah, I was really pissed, but the anger vanished quickly with the right... okay, *brat* antics, and the subsequent consequence afterward. All I remember is being caught when I fell, net in the form of Will, to save me from myself. Grayson and I laughed about it all the next morning, while we bemoaned our sore asses, no one feeling sorry for us. Everyone wanted to see the collateral, of course; we were proud to show off our spanking tokens for all the brats of the house to see.

It was kinda the best.

"I did, sir."

"Hmmm, you don't seem apologetic. I will endeavor to change your mind, brat."

There's that word again, but I deserve it in this case. As much as I wouldn't change a thing, there were far more adult ways to deal with schedule changes and my resulting inner fallout. I chose getting wasted on a school night. He rubs my back. "Brace yourself."

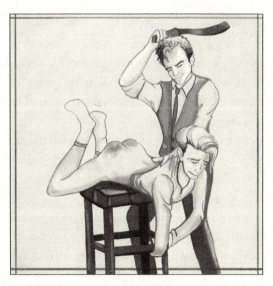

Discipline Night By Artsy Ape

I can hear the strap as it *whooshes* through the air, the

crack to my ass is white hot and far more than anything with his hand has been. I'm not near as stoic as Will, and I have to admit that even Emmery took his well considering how much it fucking *hurts*. I hate my inability to take the strapping more than the strapping itself. I cry out, I kick my legs and all around suck at this.

I'm not going to make it anywhere, not even among my own kind. At six, Xavier stops to give me a breather. "You're doing well. Remember, this is your first time. Breathe in when you hear the strap raise, exhale as it comes down."

I nod, stupid tears of frustration streaming down my face, or up my face as the case may be. I can do this. I want to do this. He moves to the other side and the next six land in quick succession, taking my breath away as I fail to follow instructions, which only serves to heighten my frustration. He stops again; I fume. He didn't have to stop for the others, he was able to carry on with a pleasant efficiency he must have enjoyed. After all, this is not just for our benefit. It's a two-way relationship; if it wasn't, it wouldn't work so well. I can't see him, but I'm sure he's growing frustrated too, with all my squirms and loud cries.

This can't be enjoyable for him. Especially with having to wait so long in between the sets of six he's decided on with me. "You've grown awfully quiet down there," he says. I have? "Are you repenting your naughty, bratty ways?"

That brings me out of whatever dark hole I sunk into. I laugh. "I really am, sir. Um, laugh notwithstanding."

"You are trouble with a capital 'T,' and this is only your first week. That is, so long as it's also not your last week?"

His voice turns up at the end, hinting at something. Might he regret it if it was my last week? "No, sir. Not my last week by far, which means, thorough as you are, I'm likely to end up in this position again." I tense a bit, realizing I've gotten wrapped up in the moment and I'm flirting. I'm flirting with the man who's roasting my ass about future roastings when really, what I should be doing is keeping this all business, especially if I'm going to discuss having a new Top.

His breath is hot in my ear. "I'm going to go just a bit slower for you until you get the hang of it. Practice the breathing I explained, or it's going to hurt even more than it has to."

Knowing he's going even easier on me, sends me back to my dark hole. I can't even be a natural at this, at taking a fucking spanking. *You fucking suck, Finnegan.* "I can take it, sir. I'm okay." Yeah, my ass is on fire, but I really am okay.

"Thank you, I appreciate the update, but I'm the one in charge and we'll do this my way, not yours. Understood?"

Wow. That goes through me and cuts through all the bullshit stirring around, even if it doesn't dissipate it. Gone is our witty banter, in its place Xavier's serious tone; it's never absent of care, but boy, when he uses it, you know you've gone too far. It's worse that it's laced with so much care, far easier to have a cold entity scold you, easier to slough off. Caring gets into you, right down to the quick. I am well and truly chastised. "I understand, sir."

I don't like it. He goes a helluva lot easier from there but he was right, I do pick up on the breathing rhythm. Not only can I take the strapping better with the breathing— even though it doesn't sting any less—I let go with more peace. All around it's a better experience, even if I'm still mad at myself for having to slow Xavier down so much.

When he tells me to stand, I know I'm supposed to thank him like the others did, but I'm too distraught over having done everything wrong. I *have* to apologize. I don't want to be his worst boy, the one he hates dealing with.

Yeah, this is where I've come. I've gone from telling myself I'll end the contract, to requesting a new Top, to I don't want to be his worst fucking boy, because the latter one is the truth. I want to be his, but I want him to be proud of me, like he is of the others. Everything else is just a façade, to give myself the illusion of control. It's easier to think you can leave something at any time you want.

The old, if you leave first, if you quit, you weren't rejected, you didn't want it anyway huh, Finn?

I can feel the apology ready to spill out of me, but I cut it off at the pass and say what I'm supposed to say. "Thank you, sir. I will carry this with me throughout my week and I appreciate you taking the time to correct me."

He nods, but he doesn't tell me I've done well and why should he? I didn't do well. I'm heartbroken all the same. I take up my place beside Grayson—at least I can stare at a wall properly—and try not to cry, while my ass throbs.

The six of us stand facing the wall, not saying a word for an indeterminable amount of time. Will's been standing here the longest, since he went first, and had to wait through on all the rest of us to receive our discipline, plus however long we'll stand here after mine. It's some feat. Already my legs are tired from the position, combined with all the other energy exerted during the strapping and the ache afterward. Plus, I know he went harder on Will than he did on me, even if no one could tell by my performance.

"Okay boys, you may redress now," Xavier says.

The quiet turns to jovial quickly; I know enough by this point to know that the discipline has enlightened everyone. There's excited chatter as they re-clothe and like within our house, they all compare asses. "Holy, William. You should see your behind," Grayson says. "It's gorge."

"I dunno, I think I like yours better. Might have my own go at it later," Will says, stealing a kiss.

"That mean I'm commandeered for the night?" Gray asks.

"Darn right you are. I'll be away tomorrow night darlin', missing you. You're not leaving me tonight."

"If I must. You're such an overbearing lout sometimes, William." But he looks over to me and winks when Will is off talking to Osh and Trevor.

Emmery takes a look at mine. "Wow, Finn. This is beautiful and uh, we're not supposed to take our eyes from the wall, but I couldn't help myself with those brilliant sounds you were making—you were born for this. Watching you take a strap was the most extraordinary thing I've ever seen."

I have to look away. Not only do I not deserve his praise, I specifically don't deserve praise from him. I want Xavier to end things with Emmery and be with me. Ani told me Xavier is the closest thing to monogamy there is around here, which means he won't see me and Emmery at the same time. "Thanks, Emmery." Emmery's not a bad guy. He's a good guy. I actually quite like him.

Grayson, who's beginning to know a thing or two about me, maybe faster than I would like, is onto me and I know I'm in for questioning later.

"Did you tell Gray?" Emmery asks.

"Tell him what?"

"The other day with the spanking?"

"Oh right. I was supposed to tell Grayson he was wrong. I don't know about what though."

Grayson does. He shakes his head. "Our dear Emmery

115

here keeps trying to convince me that he is a lot brattier than I think he is. Yes, he catches it sometimes, but not like I do, or like you Finnegan."

"So you tell people who think they're not brats they are, and people who think they are brats they're not?" I ask.

"No, I call them like I see them. Emmery's not quite an Ani, but he's pretty well-behaved."

"Who's down for an Xavier's Boys post-discipline beer?" Trevor says. "Don't worry William, I won't let the brats overindulge."

"Yeah, fine with me. I'll join ya," Will says.

"Great, I'm in and you're with me tonight Emmy, so that means you too," Osh says.

I already feel a world better with the distraction. Y'know, post-discipline beer sounds excellent.

"Have fun boys," Xavier says. "Except you. You're with me tonight."

I think for the briefest moment he's talking to Emmery, even though Osh just said Emmery's with him, and I wouldn't put it past Xavier to commandeer Emmery if he felt he needed to, especially if they're a thing. But he's not talking to Emmery.

He's talking to me.

"But sir." I almost add a 'that's not fair,' but I stop myself short. He may have gone easy on me, but that was some strapping. I'm not ready for more yet.

He doesn't address me after that, unconcerned with my protest; he addresses Will. "He'll be back by curfew, William. I know I don't have to remind you five that I want exceptional behavior at this time. It's the start of school, I expect you five to set the example."

"Yes, sir," they all say, and then in keeping with tradition, everyone gets a post-spanking hug and they're off. Nary a goodbye to me.

When Xavier spins around to address me, I've got *my* arms crossed this time. "You're an awfully pouty boy for one that just got the life spanked out of him," he says, and when he crosses his arms back at me, it totally overrules mine on principle. How does he do that?

"I wanted to hang out with them and I'm disappointed, also confused as to why I'm being kept behind."

"Mmm-mmn. Nope, nope. You do recall why you came to my school, don't you? You wrote me a ten-page entrance essay on it, which I read over several times and memorized. You're here to break open, so you can find out who you are. That's not going to happen if I allow you to avoid big topics, and right now there is something bothering you."

Yes, it's just, a lot harder than you thought it would be, isn't it Finnegan?

"You know why I kept you behind. We can talk about it now, or after you've been staring at a wall for an indeterminate amount of time. It's up to you. I'll enjoy my time either way, because you'll have your pants down and there's nothing I like more than a bare, red, bottom."

The bastard is smiling, and I want to decline him, just to spite him—which an inner voice tells me is a very brat thing to do—but I know that he *will* enjoy it and I will not. I refuse to give him the satisfaction. "Please don't make me," I say instead, the tears brimming over without me wanting them to.

Xavier takes a breath and exhales slowly, deciding what to do with me. "You are going to ruin my reputation. Come here, Finn," he says, with his arms open.

Not Mr. Brighton, not Finnegan, *Finn*.

I don't think about it, I just go. When his arms are

circled around me, he's the life raft I needed earlier. He holds me while I cry it all out to him, telling him everything I was feeling earlier. "I'm sorry I'm so bad at this. I'm sorry that spanking must have been awful for you. I suck. I suck at this. I can't even take a spanking right. I'm never going to do anything right. I'll never find out who I'm meant to be."

"Shhh, Finnegan. *Finnegan B.* I promise everything's going to be fine."

He says that, but I only feel like more of a moron crying like this over nonsense. I sniffle, forcing myself to stop crying and pull away. "You're right. I'm fine, everything's fine. There, you know now, so I'd really like to go now. If I'm quick, I can catch up with them."

The hard version of Xavier, probably the one I need more of right now, seeps back in, filling him up like a foggy day. "You're not going with them. You can leave that notion behind. I meant it when I said you're with me for the night. Turn off the light in the back office, I've got to grab something, then we'll go."

I want to complain, but there's no way I'll complain with the look I'm receiving. I give a tight nod.

"And here, take this." It's another handkerchief with an 'X' stitched into the corner. "That one I want back. I only have one more after that. You have my third one."

I do have one of these. I put it in my desk drawer where it could be secretly mine even though I'm pretty sure Ani saw it and I'm also pretty sure his eyes widened when he saw it, but he didn't say anything. Originally, I figured Xavier had multiples of them and that he must give them away to everyone. *But he only has three, Finn. Why would he give one to you?* I wipe my face with this one as I head to turn off the light. Before I return to him, I take a breath and run a hand through my hair. I'm thinking there's a chance I can turn my poor performance during discipline around. *Be cool, Finnegan.*

I head out, but I feel awkward, uncomfortable in my own skin. He's there looking bad-ass as hell in his long, black coat and his messy Superman hair, still the only untamed thing about him. He extends his hand for mine and I take it. We leave his office and head across campus, holding hands the entire time. I'm glad for it. His hand is warm and large and safe.

It's only seven, so while the light wanes, it's not dark yet. It will be soon though. Too many things are going through my head to worry about the setting sun, like: is Xavier abducting me? I suppose in a way, he is, so I decide yes on that. I can't think of someone better to abduct me though. But the other more prominent question is: what the hell is he going to do with me when he gets there? He's quiet and I can't stand it anymore. "Where are we going?"

"Somewhere," he says, coy as hell. I'm starting to think Tops have a small dose of brat in them too and insert them into my imaginary spectrum chart, which moves Ani way over from his original place on the spectrum. I add Will before Ani (well before Ani) and note to add Trevor and Osh later once I get to know them. My imaginary spectrum chart now begins with the word 'Top.' Xavier in brackets beside the word.

I can't help smiling, he's kind of adorable when he's like this and it does ruin his hard-ass rep a bit, but I know it can return at a moment's notice. We finally stop far at the edge of campus, near a large willow tree with a bench under it. "It's nice and quiet here, if you should require on-the-spot correction, there's no one around to save you."

"Hey!"

He's teasing me, but he would do it. He yanks me onto

the bench with him before I have the chance to respond and opens his jacket to wrap me inside with him. "Warm enough?"

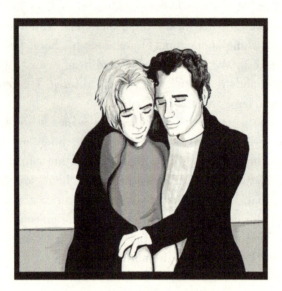

Finn and Xavier By Artsy Ape

"Yes, sir." I cozy in. I'm never leaving this spot. If being in his arms is a life raft, being molded against him like this is the first day of summer when you're a kid, with two whole months of adventure ahead of you.

"I do like *sir* more than I can tell you, but we're much less than formal right now, wouldn't you agree?"

I nod hoping we can just stay like this and not talk about anything more. No such luck.

"You know, while you think you were terrible, I'm still over here luxuriating in the feel of being the most spanking drunk I've ever been."

I peer up at him. "What in God's name is that?"

He laughs. It's a good laugh. "It's something Tops get—

the Top version of what a brat feels when he's reached the point of surrender during a spanking. A floaty, happy feeling."

I'm still confused. "Are you saying, I did that *to you*?"

"Yes."

"But how? I was terrible."

"You were *responsive*, and that's not a bad thing, it's a preference thing. I know you're measuring yourself against the others but keep in mind the following: William, Trevor and Osh are not brats, they're Tops. Discipline for them is different than it is for you, even if there are similar threads."

"What about Emmery?" I try not to wrinkle my nose at his name, but I'm pretty sure I do.

"Part of me wants to let you continue to think I like Emmery, like you think I like Emmery, so I can continue to see your nose wrinkle like that every time his name is said, but that wouldn't be right." I scowl at him for knowing everything. "I'm not interested in Emmery in the way you think I am. My interest is held elsewhere. But with regard to how he takes a spanking, some of it's practice and conditioning, and some of it's personality; each brat takes a spanking in their own unique way. I love watching personality bloom during a spanking. All the variations fascinate me."

I haven't missed that he said his interest is elsewhere, but at least it's not with Emmery. For some reason that matters. "And Tops have preferences?"

"Yes. If you look closer, you'll notice now. I'm sure you've already picked up on things Will prefers versus me and some of the various professors."

"I have."

"Professor Fraser, he's someone who doesn't prefer a lot of response. He wouldn't take on a permanent brat like that, it would frustrate him. Me, on the other hand, I *adore* it.

When it's authentic that is, otherwise, it's just a tantrum and that I won't stand for. You were wonderfully authentic tonight. I can't wait to see how you challenge me when you've had more practice."

What the...? He's pleased. I let go the invisible weight I was holding, and all the tension goes with it. "But you had to slow down for me, which is easier. I don't want you to have to go easy on me." Yes, I said it. Yes, I'll probably regret it later, but I want to be good at this.

"Going slower makes it a bit easier, but you got what the other brats got, no more, no less. That's still a challenge and quite formidable to take on your first discipline night ever. You're almost where they're at and some of them have been at this for years. You were made for this, Finnegan."

I never thought of it that way. I bite my lip.

"You and your lip biting are going to be the death of me, Finn." He runs a hand through my blond hair, running his thumb over the fuzz of my undercut. "Does that clear some things up?"

"Most things. So, you do go harder on Top types?"

"I do. They are responsible for people, and I want them to feel the weight of that, they expect no less from me." I nod. "Anything else, my churlish one?"

"Just, you told everyone else 'good job,' but not me. I thought that meant you weren't pleased, but now it sounds like you are."

"Did I not say? My apologies. I suppose I was a bit speechless. I was too fascinated with you, already playing it all over in my head and dreaming up new ways to spank you. That is no excuse, though. You, my Finnegan, are the prize of all prizes; I enjoy your responses best of all. You did exceptionally well and not just for your first discipline night, you were made for this." He uses my chin to turn my face up to meet his eyes. "Am I forgiven?"

My heart is in my fucking throat. I'm not sure I've got the breath to answer, so I nod instead.

"Good, anything else?"

"Nothing else."

"Are you still put out with me for keeping you from your new friends?"

"A bit, but I suppose I can forgive you for that too, if you promise to stay with me like this the whole time."

"I see. You still think you can bargain with me." He doesn't move though. We're quiet for some time, watching the sun go away with the sound of the birds who find shelter for the night and the general bustle of campus dies down. "I'm glad you're staying."

"Me too. I finally feel like I belong somewhere," I admit.

"You do belong *here,* I knew it when I first laid eyes on you." I'm not sure we're talking about the same somewhere. "Speaking of, I'm going to be strict with you, Finnegan. I already have a good idea of what you feel like when you spin off on a thought like you did tonight, and I'm going to help you break that pattern and form a new habit, one in which you work through your automatic negative thoughts."

"Talking...?"

"When the time calls for it, but as you know I have many ways to help boys like you."

"That sounds suspiciously like spanking to me. How many hours do I have left to say no to all this insanity?"

"None. You already said you're staying. Little did you know those words were binding."

I laugh. "They were not. I have—" I grab his wrist to look at his watch, which I plan on saying something to him about at another time (who wears wrist watches anymore?) "—three hours and twenty-seven minutes."

"Maybe if you were another boy, but you're not and time's run out."

I cozy into him more, trying to take up all the space I can in his jacket. He smells of spicy cologne. I want it to stay with me when he's gone. "Yeah, it's run out. I'm doomed," I say, glad to be doomed. "D-Do you think though, that maybe I'd be better off with - with another Top?"

"What sort of poppycock is that? *No.* You're mine and if you need reminding, I can and will spank you right here to prove it."

You're mine. He said you're mine, Finn!

But then I remember he does have another interest. He said it himself. I can't read too much into that. He has six boys to call his. Xavier runs a hand through my hair. "I had planned on keeping you longer, but it's getting colder. You should have a jacket."

I pick up on the scolding tone. "I'm not cold. Are you going to attempt to control every aspect of my life, right down to jackets?"

"Yes." He's not even sorry about it.

"I'll wear one next time. No one else wore a jacket."

"No one else is ..." He doesn't finish that sentence.

"No one else is what?"

"Nothing. Wear one next time, or else." And when I don't answer. "*Finnegan.*"

"Yes, Xavier."

"Better. C'mon. Time for me to take you home."

He takes my hand again and we walk to the other side of campus through to the section where all the Houses are. He walks me onto the porch of Alpha House, straight to the door. "I'm not going to come in, or it will cause a ruckus. I tend to elicit a particular response," he says. "Make sure someone takes care of this." He pats my ass. "I'll check."

"Yes, sir. Oh and here," I say, remembering to give his other handkerchief back.

"Thank you. My mother made these for me when she was alive." He slips it into his jacket pocket. "Goodnight, Mr. Brighton. I'll see you tomorrow."

"Tomorrow? Tomorrow's Saturday."

"I am well aware of the day, Mr. Brighton."

It's infuriating when he calls me Mr. Brighton. He probably knows that too. "What time, sir?"

"After lunch. Bring Grayson with you. I need to speak with him as well." I nod. "Until tomorrow, *behave* yourself."

"Pretty sure I can manage at least that long, sir."

"I'm not going to hold my breath." He rolls his eyes at me and then heads off into the night.

Inside, there's a lot of loud and I make the decision to try to sneak off to my room. Yes, I know I've never been successful, but there's a first time for everything, right? That first time is not going to be tonight. "You stop right there, Finnegan Charles Brighton," Ani says.

I swear that guy has eyes in the back of his head. "You look busy though." And he really does. He's covered head to toe in flour and so are the guilty counterparts standing, looking at walls near the air hockey table on the other side of the living room.

"Never too busy for you, sweetheart. Sit there, if you can."

I take a seat to where he's pointed on the couch. I was

sitting on a hard bench the last hour and a half, this is far improved. "As for you, Bellamy Brooks and Stephen Bray, none of what you did was funny. I'm telling your Tops."

"Oh, c'mon Ani. We're sorry. It was just a joke," Bellamy says. Stephen's smart enough to stay quiet, but it's all he can do to keep from laughing. I may not be able to see his face, but I can tell by the way he's shaking. They both think they're funny.

"Just wait until Will gets home. I'd deal with you myself, but I'm too mad. Do not move an inch. You can both stay like that until whenever he decides to come in the door."

They both groan and I feel for them, even ten minutes of corner time is a lot. They could be there for a couple hours still if Will stays out until our curfew (mine, his and Grayson's), which is midnight on weekend nights. "C'mon you, let's take care of you. I need to cool off. Those two are enough to drive anyone crazy sometimes."

"Um, not trying to get out of help—I've learned how fruitless that is—but you're full of flour, Ani."

"Dammit," he says, looking around for Will to catch him out for cursing. "I forgot in all the ruckus. All right, go get yourself into something more comfortable and I'll be there after a quick shower."

I slip off to my room, and while I definitely want to get out of these pants and into something more comfortable, I don't want to stop smelling like Xavier. It's comforting. I change though, and remember I have one of his handker-chiefs in my drawer.

Wait.

Wait.

Oh Finnegan, you're a dense one.

These aren't just handkerchiefs, they're ones his mother

made him, a mother that's passed and he *gave* me one. I grew up without a mother, just pictures and stories from Dad and Sam. It gives you an idealistic fantasy of what it's like to have a mother. I don't know what other people do, but Dad and Sam idolized Mom. I know they were trying to make me feel some part of her, but instead, and true to Finnegan form, I felt left out of the Mom club rather than part of it.

Sometimes I would hold her pictures and try to cry, but it's hard to cry over someone you have no memory of. If I did manage to cry, it was for what I didn't have, rather than for *her*. I did get that she was very special though, and every time I answer one of those stupid internet quizzes that asks you who'd you like to meet, living or dead, I always say Mom.

I know how much Sam misses her still.

"I'm not sure I can keep this," I say out loud to myself. But I smile knowing what it means.

When Ani enters freshly washed, flour-free, I confide to him as he rubs aloe into my ass. "I think Xavier might be, uh interested in me."

"Duh. I saw that handkerchief, Finnegan Charles. He never lets anyone walk off with those."

"Why didn't you say something to me?"

"You weren't ready to hear it. I tried to give you hints."

"Some hints. He's not soft with me at all. Do you not see how hard he spanked me?"

"You argued with him over your schedule changes in your first week and lived; that was my first tip off. When I saw the handkerchief, I knew. But now that you know, what do you think about it?"

"I was jealous of Emmery. He's soft with Emmery, so I thought he and Xavier had a thing going, which meant he wouldn't want something with me, seeing as you said he's the closest thing to monogamous around here."

"True, but also true, he's got his weak points with most brats. However, he's never let-them-off-the-hook-for-arguing soft."

"I did not get let off the hook, I got a spanking for that."

I twist to look back at him, he arches a brow. "Not the kind anyone else would have got, believe me."

He helps me with my pajama pants, and I roll onto my back. "I have the world's biggest crush on him, but he's the Headmaster of the school, Ani. I know there are no rules against it, but won't it interfere with stuff?"

"You're just trying to find excuses. Look around here, there're all kinds of romance and sex sprouting off the 'stuff' you refer to. That's exactly what it's for; a romantic relationship in this lifestyle. If you want to make it work, you will. If it needs to end for some reason, that will work itself out too, but don't think about the end before it even starts—jeez, Finnegan."

"Yeah, good point. I've just never had a relationship go all that well."

"I can't promise you the sun, moon and stars, but I can say you've likely never had a Top for a boyfriend, and you mister, you need a Top. End of story."

"You know, Ani? I really do." All of it's electrifying. I'm looking forward to things I never thought I'd look forward to, like all his strictness and scolding—not that I'll ever tell him that.

The silence is broken by the sounds of slaps ringing off of bare ass cheeks. "Sounds like Will's home. I'd better get down there. I'm excited for you, Finny. Xavier will be good for you."

"Who will be good for what?" Grayson says, pouncing on me.

"He'll tell you all about it, but only if he wants to, Grayson, no pestering him."

"You'd better tell me everything, Brighton," he says, when Ani is out of earshot. "I knew there was something going on. Your face tonight gave you away. You have a terrible poker face."

"I will, I will, but first, Xavier wants to see you tomorrow."

"What? Why? I haven't *done* anything."

I shrug. "Guess we'll find out tomorrow."

———

As soon as the clock strikes midnight, Will is on me and Grayson. "Grayson, why aren't you ready for bed?"

"Finn and I are talking."

Will doesn't care. "Teeth brushed, now. You too, Finn."

I'm in too good a mood to complain. I don't even mind being sent to bed so much, I'm tired anyway. "Yes, Will." I grab Grayson's hand, who's looking at me like I've lost my mind.

I brush my teeth smiling, Grayson scowling away. "It's too early for bed, Finn."

"It is, but I think we owe him some good behavior. We're the reason he earned the strap tonight."

He rolls his eyes, but I can tell he agrees. When I try to put my toothbrush into my toiletries bag, Grayson stops me. "What are you doing? You live here now." I glance at my phone on the counter, twelve oh nine. It's officially day eight, which means my grace period is over. Grayson grabs my toothbrush with purpose and drops it into the communal toothbrush holder. "C'mon. I'm gonna convince Will to let me sleep in your bed tonight."

"Do you ever sleep in your own bed?"

"No. Not alone anyway."

I spend my first official night as part of the House with an octopus named Grayson wrapped around me.

CHAPTER SIX

M y hand *hurts*. The painkillers the hospital gave me wear off as Gray and I try to figure out how to get out of this room. All I want to do is run to Xavier and have him fix all of this. I know he can't fix my broken hand but being pressed up against him would be better all around.

"We can't do this, Grayson. Let's call someone to come get us." We'll be given the spanking of our lives and grounded forever, but then it will be over. Really, that's not the part I'm avoiding.

I slipped right into the domestic discipline aspects of the House. For me, it was natural, a manifestation of what I felt inside. Sure, I question things, like, *why am I like this?* and *why do I need this?* which seem to be the world's most unanswerable questions, but there is no doubt that I am like this and I do need this.

In part because of the avoiding.

I avoid rather than deal.

When I signed on for this school, I knew what I eventu-ally wanted was a domestic discipline relationship with someone. Even though I didn't understand everything about it at the time, I knew something in me was wired that way. I wanted the kind of consensual-non-consent that a domestic discipline style relationship could give me. I wanted someone I could trust to make the decisions, ones I could follow, with consequences if I didn't.

Because I need that. I won't do things on my own, I *won't*, and when I don't, that leads to consequences much worse than spanking. Spanking heals me. Sometimes a spanking isn't punishment, it calms me down, helps me think. The threat of spanking reminds me to *do* something.

It connects me to myself.

"You can't give up now. Pull it together, Brighton. Lookit all the stuff I found; we'll totally get out of here, just one problem."

"Oh?"

"My phone's not getting a signal. How's yours?"

I take a look, and oh fuck. "It's dead."

"Now we can't throw in the towel. Xavier is really not about boys who let their cell phones go dead, especially if that boy is the love of his life."

Yeah, Xavier really is going to freak about that. He *hates* that. "We don't know how to pick this lock. Without the internet, we're stuck here unless one of us climbs back down and opens the door from the outside." And that person's going to have to be him. I made it up, barely. Climbing up is different than climbing down. I won't make it down without breaking more bones.

"If it comes to that, I will. Let's just take a quick breather and think. How hard can it be to pick a lock?"

Turns out, really fucking hard. We try, using bobby pins and all kinds of other thin instruments we can jam into the door handle, but no such luck. They make it look so easy on TV.

While we fiddle with the lock, a loud slam sounds behind us. Both of us turn to look, mouths gaping at the window that's slammed shut of its own accord. Grayson runs to it and tries to pry it open, but it won't budge. "Um, Finn? Now we're totally stuck up here."

I slump to my ass on the floor, the back of my head hitting against the locked door. I don't want to face *him*. I can't face *him*. "How long can we live up here for?" Please say forever.

"Not long. We won't last without water, Finny." He plunks himself down beside me, wrapping around me in the way that's familiar, with both his arms around one of mine, his leg hooked over my thigh. He nuzzles against me like a cat.

"How can you be so calm about this?"

"We're not going to die up here."

"There are worse things than death—like Xavier's face when he finds out. How could I do this to him?"

"He will forgive you, Brighton. And Will is going to forgive me." He picks up my casted hand. "How's this?"

"Hurts, but I'll live, well until I get murdered."

"Yes, we will get murdered, but won't it be a good one? This is the worst we've done."

I should know better than to chat things like this over with a brat as bratty as Grayson. They live for this. Me, I can't see past my beating heart and the sour twist in my gut at the thought of Xavier's eyes turned down at me. Grayson's right about one thing though, we will be forgiven. We will be fine. I breathe easier remembering that.

Gray finds my lips and I close my eyes as his tongue slips in.

"That's it, Finny. Relax."

The kiss gets heated, his small hand moves over my crotch. "We don't have any lube, Gray."

"Dammit. I could suck you, least I'd get something to eat," he jokes.

"Let's just do this." I pull his face to mine with my good hand, ignoring the throb of my other one. *Take a painkiller, Finn.* Yeah, I'll get to it.

He nods. "Okay. Did I ever tell you your jaw is bitable?" he says, between kisses.

"You have. You've also said it's sharp as a blade. What you doing wanting to bite stuff sharp as a blade, huh?"

I don't mind his nonsense though; he's got my favorite kind of nonsense. When we tire of kissing, he lays against my chest and closes his eyes. "I'm not fine about being locked in the attic, Finn. Far from it, but I've got you. You keep the monsters away, like Will does."

I know that. He's never said it, but I know it. I kiss his feathery head. "Sleep, Graysie. Nothing we can do for now but wait till morning."

He doesn't answer, already out.

W hen Xavier has us seated on our still tender asses in the large, brown leather chairs in his office, none of what he has to say has anything to do with me and him being a couple. Instead, it's him giving us more rules. "Will's off campus today and tonight, everyone else has another place to be except you two."

"We can handle one night by ourselves, Xavier," I say forgetting that we're in his office and not out on a bench, under a tree with me wrapped in his coat. His eyes darken, unimpressed. I backtrack quickly. "What I mean is, where would you like us to go, sir?"

"Better, but you're a hair away from a trip over my lap, Mr. Brighton."

"Noted, sir."

"Unfortunately, I don't have a place for you tonight other than the house so you will have to 'handle one night by yourselves,' which is why I've brought you here to instill the fear of God into you both."

"What is it you think we're going to do, sir?" Grayson asks. Grayson is good at pulling off a thread of sarcasm, in a way that amuses Tops, without pissing them off—most of the time.

"The Gamma party, Will told you not to go, I'm telling Finn he can't go. That's the place I think you're going to go."

"Hey, wait a minute, why can't Finn go to the party?" I say. Not that I had any desire to go, but now that I'm being told I can't, I want to.

"Because I said so," Xavier answers.

"That's not a reason."

"It's the only one you're getting."

I glare at him, and we have a stare down until Grayson interrupts. "Because your best friend can't go and you're going to sit at home and watch Netflix with him in solidarity. Sir, of course we're not going to the party. Will would skin me alive and Friday night discipline would be even less fun than usual when you got hold of me."

"Not just Friday night discipline. I won't just punish Finn, I will personally punish you too," he says.

I cross my arms and slink down in my chair. Everyone wants a brat? Fine, I'll be a fucking brat, because, "This isn't fair."

"I'll remind you, Mr. Brighton, seeing as you're still

new, I don't promise fair, I promise what's right and what works for the balance between Top and brat. Unfortunately, it means missing a party now and then. I do have a reason, I'll tell you at the end of the weekend; consider this a trust building exercise."

"I'll explain it all to him, sir. Any other instructions for us?" Grayson is being way too agreeable. Why isn't he as pouty as I am? He's the one who destroyed the house over this party only a week ago.

"No, other than run any plans you might come up with tonight by me rather than Will. I want him to have the night off completely to be with his brother."

"We will, sir. But I really do think it's Netflix for us. And maybe a pizza, but don't tell Ani, he'll have my head. He's probably left some healthy crap for us to eat while he spends the night with Tom," Grayson says.

"Here, I'll spring for the pizza. Then at least I know you two will eat," Xavier says.

That moves me to action. I stop Grayson from taking the money. "We don't need pizza money, sir. We'll buy our own pizza or eat whatever kale-laden thing Ani left us."

Xavier and I proceed to have another stare off as he taps his fingers on the desk. "Leave us, Grayson. Please wait outside for Finnegan. Heed my warning," he adds.

"Of course, sir."

When Grayson is gone, "Is this about my brother not coming this weekend?" I figure out. I'm starting to see how Xavier works and I know Will had to tell him my plans for the weekend changed.

"Yes, mostly."

I think about it; nothing comes, but something about the tightness of his jaw gives him away. "You're jealous." I can't help it; I'm already swooning inside about that, butterflies doing somersaults in my stomach. I've always liked a little jealousy.

He doesn't say anything for several heartbeats and then he slams his fist on the desk. "Fine. Yes. But only a bit. Mostly I'm beside myself with worry about tonight. I know you're not okay about your brother not coming, the possibility of you doing something rash is high, and I would cancel my thing if I could, but I can't. I've even considered bringing you both with me—I still might."

Wow. First, he's *really fucking hot* jealous, even if it's only a little jealous. It's low-key adorable, especially since we aren't a thing yet—our only 'thing' so far is us dancing around our thing. Second, he's a whole other something when he's concerned about me like he is now. "It's nice of you to worry, sir, but you don't need to. I promise we'll be okay for one night. Would it make you feel better if we stayed in?"

"Yes, hence the pizza money. A bribe."

I laugh. "Well this may surprise you, but only a week ago, I stayed home on my own all the time. Been doing it a lot of my life even."

"None of that comforts me. Not only is that part of the problem, I am responsible for you now. If something happens to you tonight and I'm not here to deal with you, some of that's on me."

"What's your unavoidable event?"

"A charity auction," he says, wrinkling his nose.

"Oh my God, that's such a rich person thing to do."

"Yes, and not something I enjoy, other than the donating to charity part, but it's a necessary evil when you run a school. Networking."

I nod. "We'll be okay, Xavier. I promise."

"If I find out you two did go to that party, I will be

relentless. Neither of you will be leaving the house for anything aside from school obligations for a month," he says. He means it. "Sitting comfortably will be a thing of the past."

"No party. Scouts honor."

"You were never a scout."

I sigh. "Figure of speech. No? Okay, we'll stay in, sir."

He nods. "Thank you, Finnegan. All right, you may go."

I'm disappointed there's no more touching, or snuggling into his jacket, but I get the feeling the only touching he wants to do right now is his hand smacking onto my backside, which I'd like to avoid at this juncture. It's the language Xavier knows, and it soothes him every bit as much as it does me—that much I've figured out—because it's the language the House speaks and the comfort it seeks too.

Dammit. I know what to do. I need to do it. As much as Tops are drawn to soothe us... oh fine 'brats,' us *brats* are drawn to soothe Tops. I've watched Grayson do it a ton, Chris, Bellamy and Johnny too. Even Bray when he's in the mood. I swallow. "Oh, sir? One more thing. We can still have people over, right?" It's not against House rules for each of us to have one friend from another House over. If it's more than that, it turns into a party, which would require permission, but as the rules stand, that means one for me and one for Grayson.

His eyes narrow. "Who?'"

I shrug. "Haven't decided yet, but there is this hot Top, Nikolage, from one of my harder classes. Maybe he can uh, help me with my homework?" I waggle my eyebrows, suggesting that yes, fucking Nikolage is what I mean.

His chair slides out, he stands, hands flat on the desk and my heart's beating so damn fast. I have to take a stealthy breath. Maybe I should abandon the whole thing—I'm poking at a fucking lion and I know it—but I also know in my bones it's the right thing to do.

"No."

"Why?" I dare to cross my arms at him—a, *God* ... a *brat's* red flag, okay?

"Come here, my little Finnegan." He flashes shark teeth at me. He is predator, I am prey.

I want to buckle, I want to tell him I'm just kidding, but I'm in too deep now. I commit. "So you can spank me? Forget it. It's not against the rules. I was kind enough to even run it by you. I'll be leaving now."

I went too far didn't I? Yep. Too far.

Xavier clears his desk in a smooth, panther-like leap. I'm quick to respond, gripping either side of the leather chair I was just sitting in, catapulting myself over it. But I was a hockey player, not a gymnast and though my response is quick, my catapulting skills aren't graceful. I catch the chair and hit my knee, landing like a rock on the other side. "Fuck!" I roll on the ground behind it, licking my wounds.

How is it I can take one helluva spanking, but this paralyzes me?

Xavier's there fast, reminding me of Superman with the way his jacket flares. He crouches beside me. "I'm sorry. I didn't mean to scare you. Are you hurt?"

I laugh. "I'm fine. I wasn't scared."

"You were a bit, but - well I thought you wanted me to chase you." I've never seen the man blush, he does now. He can't even look at me.

I wait until he braves my eyes again. "Xavier, I *did* want you to chase me."

He stares frozen, my words sinking in, as my heart thumps loud drumbeats into my ears. While I wait for him to come to, I rub my sore knee. It is fine, but there's gonna be a nice bruise I'll have to explain to Ani later. I smile thinking of the arnica he'll insist he has to apply to it. Xavier notices my rubbing.

"Your knee."

"No, Xavier—"

But it's too late. He scoops me up and it's fucking embarrassing how easy it is for him to lift me. It's not like I'm small, he's just that large. He's got me bridal style and he swings us around, placing me in the chair and bending down to inspect the knee. I wore loose jeans, he's able to roll them up to have a look. "Doesn't look to be swelling, but you'll ice it anyway when you're home. Understood?"

He's holding my knee in both of his elegant hands, which are hot against my skin. I have to look down at him. "I will, sir."

I'm kicking myself now. This was a disaster. One point to me on not being a brat. A real brat would have pulled this off; I end up injuring myself.

"Now that it's established your knee will be fine, we will address Nikolage." His nose wrinkles, his form takes up all the space in the room once again.

Shit. Already forgot about Nikolage. "There's no Nikolage. I only said that to—"

"—I know Nikolage."

"I meant there's no Nikolage for me, sir. May I go?"

He's staring at me for a new reason now, a smile spreads slowly, reaching his eyes. He yanks me up. We're close, my lips aren't far from his. "I want to spank you so badly right now."

That was the goal. "You uh, you can, sir." My voice is just above a whisper.

"I know. I can spank you whenever I want. But that would not be a good idea. It's day eight, Finnegan."

"I am well aware of the day, Headmaster Harkness," I say, boldness returning. Two can play the game of cheek, but only one of us will win. We both know it's going to be him.

"All right, that's quite enough cheek from you, brat."

I light up everywhere. Maybe him calling me brat isn't so bad?

"I don't date people, Mr. Brighton. I own them. Do you want to be owned?"

"That depends, are you going to call me Mr. Brighton during sex?" It's too far. Only, I don't figure that out until right after it leaves my mouth and I can't take it back. I expect the smack I get. "Ow!"

"Think about it. *Seriously*. I won't settle for less than all of you. You've gotten an idea of what kind of person I am, and you know the rules. None of them would change, other than to get stricter. I'm quite possessive."

All of that takes my breath away, in the best way. "Xavier I—"

"—no," he cuts me off. "*Think* about it. Tell me tomorrow when you've had the night to think about it. You'll have time because all you're going to do is watch Netflix at the house and eat junk food Ani won't like."

"I'll think about it."

"Good. And no one over."

I roll my eyes. "I don't have a thing for Nikolage."

"He's your type." Everything about him is intense right now—his eyes, his body, even the line of his jaw as he chews metal with his teeth.

"No one over." Grayson's going to kill me for that one and there goes my 'I'm-not-a-brat' point.

141

"Very well. I release you and for God's sake, behave yourself, brat."

Yeah. Y'know, maybe brat isn't so bad, so long as I'm *his* brat? It's starting to grow on me. "I'll be a perfect angel, sir."

He looks skyward. "Heaven help me." He pats my ass, lighter this time, but in a way that relays how much he would like to spank me right now. "Go, before I put you over my knee on principle."

See? I get out of there fast after that and I swear I hear him chuckle from behind.

"Well, looks like our night just got cozy," I say to Grayson as we walk back from Xavier's office. "We're going to that party, Finnegan, if it's the last thing we do."

Oh brother. It very well might be. "What was all that stuff in there? Aha! I knew you couldn't be that agreeable." When we get home, the living room is empty for once. We're able to bypass any Top ears and head to my room where we can talk in private—after I grabbed ice for my knee of course, even though it's total overkill.

Grayson throws himself down on my bed, wiggling against the soft blue comforter, as I pull out a pair of sweats to change into, to make icing easier. "I had to throw him off the scent. He was onto me. I actually think he was more onto you," he says.

"Why was he more onto me?"

"Because you're a terrible liar. We're going to have to work on that."

"I wasn't trying to lie. I'm not planning on going to the party, not after that kind of warning."

"So then you do believe you're fine," he says, more to himself.

I answer anyway. "I believe I'm fine, because I am fine."

"Whatever. I have a plan and I think now you'll actually help me."

"What makes you think I'm going to help you? I'm staying in. You heard Xavier, didn't you? You're acting like you didn't hear a word he said."

"Oh, I heard him all right. Are you going to let him boss you around like that?"

"I was planning on it, yeah. I like having the option of a social life and sitting comfortably." When I get my sweats on, I take the plunge this time and slide in beside Grayson, leaving the ice pack near us on the bed for after. Can't believe I'm going to say this, but I want to cuddle first. We fit together, like we live in the same egg carton and I guess we kinda do.

Grayson settles his back into my chest and adjusts my arms around him how he likes them. "If we don't go, how will we prove we've changed our ways and are responsible enough to go to future events?"

"I'm guessing when they say we are? Isn't that why we came to this school and sought out Tops to begin with?"

"Oh, I see. Poor, delusional Finnegan. That's not how Tops work. Once they've watched their evil plans in action, *working*, they pat themselves on the back for a job well done and decide it's clearly what their brats need, and do more of it. Trust me. You've got to act now with this kind of stuff before it gets out of hand."

"Xavier seemed worried." I run my hand through his feathery hair, and he relaxes, reminding me of a cat Sam and I once had, who was always on edge until one of us ran our fingers from the top of his head to the base of his neck.

"I'm sure he is; so is Will. They're paranoid, nothing more. Tops get unreasonable when they worry, so this is the best time for a brat to push back. They expect it even."

Is that true? Grayson is more experienced than I am with this kind of stuff. "This one feels big though."

"They all do in the beginning. Like the first scratch on a brand-new car."

I think about it. "No. This thing with Xavier is new. I don't want to fuck it up."

"Let me put this in terms your love-addled brain might understand. If not for this 'thing' with Xavier, if he were just your Top and disciplinarian, as before, would you have come with me?"

Would I have? There still would have been consequences, the pleasing component would have been there for me, but truthfully, with Sam not coming, I need the distraction. I understand Sam having to work on a logical level, but the less logical part of me is upset he's not coming. "Okay, yeah fine. I would have."

"Exactly. Come to the party with me, I'm going with or without you."

And then you'll be alone, Finn. "Okay, fine. Ugh, but only for a little bit, okay?"

"Yeah sure, Finny. A little bit." He closes his eyes.

"Hey, what are you doing?"

"Shhhh. I'm resting my eyes. Keep doing that with your hand."

"Did anyone ever tell you you're a bossy little thing?"

"Everybody, all the time." He's unapologetic and I can't help giving him what he wants.

CHAPTER SEVEN

G rayson wakes up, rubbing his eyes. "Did you sleep?"

I shake my head. "It's getting cold though." The window's not open, but there isn't much heat up here.

"I saw some blankets over here—wanna make a blanket fort?"

"Definitely." Before we get started though, I swallow a couple of painkillers. They're bitter going down dry and they'll knock me out, but it'll be a blessing at this point. We construct our tent-shaped blanket fort, hanging sheets from the rafters, tying them with string to hooks in the floor and I ponder the idea that maybe once everyone sees our kick-ass fort-making skills, they'll reconsider our early deaths.

Not likely.

We find a mattress pushed against the wall. I use my one hand and with Gray's help, we install it in the fort, piling blankets and pillows on the surface and then collapsing on top of it. It's creeping close to three am. Maybe we can catch a couple hours before the House wakes up. We strip naked, how we like to sleep and meet under the pile of blankets. Grayson can't help himself. He traces over my cock with his fingers, even though it's dead to the world right now. Feels nice, though. "Finn? Will you talk to me?"

"About?"

"You know what."

"I don't."

"The thing you're avoiding. The reason we fucked off like we weren't supposed to tonight."

Oh, that. Grayson is far better than I am at racing off on a brat adventure with me, no questions asked. I usually grill him and make him give me some idea of why I'm putting my ass on the line. I owe him an explanation, but I can't.

"Talking is the opposite of avoiding."

"*Brighton.*"

"Look, it's fucking stupid, okay? I'll get over it."

"Hah. You think that's gonna fly with anyone? Xavier's going to make you talk. Why not practice on me?" He wiggles, trying to get closer to me. He's thin—I keep track of how thin. He's the okay kind at the moment.

I kiss his feathery head. "Fine. I'm freaking jealous of Max. There I said it."

"Will's not here, you can swear."

"Force of habit. Did you hear what I said?"

"I did. I knew it, and if I know it, Xavier knows it. Why do you think he wouldn't let you go to the party in the first place?"

I'm not sure he does though. Grayson and I live in each other's pockets. In some ways, he might know me better than Xavy. "Then why didn't he say something to me about it?"

"Because he was giving you the chance to process it, dumbass. Tops do try to let us handle things on our own.

You know it too. It's not Xavier's fault you went from zero to sixty on this one. Even I wasn't sure Finn and I know you."

He has a few points. The goal of Xavier's and my relationship isn't for Xavier to solve all my problems for me. He steps in when it's time. Leaving a brat to their brat fit is a necessary evil. I doubt he expected me to do something this monumental. He couldn't have predicted I'd go this far.

"What am I supposed to do?"

"Lord Christ almighty, Finn. Talk to him."

"You've been with Will too long." Will rarely swears, but he'll say that when he's really fed up.

"I see why he says it now. When you gonna learn to talk to people?"

"I do. Usually." I haven't always been good at it. His assessment's fair. Still rankles me. "Even if I did, nothing I can do about it. It's not like I want Xavier to kick Max out of the school, or assign him another Top, and I just know he'll do something like that. He's a good kid, I'm the one with the problem." Max is a twenty-five-year-old man, not actually a 'kid.' only four years younger than me. But he comes off young.

"You don't get to decide that, or have you forgotten where you live?"

"You're one to talk."

"We're not talking about me right now."

"Maybe we should." I breathe hard, staring at the dark blanket ceiling.

"Sorry, Max is a nerve. I shouldn't push, but I care about you, asshole." He returns to fondling my cock. Then he gets on his hands and knees, straddling me, kissing down my body.

"What you doing?" I ask.

"What I shoulda done earlier. What you really need is a

147

spanking, Brighton, but I don't give that shit out. This I can do."

He swallows my limp cock, which doesn't stay limp for long with his hot mouth on it. I pant heavy, arching my back. "Gray. *Gray*." He's too fucking good at that.

He pops his head off my dick, smug as fuck. He knows how good he is. "C'mon. Come down my throat, Brighton."

I do, holding onto his soft hair. Moaning, as relief floods through me. Between the post-orgasm energy depletion and the painkillers, my eyes droop.

"Your turn, Finny. Go to sleep. You need it."

Couldn't stay awake any longer if I wanted to.

I dream about lemons and fresh rain and men in long dark coats.

"Here, you're gonna need to put this on," Grayson says, waltzing into my room and handing me a pair of jeans and a t-shirt, which I'm pretty sure is salmon pink.

Everyone left. They all had other places to be, which means Gray and I are alone. Neither Ani nor Will liked leaving us, that we are both grown men of no comfort to them. But they both had to go, so eventually they left with lovingly stern warnings.

"Oh my God, Grayson. The nineties called; they want their wardrobe back. These are three sizes too big!"

"Which is why no one will recognize you. Also, your hair is way too blond, you'll need a wig."

He slaps one in my hand and turns to leave from my room. I stop him with a hand flat to his chest. "Grayson, this is starting to seem like a worse idea all the time."

"We need disguises. In some ways, this campus is too small. There's the off chance we'll get recognized by a Top and that Top will mention our presence to our Tops in passing."

"I'm not sure these disguises are good enough."

"Don't worry, I got us covered. We're safe from being ratted out at Gamma House. No Tops, remember? But to be on the safe side, we're gonna head straight upstairs to Brat Central when we get there."

This is sounding complicated, but I put the 'disguise' on. "I look ridiculous."

"You're good enough for a quick run up the stairs. Trust me."

"That's the problem, I don't." This one hundred percent spells disaster.

When we arrive, things look hopeful. The thrill of adventure takes hold. "C'mon guys, up this way," Emmery says.

I don't get the chance to look around much as we follow him up the stairs, but I do see that this house has a more open-style concept than our house does. You can view into the living room from the hallway at the top of the stairs, which isn't blocked by a wall, only a railing.

We're led to a room with seven other guys in it. I might be imagining this, but it's like they've got brat vibes coming off them. And dammit, I might fit in here. "You weren't allowed to be here either?" I ask Emmery.

"Oh no, I have permission, are you kidding me? Only Grayson is brazen enough to do something like this and uh, you I guess." The waves of his gorgeous dark hair bounce as he moves; he's pretty.

I look to Grayson, because none of that matches the tone of his advice earlier. He shrugs. "Would you have come if I opened with this is really risky and only insane people try to teach Will and Xavier lessons?"

"No. No, I would not have."

"See? What was I to do?"

I have a few suggestions for him, but I don't get to say any of them, as he walks past me and further into the room, grabbing a beer from a cooler on the way by. "Why were you given permission and not me?" I ask, Emmery. I know why Grayson wasn't, which means I'm going to have to watch him with the beer.

"You must be his favorite. He only gets that paranoid when he's smitten. You should have seen him with Trenton. It's how Xavier shows care, by being an overbearing, over-protective, ox."

Joy.

But at this stage it's somewhat comforting, and even though Emmery's poking a bit of fun at Xavier, I can tell those are things he appreciates too. Since we're in the room, I remove my wig and stuff it in the pocket of my oversized jeans. "Where are Trevor and Osh tonight?"

"Trev's off campus and Osh stayed back with the other brats of our House. They run a busy ship over there."

"How many brats are there in your House?"

"Including me, seven, which is why there's two full Tops. Will's the only one on his own with seven brats. I know Ani's Top-like himself sometimes, but it's not quite the same thing. Trevor is rough. People generally try not to give him cause to punish them and Osh is his own kind of force," he adds, his adoration seeping through. "If you live through this, you should come hang out. We have fun over there, even with three professors, a headmaster, a Trever and an Osh between us."

"That's a lot of Tops."

"It is, but we mostly only have to worry about Trev and Oshie directly, since the professors don't live at the house, and then Xavier between the three of us that belong to him."

Right. I suppose I've never had any run-ins with the Tops of the other brats in our House, but I also know that doesn't mean I'm immune. They would be owed proper respect should they happen to stop by.

"Anyway, you're here now. Come in, have a beer or ten and have fun."

"I'll have one beer. We're not staying long."

"Yeah, okay." He doesn't believe me.

I talk to and get to know a few more brats, all the while keeping an eye on Grayson who's three beers in—Will wasn't wrong about him. I do okay and take pride in how well-behaved I am. Maybe once Xavier gets over the fact that I've blatantly disobeyed him, he'll see that I can be responsible at a party. I really don't see what he was so worried about.

Three beers in, I cut myself off. I've had my fill, and it's time to break the seal and have a piss anyway. "Hey, Em? There a washroom I can use?"

"Yeah, down the hall."

I don't bother putting my 'disguise' on, since I'm just going down the hall. I have to wait in line and while I do, I see a familiar head down below. My heart swells, *Sammy came after all.* How did he know where to find me? I head down the stairs to greet him, tapping him on the shoulder. "Hey broth—oh." It's really, really, not

Sammy. "Uh, sorry man. I thought you were someone else."

"Someone handsome? You're a stud. I'm sure I can be your someone else. We can find a room, plenty of 'em here."

I'm so gutted it's not Sammy, I almost say yes, but everything's constricting, my muscles, my clothes, there's a weight on my chest and it's hard to breathe. *Get out of here, Finnegan.* I head outside for air, leaving buddy hanging, and pull my phone out of my pocket to dial my brother, but it goes to voicemail. *'Hi, you've reached Samuel Brighton and Associates, please leave a message at the tone.'*

Samuel Brighton and Associates? Did he make partner already and not tell me? That would mean he's been working at this awhile, that it's not a recent thing like he said on the phone. I bet... I bet he kept it from me because I'm always so fucking needy. He probably didn't want to upset me and have me think he's leaving me so he can live his own life. Which, he really should do anyway. I'm twenty-seven, I shouldn't need my big brother anymore.

I almost call his phone back, just to hear his voice again, but I don't want to hear about his life without me. Instead, I head inside and grab a beer from the first cooler I see. I want to break rules suddenly. There's no official rule on drinking beer, but I'm not supposed to be here, and if I'm totally honest, coming here was probably my first act of rebellion over the Sam thing. Getting drunk won't lead to anything good or responsible. Perfect. I'll get in trouble when I get caught.

Maybe Xavier will kick me out of school and things will go back to the way they were with no changes.

I get another few beers in, and then find Grayson who's six sheets to the wind, dancing with several someones. They're happy for me to join them.

That's the last thing I remember.

I wake up to the rising sun, poking through the window, shining in my eyes so I have to cover them. I'm on a couch, a couch that *isn't* the pale green one with cherry blossoms on it—it's some kinda royal blue with silver trim—on top of, "Grayson?"

"Huh, what?"

"Shit. I think we fell asleep. What time is it?" My voice is groggy as fuck.

He scrambles off the couch and steps on a sleeping Emmery. "Ow! Oh, fuck. Where are we?" Em says, waking.

We never went home. We're still at Gamma House, on the couch, surrounded by the stench and empty bottles of last night. We all come to this realization together. "What are the chances we can still get away with this somehow?" I ask.

"Ugh, about zero," Grayson says. "I think a cat died in my mouth."

"Ew!" Em says.

"Well, it's true. God dammit, do we have to go home?" Gray says.

"I'm all for running away to Mexico," I suggest.

"Mexico?" Em says.

"Yeah, because I don't think we should go home, I think we should get far away from here. We are so dead." I *thunk* my head backward onto the couch. As much as I am truly dreading all the trouble we're in, there's something fun about being in it together.

The three of us laugh. "Well, we really should get back.

Someone's likely to have called the national guard by now," Grayson says, his droopy eyes barely open.

"It was nice knowing you both," Emmery says. "I'll make sure to visit your graves daily."

"You know what Xavier's like about curfew, Em. You're not getting off easy either, plus you're an accomplice," Grayson, points out.

His eyes widen. "Mexico it is."

Grayson and I finally peel off the couch to leave. "Ow!" A pain shoots through my wrist, as I push myself up. It's swollen and bruised. "What the fuck?"

"You don't remember falling?" Emmery says. I shake my head. "Yeah, you fell pretty bad by the pool, tried to catch yourself by putting that hand out."

God dammit, Finnegan.

Grayson winces. "Xavier is not going to like that."

"He's not going to like any of this." I run a frustrated hand through my greasy hair. Even the fuzz of my undercut is greasy.

"Yeah but, well, you'll see."

That reminds me. He freaked about my knee and it wasn't even a real injury. What's he going to say about this?

We hug each other goodbye and then split off to go our separate ways. When Grayson and I reach the door, I see the note, and every crook and cranny in my body cringes.

Turn around and come straight to my office, Mr. Brighton.

Xavier

Fuck he makes my heart race, even in a note.

I look down at my clothes. I'm still wearing the over-sized jeans and t-shirt from last night. I'm nowhere near presentable, but this note tells me a lot. He was here. He could have texted me to say to come by, but he left the note so I would know he came to the house personally. He doesn't want me to go in and change; he wants me to come as is.

"What are you going to do?" Grayson says.

"I'd better go."

"Like that?"

"Like this. Let the rest know I'm still alive, for now."

He nods, slinging arms around my neck. "Finn, I had the best time. I know we're in a lot of trouble, beyond trouble, but..." he looks to the ground. "I needed to do this. Thank you."

Something aches in him. It's the same thing that aches in me. I press my lips to his and squeeze him before I head to see Xavier.

When I enter his office, our eyes lock in a stare down, which is starting to become our thing. I back down first. I'm the one who broke my promise, I know I'm here to get wrung out. What I don't expect is for him to burst with laughter. "What on Earth are you wearing?"

I look myself over again, remembering the 'disguise' Grayson concocted—a lot of good that did—and run a hand through my hair, which must look a sight. My head is still pounding a bit with the hangover that's making itself known and I'm going to need greasy food and coffee stat. "It's a long story."

He shakes his head. "You went, after you promised me you wouldn't."

"I know, sir. I'm sorry. And you were right," I tell him sitting in one of his large, brown leather chairs, curling my legs up and resting my head on the tall back wanting to close my eyes so badly. *What are the chances he'll let you sleep here before he wrings you out, Finnegan?*

"I know I was right, but what did you come to the conclusion I was right about?"

"Going was a bad idea. Nothing overly terrible happened, but it turned into another night of me drinking away my sorrows, a habit I came to this school to stop. Plus, I'm a terrible drunk and I think I sprained my wrist."

"*Finnegan.*"

"I know, okay? And I know I'm in trouble for breaking several rules. I fully accept all consequences." At this point they'll be a relief.

He sighs a sigh that says he doesn't know what to do with me, which is probably weird for him, the man who knows what to do with everyone and everything. "Come here," he says. "Let me have a look at that wrist."

"It'll be fine."

"Wasn't asking, Finnegan. Get over here." When I get there, he pulls me into his lap by the waistband of my too large pants. *You're on the other side of his desk, Finnegan.* I settle into his large form, getting comfortable as best I can—I'm a medium height and he's six and a half feet tall and we're in one chair—and I'm self-conscious because I must reek of alcohol and partying. He takes up my wrist carefully and looks it over. "This is swollen. You'll need ice."

"Yes, sir."

He pulls my wrist toward him, pressing soft lips to it ever-so-gently, like it's an egg. "Did you have time to think about what I asked you to think about in all your drunken debauchery?"

"That's still on the table?"

"Why wouldn't it be?"

"I said I wouldn't do something and then I did it anyway."

"Which sounds exactly like a brat to me. Just don't expect me to feel sorry for you when you want to go out next weekend and you're stuck in the house. I meant what I said, you and Grayson aren't going anywhere for the next month."

I should be pissed about that, but I'm not. I'm fucking glad I haven't ruined everything, and I'm comforted by the restrictions rather than bothered by them. My face cracks into a smile. "Xavier I..." I need to say it, but it's hard to say. I'm not good at this. I make myself do it anyway. "I want to be yours." No, I didn't think about it *during* said debauchery. My mind had already been made up, because I had plenty of time to think about it yesterday after Grayson and I met with him.

I thought over what being his could mean, and while there's no way to truly know, I know in my heart of hearts how much I'll regret not even taking the leap to find out. Especially when I feel the universe has been conspiring to pull us together, as foo-foo as that sounds—I have Sam to thank for that kind of thinking—and every cell in my body *wants* him.

I don't know what possesses me—this man does something to me—I throw my arms around him, like I saw Grayson do my first night at the house and he hugs me to him. *You might officially be a brat now, Finnegan.*

Nope. Not saying it yet.

I squeeze him and he holds me, and everything feels right again, *almost.* We've still got to chat in the language we speak, but for now, *this.* "What happened? I do understand something of you, even if you've not been here long. You're a brat, but not this kind of brat."

"I needed a distraction."

"I see. From what?"

"You were right," I repeat. It comes pouring out of me. Everything about my brother and feeling like we're not close anymore and that I've become a burden. Then, as soon as I say the words, I feel like an idiot because I've said all of these things to him. *Him*, practically a stranger, but whose approval I desire, and now that he knows one of my innermost fears, I'm terrified it will drive him away from me. And yeah, I know that's stupid, I know Xavier's made of the toughest stuff imaginable, that he can handle the likes of me, but the feeling is there whether I want it to be or not. "When I heard his voicemail, it was the thing to break down the fragile dam I had in place. That's when I really started drinking."

He nods, and he's quiet, letting me cry, running his hand through my hair, which is probably gross and fucking oily. "I knew I shouldn't have left you last night."

"How did you know?"

"A feeling that gnawed at me. I seem to have a bit more of a sixth sense with you. I knew your brother cancelled his visit. I should have brought you with me; I shouldn't have left you alone. But your disobedience is on you, Finnegan."

"I know, sir."

"How are you feeling about your brother now?"

"I want it not to bother me, I want him to have a life, but it does bother me some."

"I think your brother, and everyone in your life for that matter, chooses exactly the relationship they want to have with you. Remember that, Finnegan, the next time you feel guilt over being vulnerable with someone. People listen because they love you." I nod. "In the meantime, because I have every faith you'll talk and work things out with your brother *when you talk to him*," I hear every bit of instruction in those words, "you and I have something to work out. But it's hard for me to take you seriously, looking like this. Is that a wig in your pocket?"

I look down, and the black wig's there sticking out of my pocket. I laugh. "Yeah."

"C'mon. You're getting showered and changed."

We leave his office, but this time, instead of walking, we hop into one of the campus golf carts and drive to an apartment block. We take the elevator up to the penthouse and holy shit, I'm going to Xavier's apartment, aren't I? The space is large and open, with a kitchen immediately to our left and living room to the right. Across the space is the bedroom with an ensuite bathroom that he ushers me into. "Shower. I'll put clothes on the bed for you. Dress and then come out to the kitchen."

I get the oddest sensation of déjà vu, like I've been here before, like being in Xavier's apartment is the most natural thing in the world. I shower and when I come out, on the bed is a white t-shirt I smile at—he's noticed how much I like to wear white t-shirts—I'm surprised at the grey sweats, but I put them on.

I patter out in bare feet to the smell of coffee and bacon. He sets an ice pack and a cup of coffee on the white countertop for me and continues on with his cooking. I set myself on a barstool to watch and admire, while I ice my wrist as he's wordlessly instructed. He's changed too, into a less formal button-up shirt in blue, the sleeves rolled up to mid-biceps, the top buttons open and the skin of his chest showing. He's not just handsome, he's the kind of handsome you need to analyze, because you're not quite sure it's real. *What's a guy like him doing interested in you, Finnegan?* I don't know. Someday, I'll lose whatever intrigue has caught his eye, because he'll realize it was never really there to begin with. He'll figure me out and realize I'm nothing special. But for now, he seems to think I hung the moon. "I didn't think you owned sweatpants. Isn't this against the rules?"

He smiles. "I'm not allowing you to go anywhere like that, it's just for me. Somehow, you manage to make sweatpants indecent. Also, it's all I had that would fit you. How's your head?"

"It's been better."

He comes up with two Advil and a glass of water, then returns to his cooking. "So, what is it we had to work out before you make true on your promise that I won't be sitting comfortably for the next few weeks?"

"You may want to refrain from reminding me of that. I'm putting it out of my mind, so we can do this, and I'll deal with you and Grayson tomorrow. The thing I want to work out is us," he says, gesturing from him to me. "I told you, I don't date people, I own them."

I lean in, putting my elbows on the counter, and grasp my hot coffee mug with one hand, while keeping my bruised wrist on the ice. Xavier is fascinating; I could stare at him forever. "What's that mean? You want a kinky sex slave, or somethin'?"

"As fun as that does sound for a night or two, no, I don't want a sex slave. Besides that's not you and I quite like who you are. I engage in a domestic discipline lifestyle with my partners. That much is a given and it's why you're here anyway; you knew there was something in you that would respond well to such a structure. But it's one thing to come to my school and have me be your Top and disciplinarian, it's another to add romance."

"Ani said lots of people do that here, that it's the whole point."

He nods, turning the bacon over. "It is. And I know you mentioned in your forms that you hoped to find a partner while you were here, but did you imagine the responsibility of being *my* partner?"

"I imagined the hope of getting through the first week without having a run in with the Headmaster, but that didn't happen. At this point, I've let go of expectations, sir." I give him a cheeky smile.

"Point, you. What should and shouldn't happen is usually moot anyway, and it's just as applicable here, because you already said you're mine and I'm not letting you go easily."

My heart lifts and I drink my coffee. I already like the thought of being his.

We eat together and it's all easy. The conversation, the banter, even the casual touches that happen, like my foot finding his ankle and twining around it. I might be as possessive as he is, maybe more.

"You should know, Finnegan, I'm not quite as polyamorous as some. I don't take on other partners, and I would prefer to focus on you, romantically, especially when I have so many other boys who need my attention in other ways."

"Ani mentioned you're the most monogamous of us all."

He laughs. "It's still not monogamy by far. And I want you to take other partners, I encourage it. Brats like you need that kind of touch and intimacy from your spanking circle. Everyone in the house and my other boys come pre-approved, but if you want someone else, we'll need to discuss it. As you know, all of us on campus, including myself, since I am close and personal with many bare bottoms, are tested frequently, but it's more of a commitment thing for me."

"Of course. I know that 'poly' doesn't mean 'sleep with whoever you want,' but it seems unfair if I have multiple lovers and you have just me."

"Equal does not mean the same. We have different needs. My need is to take care of you, and taking care of you includes making sure you get what you need. There might be some people I'm not comfortable with, I'll let you know."

"I'm going to guess Nikolage isn't on the approved list?"

His eyes darken. "He is not."

God that gives me the best rush.

He pours us both more coffee, and I note how much his demeanor changes as the morning turns to afternoon. He's still firm as ever, but he's the most relaxed I've ever seen him. He leans back in his chair, spreads his legs and holds his coffee mug in two hands, letting the mug sit atop his chest, while laughing at everything I say. *Are you that funny, Finnegan?* Xavier seems to think so.

He never loses his stern, Headmaster of a Discipline school countenance, but he's also just a guy right now, a guy who's interested in me, of all people. Like, downright fascinated. He's so normal, it's almost unnerving. But then we return to familiar ground. "I would have liked to take you for dinner tonight, but unfortunately you're grounded."

Warmness spreads to my forehead—well that's embarrassing. This has added a whole other level to our relationship. "You can't make an exception for that?"

"I will not." Even with that, his refusal to budge, it brings me peace inside and the feeling of having something solid increases. "But it is time for you to get back to the house, before they think I've eaten you. Fair warning, Will and Ani may have a few words for you."

I wince. Right. Dammit. And in that house, they are never just words.

He won't let me leave without wrapping my wrist in a Tensor bandage and telling me I'm to visit the school's infirmary later today. He walks me to the door of his apartment, and I slip my shoes on. I like that I can feel an energy between us, it's unlike anything I've ever felt before and I know that energy's going to be the source of both hot passion and explosive disagreements. "I guess I'll see you tomorrow so you can, you know..."

"Spank your naughty bottom?" *Whoa*, the rush. "You will. Four pm sharp, bring your partner in crime."

"Yes, sir." I turn to leave.

"Finnegan, wait."

"Yea—"

His large hand slams against the wall beside me, his arm trapping me there and then his lips are on mine, hot and savage. The most electricity I've ever felt in a kiss runs through me and I respond in kind. He's become that life raft again, holding me afloat, while I grapple for something; all I find is him and I'm okay with that. When he pulls away, we have a new kind of stare down, as we look at each other in awe. *Did that really just happen, Finn?*

We both pant and try to catch our breath. "Wow. I don't know what I expected, but not that," he says. "I shouldn't have done that."

"Why?"

"Because now I want you to go even less." He grazes the back of his hand along my cheek.

"I'm okay with that."

"If you stay, I will bring you to my bed."

"I'm *really* okay with that."

"I won't be able to resist spanking you and your arse needs to be in top form for tomorrow."

I groan. "Okay." But fuck is my cock hard.

He kisses my forehead and sends me off with a hard smack to my ass; I float out the door.

I stand on the porch and hesitate going inside. I already know what awaits me. There's something comforting in it, but I'm going to hear it from Will and Ani, and knowing how upset they're gonna be twists my stomach. Part of me hopes Will is dealing with Grayson or is too tired from the dealing with him. The phrase I've heard used around the house: 'no honor amongst brats,' comes to mind. In fairness, this was all Grayson's idea, even if I willingly went along.

Are you saying you're a brat, Finn?

No. *No.*

"There you are," Ani says soon as I walk in the door. "March. Into the kitchen. I'm having a word with you."

Spank me with his wooden spoon he means. "But Ani, Xavier is going to spank me plenty tomorrow, and I'm already grounded. Isn't that enough?"

"All that's between you and Xavier. We have to settle up between you and me," he says, still pointing toward the kitchen.

Bray, Johnny and Christopher are there, but Ani doesn't pay any mind to them, or tell them to leave. There's no such thing as privacy in this house when it comes to spanking. You choose to forgo the rules, you can be spanked with an audience. Even though I'm the only one about to get spanked, the dread from everyone is palpable

—Ani's spoon and hairbrush are legendary in this house. He picks up my bandaged wrist, carefully. "What's with this?"

"Sprained it. Xavier took care of it. Iced and wrapped. I've got to visit the infirmary later."

He nods. "Get yourself over here, good hand on the counter. I'll be careful of your wrist."

"C'mon, Ani. I'm sorry."

"You want to forget to come home and worry us, that's fine, but you're gonna know how I feel about it."

I groan, but place my hands on the counter, making sure not to put weight on the injured one.

Ani Spanks Finn By Artsy Ape

His fingers are quick to climb under the waistband of Xavier's sweats and my boxers, tickling just the slightest bit. Then it's cold air on my bare ass, out and vulnerable for Ani's spoon. "You," smack! "do," smack! "not get to take off like that anymore," he says, all punctuated by sharp whacks with his nasty little spoon.

"Ah, ow. Ouch! I'm sorry, sir," I say, because Ani is sir right now. He might be gentle and soft and less stern, but he's still a force and he's still in charge.

"The rules of this house will be obeyed, Mister Finn. For you, that's your butt in this house by midnight on weekends and eleven on weeknights. Do I make myself clear?"

"Yes, Ani. Sir! Ow, yes sir."

It's painful, but fast and then it's over. My ass *stings*, as Ani pulls me into a tight hug as I rub with my good hand. "When we got home this morning and neither one of you were here, we were so worried about you," he says, crying plump tears.

Ani crying is the worst; I'm an ass. "Ani, I'm sorry. We won't do it again."

"You won't. Now sit in that chair and no moving until Will gets down here. Did Xavier feed you? Tell us what happened?"

"Yeah, some of us are dying to know," Chris says. "He was here looking for you this morning. We all saw the note, but here you are alive. What kind of sorcery did you pull?"

Have I got a story for them. "Well actually, these are his clothes, and he kissed me."

The kiss ends up being the least surprising thing, everyone already sure this was a thing that was going to happen, the bets not placed on if, but when. Everyone's more surprised I lived to tell the tale, and even more surprised that he's refrained from punishing me until tomorrow. "Not totally," I complain. "I'm not allowed to leave the house."

I relish in the normal of that sentence. Other places it might sound weird, but not here. Here it's a thing, and it ties in with belonging for me. No one's fazed by the spanking either, other than glad it wasn't them on the chopping block; it's normal and happens several times a day in this house.

I dread the look on Will's face. If it was anything like Ani's tears, I want no part in it. While I wait, my phone rings. It's Sammy. "My brother, Ani. Can I take this?"

"Yeah, go ahead, sweetheart."

I'm going to be mature about this. I want this for my brother. He deserves to become partner. "Hello?" I say, slinging myself down on the now familiar green couch with the cherry blossoms blooming in various phases of life all over it.

"Finn! I saw you called last night. God, I miss you. I'm sorry about the work thing, I feel like such a heel. I should have come. You're more important to me than work."

"It's okay, Sam. I... I heard the message. I mean, I wish you would have told me yourself, but I'm still happy for you."

"Message?"

"Samuel Brighton and Associates?"

He's quiet for a moment. "Oh. Oooooh." He laughs. "No, that was me and a guy at work goofing around. Shit. I've got to change that back. Just dreaming, I didn't make partner yet. You'll always be the first one I tell something like that too."

I tear up. I would have found a way to be fine with it if he hadn't told me first, but I'm glad it's not a thing yet and I get to be part of the journey with him. "You'd better."

"I will."

"And Sammy, please come visit? I fucking miss you, man." It comes out. That's not something I would have just said a week ago. We both know it.

"Wow, Finn. What're they doing to you over there?"

"I'm not sure, Sammy, but I think I like it."

We chat and it's just when I'm getting off the phone, Will's there. The tall cowboy's hurt, I can see it etched into his body language. Grayson and I really crossed the line last night. For whatever reason, Grayson had to do it though, and I was hard-pressed to let him go alone, but now I wish I'd let that one play out between the two of them. It was too soon for me to do something like this.

"Will, I'm sorry. I know that's not enough, but I'll make it up to you. Promise."

He analyzes every inch of me. Knowing what I know of him, he's looking me over to make sure I'm all right. I've been absorbed into this family quickly, maybe by Will most of all. I'm one of his, now. His eyes brim with tears and I want to die. "I came home this morning and noticed y'all weren't here. We looked everywhere, and it wasn't long after someone located you both at Gamma house. I was about to head over there and wrangle you both home by your necks like naughty kittens, when Xavier showed up. He convinced me to let you two saunter home on your own, since we knew you were safe."

I want to tell him I'm sorry a thousand times more, but my apologies feel worthless. I know I'm never doing something like this again. Which means I'm not a brat, not at all. Sure, I can be Xavier's brat, it's like, a figure of speech or something, because if a brat's a someone who puts this look on Will's face, count me out.

He sighs. "C'mere, naughty kitten."

Will's torso is a good torso for hugging. It's solid, and familiar, the kind that holds you up through anything. His arms are thick and hold me in an owning way, a way that says, 'you're mine and I will keep you safe, even if that means saving you from yourself.' "What happened to your wrist, darlin'?"

"Sprain. It'll be all right. Xavier took care of it. I have to head to the infirmary later."

"I'll be taking you. Jeez, Finn. Next time, I'm getting y'all a babysitter, or taking you with me."

"You sound like Xavier."

"He did teach me all he knows."

"How's it fair we get two of you?" I smile up at him. "I'm kidding. We're lucky to have two of you."

"Flattery ain't getting you out of what you have coming. Speaking of, upstairs to your room. I'll be up in a bit and we're gonna talk all about going to parties you're not supposed to be at, staying out all night without a word."

"Ani gave me the preview of that chat."

"Good. I don't feel sorry for you. Go."

"Yes, sir."

I shouldn't be surprised at this point, but I am when I see Grayson in my room. "Finn, you're alive!"

"Do people really think Xavier eats people?"

"Yes. Hey, you're not wearing the lovely disguise I gave you."

"Nope. Oh, how I miss my Kris, Kross jeans." I lay on the bed with him, wrapping myself around him. Grayson has quickly become an anchor for me, a place I can sink into and stay while the ocean storms around me.

"So, you and Xavier, huh?"

I get shy. "Yeah. What about you? What can I expect from Will?"

His eyes widen. "Nothing good. There's a reason I've been laying on my stomach."

"Yet still not enough to keep you where you're supposed to be."

169

"Who says I'm not supposed to be here? Will said I could. He knew that it would be cruel to keep me from you. Remember, we brats gotta stick together. I had to make sure you survived Xavier. And Finn? I owe you an apology. I knew you were chasing a spanking. I'm not sure you knew it then, or even if you know it now, but I did. I took advantage of that."

"Gray, you're gonna have to explain that to me in English." There are all these brat terms they use, and I'm still catching on.

"Chasing a spanking is something Will says. You get riled inside about something and you can't sort out your feelings on your own, so you throw a brat fit to push. What we really want—ugh, can't believe I'm going to say this out loud—is a spanking. But we won't ask for one, instead we brat it out so we'll get spanked. I knew you were upset about your brother not coming, that you were on the verge. I took advantage of that."

"I... oh." Yeah. That's... was I? Something about all of that feels right. I can't deny it, but I also didn't decide any of it consciously.

You might be a brat, Finnegan.

Shut up, brain.

"I forgive you, Gray. I made my own choices. I wanted to go. My behavior's on me even if you egged me on. By the way, we see Xavier after school tomorrow."

"Fuck me, why do I do these things?"

"We can't do this again, Gray. It was horrible. Will's face, Ani's face, Xavier's face."

"I know. I regret it all too." He rolls on his back, away from me, wincing when he hits his sore ass.

"You do? I thought this was the sort of thing brats did?"

"Well yeah, but it doesn't mean we don't feel guilt and

170

regret. What I really needed was that spanking Will gave me. I wish I could just say it instead of making him go through all that, but I can't. Not yet anyway, maybe one day. So you're still in brat denial, eh?"

"Denial? There's nothing to deny. There's a spectrum. I might do the odd brattish thing, but I am far to the low end."

"I agree, there is a spectrum, but being on it, still means you're on it. I would argue that you're further toward brat versus good boy than you think, but you'll have to figure that out for yourself. We're the same, Finn."

I'm not so sure we are. I know he wants us to be.

"Anyway, doesn't matter for now. I just wanna cuddle awhile. My ass hurts."

I'm happy to do that, accepting him when he rolls back toward me, shoving my hand down the back of his pants. "Wow, this is still warm."

"Wait till you see. It's awesome, but I'll wait till later to do the big reveal. Once Will's spanked you."

"Joy. Why is that a thing again?"

"Don't even with that, Brighton. You enjoy it too." He burrows himself into me.

And yeah, he's right about that one. I totally do.

CHAPTER EIGHT

"I don't know why you've wound yourself up about Max and frankly I don't want to know, but for what it's worth, Xavier's gone for you."

Grayson's rolled off to the other side of the mattress, lounging on his back, staring up at the dark, blanket ceiling in our hastily constructed blanket fort. His legs are kicked up the wall, feet tugging at one of the main blanket walls. I woke up a few moments ago, and I think that yellow haze beyond the blanket is the first dredges of morning sunlight coming in through the window, casting a gnarled shadow of tree branches.

I throw a pillow at him. "Gee, thanks. All better, asshole."

"Did you hear the last part I said? Xavier only has eyes for you."

"Yeah, I... yeah I know."

"But you're still waiting for the other shoe to drop, even after two years."

Yes. "I told you it was stupid. Can we talk about something else?"

"Xavier's gonna love hearing about how your cell phone wasn't charged."

"How's that supposed to help me?"

"Just give it a second, Brighton."

When Xavier finds out I didn't call him from the hospital, when he finds out I let my phone die, when he's spent time wondering where the fuck I was, worrying, he's gonna kill me. Know what? I should live here now.

And ... *oh*.

That feeling doesn't happen by accident. It's created.

It's knowing that Xavier will kick my ass if I miss curfew. It's his scolding voice when he says, "I wouldn't do that if I were you, Mr. Brighton," or even his personal favorite of, "Someone's going to have a very sore bottom if they keep at it."

It's in the follow through. When I'm getting a spanking, I'm *getting* a spanking—there's no such thing as sweet talking my way out of it. There's a look, with irises made of torrents, and a brow that arches higher than any brow should. Little things to swirl within me, stirred by each other.

But rules.

Maybe rules most of all because they are the most far reaching. He doesn't have to be there to look or scold or spank when everyday occurrences remind me of the rules.

Out in the world at large I know I'm his, I know he's imprinted within me, because of rules. Rules I choose to obey.

Xavier's gonna love hearing about how your cell phone wasn't charged.

A knot releases.

"You sure there wasn't water in those boxes, Grayson? Maybe once we get the window open, we could figure out a raven system with Emmery and he could get food up to us."

He smiles a smug smile, reaching his arm across the mattress and slipping his hand into mine. "There you go, Finny. I knew you were still there."

Will comes up and I'm grateful just to have a visitor, even though I know what he's up here to do to me. Grayson got kicked out hours ago via text message. I watch Will shut the door with purpose, his whole demeanor somber. I know Tops enjoy spanking, but I suppose there's some amount of regret in having to do it, because of what disobeying the rules means. It's disrespectful and Will is big on respect. I sit up quickly, remaining quiet so he can speak first.

"You know what this is going to be for, so why don't you tell me?" he says, crossing his arms.

I bite my lip. "Even if we had permission, which we did not, we should have been home by midnight, we should have told you where we were going to be."

He nods. "It's nice to hear you know what the rules are."

"I'm sorry, Will."

He nods and I should be thinking of so many other things, but I admire his legs in his soft, ripped jeans. They're thick and strong and ugh, I'll be over them soon. *Finnegan, why do you do the things you do?*

He sets his white Stetson on my desk. "I suppose sometimes our rules don't make much sense when you're new. As Grayson pointed out, it's not like either of you almost killed yourselves, but it's not about that sometimes. There are

174

rules and they aren't there for the heck of it. You're expected to follow them to the letter—the habit of following them's just as important as anything else you'll do at this school. It keeps the circle intact, the one you form with your Head of House."

"I think I get it, sir. It's the lack of respect. Yeah, it is a bit of a circle, isn't it? Breaking the rules breaks the circle."

"That's right. The rules and the consequences for them create the feeling, *that* feeling, the one we all look for, but that's not the only thing. The small rules, like curfew, speak to the larger rules that do have extraordinary benefits to your psyche. Holding a brat to small rules, says we'll hold you to bigger rules. Each is a cog, affirming the existence of the next cog. Not to mention, just because something didn't happen this time—though I would argue that it did with your sprained wrist, Finnegan—doesn't mean anything."

"I'm starting to really get that, all of it, on the larger scale."

"Good, which means you'll get why I can't go easy on you. Obedience is big around here, whether you agree with a rule, and its severity, or not. Being where you're supposed to be is a big one for me. If I don't know where you are, I can't come save your foolish butts. We're lucky nothing happened this time, but next time, we might not be so lucky."

He comes over to my bed and extends a hand for me. I take it and let him pull me off the bed. I'm still wearing Xavier's sweats. They get pulled down pretty swiftly with my boxers and I'm guided over his lap. "You will follow the house rules, end of story. Am I understood?" he says, when I'm good and uncomfortable, my ass bare, and in the air.

"Yes, sir."

He starts in with his heavy hand, and it's not terrible,

yet, but I know he's only just begun. "We care about you, Finn. I know you only jus' got here, but we're quick to caring in this house. You're one of us."

"I ... Yeah. I know." I do. I've gone from not feeling like I belong anywhere to knowing I've always belonged here.

"And I think you were testing a bit," he says, still spanking away on my poor ass, who is beginning to want to move out of his target range. "Brats always test the first week and that's fine, test all you like, but you'll end up with a sore bottom every time."

"Ahh! Ow, yeah. Okay, I got it, Will."

The spanks get more intense, I have to look back to see that yeah, it's still just a hand. Will's hand isn't just any hand though. It's thick and meaty, it packs a heavy sort of spanking, I fidget without wanting to. Will puts one strong leg, of the same ones I was admiring, over my two squirming ones. "Your curfew will be strictly respected. This is what happens when you go to parties and drink too much. A habit you could do without in my opinion. Lucky for you, Xavier makes that final call for you, but if it were me, I'd put a full stop on drinking for you for a bit."

It's at about this point in the spanking it seeps in. I don't know why it takes time during some spankings and other spankings it's just there all along; I feel it now though. Maybe it's that thin slice of disappointment I detect in his tone triggering it. I don't like knowing I've disappointed him. I don't like that I've behaved badly.

The swats come faster, with less breaks in between, I'm panting heavily, and the yelps and sounds come out of my mouth without me wanting them to. I'm responsive, like Xavier says I am. I keep trying to hold it in, thinking I should take the spanking with indifferent poise, but I'm not capable. I squirm and fight.

I get a break, as he takes the time to pull my pants down further, exposing more of my thighs. I know what he's going to do. "Will please, not the thighs."

He takes the time to rub my sore ass. "What part about displeased did you not get the memo about? Yes, the thighs. Don't disobey me or Xavier next time."

Ooooh!

He's relentless and by the time he's done with the tender flesh of my thighs, I'm swearing on my life I will never set a toe in the house past curfew again, nor will I ever be where I'm not supposed to be.

And then he's done.

He stands me up and lets me stand there with my pants down taking my hands (my sprained one gently) so I can't reach back to rub anything. The sting radiates outward and down to my thighs. "Actions have consequences around here. You and Grayson might talk yourself up into the kind of trouble you end up doing, but we'll always be here, and we'll always hold you accountable. Remember that."

I have to think about that one. I understand the words, but there's more to it than words. I nod, letting the burn of my flaming backside sink in. "We love you, Finnegan."

The spanking didn't elicit crying, but that does. Tears flow, he pulls me to him, and I cling to the large cowboy with arms around his neck.

Will Spanks Finn By Artsy Ape

"You two are fecking silly, you know that? I've got to keep a better eye on you. On your own, you're not so bad, but the two of you together is one Bellamy, maybe worse than."

He helps me with my sweats. "So, this is how grounding works in this house; you have early bedtimes, nine-thirty on weeknights, ten-thirty on weekends."

"Nine-thirty?"

"You having trouble hearing? 'Cause if not, that'll be a yes sir, or you can go back over my knee."

Wow. He is not fucking around today. I sigh and let myself melt into him, almost as if his sternness is what I was looking for. *What I was chasing.* "Yes, sir."

"Good. There's also a screen time limit. Being grounded doesn't mean scrolling on phones or video games. It's not supposed to be fun, it's supposed to deter you from misbehaving. Maybe I'll even send y'all up to the attic to dust."

"This month's really gonna suck isn't it?" I say, not leaving his shoulder.

"Yep, but you'll live. And by the way, I would have only grounded you both a week. You have Xavier to thank for the extra three—don't cross him when he says don't do something."

"Or he will be relentless; he said that. I should have written it down."

Will runs a hand through my hair and kisses my crown. "When he's done with you, won't need to. Now, you have some corner time to do for me. That corner there. You can do hands by your sides considering your wrist, pants down. I'm gonna trust you can follow my instructions and stay where you're told. If I think you're not, you can do your corner time in the kitchen, am I clear?"

"Yes, sir." I am happy to avoid corner time in the kitchen, if possible.

"All right get moving. I'll come get you when lunch is ready."

I move to obey him, and it's not long before I'm staring at a wall with nothing on it—I've got to put something here, so at least it's not so boring—and have my hands by my sides like he asked. "The corner is for thinking. *Think.*"

He leaves quietly after that and I do think. I also notice how calm I feel, the spanking is not just fire in my ass, but a buzz through my body. I think about what drove me to that party in the first place. I don't even go to parties, not really. I'd like to think that I'm not so childish as to test boundaries, but truth is, I haven't had firm ones for a long while.

I feel like Sam is the sort who could have firm boundaries but didn't with me because of misplaced guilt. He gave me too much of what I wanted, instead of giving me what I needed. Talking Sam out of a curfew was easy. The good old, "nothing bad's going to happen," did the trick.

But not here. The rules are going to be enforced and I can try to get around them, but that kind of behavior's just going to get me here, staring at a wall. *Okay Finnegan, you need to shape up.* Except something tells me this is just the beginning. I am stirred inside, more stuff churning, needing to work itself out. This is going to require a lot of thinking time.

Yeah. I'm gonna need something to look at while I'm here, in the future.

"How about the vent? We could Die Hard our way out," Grayson says.

"Yeah, we might have to."

"Finn, I love you, but I think we need to cool it on the rebellion."

"I'm in complete agreement with you. Let's get out of here, so we can tell them all about how we've sworn off trouble forever."

"That's what we said the last time."

"We'll really mean it this time."

"Said that the last time too."

Yeah. Guess we did. When you're in said trouble, staying away from trouble seems plausible. Until trouble finds you again.

I dread four pm all day. I know this is going to be the least amount of fun it can be. Not to mention, things feel different knowing I'm in trouble with *him*. I don't like it at all. I can't shake the feeling all day and I almost get a spanking in Professor Hornwheeler's class for not paying attention even though I have something which should keep me focused: my sore ass cheeks, still complaining about the spanking Will gave me.

When Grayson and I are on our way to see Xavier, it's almost a relief. Almost. There's still facing him. *Admit it Finnegan, you need to see him make you own up, you need to see he'll do it. You won't admit it, because you know that's what a brat does, and you don't want to classify yourself as a brat.*

Ugh, maybe. I can be his brat, I might even be a house brat, but can I be *a* brat?

We're in our school uniforms, the confining jackets and shorts that feel too short even though they go well to mid-thigh. I am acutely aware of the socks clinging tightly to my calves. "Don't be too nervous, Finn. I know it's hard for brats to face their Top, but I'll be right beside you."

"You say that like he's not your Top too." I remember how upset he was that first night, for Xavier to find out about his tantrum.

"He is. I'm one of Xavier's boys, and I'm accountable to him in every way, but it's not in the same way as you. There's still another level, and that's a level only you have with him."

"Like what you have with Will?" He doesn't answer. "Grayson, I can see what you and Will have, any idiot could."

"Yeah, look, Finn? I don't like to say it out loud, okay?"

"Yeah, yeah, that's fine." I'm fucking curious as to why, but I don't want to pry.

Even though we're here to get our asses handed to us, I'm excited to see Xavier. I haven't seen him since breakfast yesterday. He did text me though, which was way more fucking exciting than it should have been, even if was mostly to scold me.

Are you being a good boy? You'd better be in bed.

It made my heart race; I read it several times to make *that* feeling last. I think I'm getting addicted to *that* feeling. *Yes, I'm in bed,* I answered. *How can I not be in this house? I'm no longer allowed to sneeze without permission.*

He did not feel sorry for me. *Glad to hear it. Will told me your wrist was looked at by a medical professional and that it was going to be okay, but how does it feel?*

I update him. Of course it's fine. The physiotherapist saw it and told me to rest from lifting heavy things, but to do some movement-based exercises to keep the blood flowing. Ani also put some arnica on it for the bruising and circulation. I tell him all this and add a second time that it feels fine in case he missed the first it the first time.

Good. Goodnight, My Finnegan. xoxo

My heart lifts when I set eyes on him, but he remains austere. It makes him even more beautiful. And while he maintains some distance, because well, I am in a lot of trouble, there's still a pull between us energetically that remains intact. I have trouble speaking, even though what I want to do is throw myself at his feet and beg him to stop looking at me like that. He really was soft yesterday. I see that now. He shelved all of this, so we could have our first moments as whatever we are, but now he makes the full force of his displeasure known. "I did not give you leave to sit, Mr. Worthington," he says to Grayson. "You know better."

"Sorry, sir."

I stand a little straighter, glad I didn't follow suit and sit too. All the mischief has left me, and I'm on my best behavior now. "Tell me gentlemen, was there something unclear about our meeting on Saturday morning?"

"No, sir," we both say, together.

"Then it's a simple case of disobedience, which I abhor most of all. If you didn't know I don't tolerate it, Grayson, Finnegan," a hot thrill goes through me hearing my name in such deep, chastising tones, "you're about to. Both of you can spend the next hour looking at that wall, pants down and in position. I've got other meetings to attend to, they can see what naughty boys I've got and what happens to them when they don't follow the rules."

Ugh. More corner time, but I'm not arguing, and I am never, *ever* disobeying Xavier again, or Will for that matter. It's total silence in the room, except for the sounds of belts unbuckling and zippers unzipping as we prepare ourselves as instructed. Grayson smirks at me. "What's so funny?" I whisper.

"You," he whispers back.

"Gentlemen. No talking. Finnegan, you may opt to place your hands at your sides, considering your wrist, Grayson, hands on your head."

When I'm in position, my school shorts halfway down my legs so all of my ass shows, I start praying no one comes in.

Finn in the Corner By Artsy Ape

There's every possibility it will happen and knowing Xavier, the likelihood is high; he wants this to be embarrassing. At the same time, it's nice going through the process with someone, especially Grayson. He stands tall, almost proud to be here, serving his sentence. I try to mimic him. I want Xavier to be pleased with me. I can do this right.

As predicted, Xavier takes other appointments while we stand as we are. We can't see, but we overhear his short meetings. One with another student, and two separate ones with other professors at the school. An hour becomes a long time and my legs tire. The anticipation of the spanking to come rises. I know it will hurt, but that's not what's stirring inside me; I'm going to have to face him in the most vulnerable way and I don't mean because my ass will literally be exposed. Xavier seems to know how to cut to the heart of what I'm going through and help me stop the bullshit.

It's always worth it in the end, but going through it's not fun.

"All right you two, over here," he says, when his last meeting finishes.

I watch how Grayson holds his shorts so he can walk and then resumes standing before Xavier with his shorts still down and I do the same with my good hand. "I am disappointed," he says. That fucking guts me, and it hits me why punishment is so much worse than discipline. With discipline it's *potential* disappointment, a thread of it maybe, but not enough to feel this heavy. Punishment has the full weight, which means the headspace is different. "My rules will be obeyed, gentlemen. As you cannot be trusted, next time you'll either come with me, or there will be a babysitter." Will said the same thing, they think too much alike. "You'll both take my strap, over the desk. Please take care of your wrist, Finnegan. Tell me if you need to adjust for it."

"Yes, sir."

Again, I look to Grayson for guidance and mimic how he sets himself over the desk, belly down, gripping the other side with his hands. Xavier's hand on my tender flesh sends a shiver through me. "This is a lot of spanking in one week, Mr. Brighton. Do you plan on sitting at some point during your stay here?"

"I do, sir. I'm sorry," I finally get to say. Yes, I said it yesterday, but I want to say it now too when he's showing all of his displeasure.

"Grayson, Finn is still new. I'm disappointed to learn you egged him on. Not that I don't hold him accountable, he's still a big boy and capable of telling you no, but you also have a responsibility to him. I expect better."

"Yes, sir. I know I shouldn't have, and yeah, I went pretty hard on the peer pressure. I was pissed at Will." He turns to me. We've already had the conversation, but he needs to say it again. "I'm sorry I dragged you into my bullshit."

"No. I could have stayed home."

"Yes, you could have," Xavier underlines. "You will both be getting the same. I'm not going to differentiate between instigator and instigatee in this case."

Xavier starts with me. "Finn, I know you're testing. You want to see if there's really a net to catch you when things spiral out of control. We are here and we will catch you." He punctuates that with five stripes of his strap.

It's surprising and sharp, much sharper than Friday night discipline had been with the *same* strap. "Ow, ah! Sir! Okay. I'm sorry."

Thankfully, I get a break, but hearing the strap against Grayson's ass has me flinching. It sounds like it hurts. Too soon, it's my turn again, for another five. I tense, gritting my teeth, crying out, never meaning to, but it's there. It almost feels good to let it all out.

"Grayson, you act out to get William's attention. I understand that on some level. You have a hard time asking for what you need, but there's brattery, and then there's too far. This was too far. You *won't* do this again."

Grayson's crying. "I-I-I won't, sir. Will and I talked about it. I know it was too far, I hurt him, and I hate that."

I don't know if it's allowed, but I reach to grab his hand with my good one and squeeze it. I hold it while Xavier lays down another five. His body contracts and relaxes in time with each crack of the strap. Xavier doesn't tell us to stop.

Then it's my turn. It's back and forth like that a few times, until, "Last five, Finnegan. I'm really going to drive this lesson home. I cannot have my boys out at parties, drinking to excess, missing curfew. My boys are more well-behaved than the rest, end of story. Brace yourself."

I try, but there is no bracing myself, especially when the place he decides to paint my last five are the backs of my tender thighs. *Mother fucker*. Even when they're done, I can still feel the burn of them. They seem to light anew, when Grayson gets his. I squeeze his hand tighter, and he squeezes mine right back. "It's over now, you may stand and dress."

It wasn't a long strapping, but Xavier went hard, and it already aches. Plus, it was a spanking over the one Will gave me and the buildup is real. I'm having a long, hot soak after this. Grayson's eyes are tear-filled. "Thank you, Xavier. I really will be on my best behavior."

"Yeah, until the next time, brat." Xavier pulls him into a hug. "Will already told you both the rest of your punishment and how it works, so I'll spare you repeating it, but I trust you never to do something like this again. I mean it. This one was serious. Considering what did happen, we're lucky nothing more happened."

Yep. And we got that speech from Will too.

Grayson nods. "I deserved what I got. It won't happen again."

"Good boy," Xavier says, kissing his forehead. "You may head back to the house now. *You*, sit in that chair," he says to me.

Sit? At least the fine leather is soft, but I'm not pleased to find out I'm staying. Grayson smirks at me before heading off.

Once he's gone, Xavier spins around. "Why do I have to stay?" I complain. And not because I don't want to stay with him, I do, but my sixth senses are telling me it's a conversation I'm not going to like.

"Because, my boy, we need to have a conversation."

His eyes are the dark torrents right now, and I know this lecture isn't quite over. My heart's still beating a little faster than usual and I watch him carefully. He's tidily put together, as per usual, his tie is bright blue to match his eyes, everything in its place except his dark hair. "We are at the beginning of something I hope will grow into more, Finnegan. I found this hurtful." I didn't cry through that strapping, but now the tears come. "I'm not telling you this to make you feel bad, but it's important you know what does and doesn't hurt me, like with William and Grayson."

If I were Xavier, I wouldn't continue with someone already showing red flags like I am. *Leave him now, end it now, before you're rejected, Finn.*

That's my brain, but my heart doesn't want to.

"Being with me comes with the added responsibility of setting an example. You need to remember that when you make decisions, Finn. When in doubt, come to me. When you're struggling, come to me. I know that's hard for you, and it's going to be the first thing we work on together."

I nod, unable to speak. I want to repeat how sorry I am over and over.

"Okay, Mr. Brighton. It's over. You are no longer in trouble, other than to fulfill the rest of your punishment. You can relax now."

"How? I don't like that I've hurt you."

"You've apologized, and I will live. You're a... well, you're wired in a way that leads to this behavior. I know what I'm getting myself into." He's smiling.

"You were going to call me a brat."

He smirks. "Yes. I am of the opinion that you are, but it's not fair to push an identity on someone. If you truly don't feel you are, I will stop calling you that. Your identity in this realm is for you to discover."

"You'll stop calling me brat out loud," I say, wiping my eyes. "But not in your head."

"You've got me dead to rights."

Something happens in that moment; something makes sense to me. I've fought the brat thing all this time, but now that it's being taken away—in a matter of speaking—I want it. Not just because everyone else thinks so, but as I've observed and participated in house antics, I realize I am like them. Not just in behavior, but on a deeper level. We're wired the same way. We get each other without words. We understand each other in a way no one else ever could. There are things we need and want (even if no one will admit that out loud), things that work for us. In this way we are the same.

I see that 'brat' isn't a term of reproach, it's an honor and it's an even greater honor to be someone's brat. I'm not quite a Grayson on the spectrum, this instance notwithstanding, but I am a brat all the same. "You know, um, I think, I *know*. You've got me dead to rights too."

He smiles. "Come, my unbelievably naughty brat. You're coming home with me tonight."

"I am? But I thought I was grounded?"

"You are. This is not going to be fun. You'll do home-work and go to bed early, but..." he looks at my wrist. "I can't stop thinking about it. I have to look after you. I didn't think you'd mind."

"I don't." I smile. "But I don't have my things for class tomorrow."

"Text Ani with what you need, and I'll allow him and Grayson to bring the items over. There's grounding him, and then there's stealing his new favorite teddy bear for the night. If I don't let him say goodnight, I'll never hear the end of it."

That makes me laugh. He's right though.

Xavier takes me by the good hand, and we leave his office, taking a campus golf cart back to his place again. I text Ani using the voice command option, which is easier on my wrist. It's amazing how connected the use of your thumb is to wrist action. When we get up to his place, he's full of orders for me. "Blazer and shirt off. I want to ice and then rewrap your wrist. Ani should be here by the time we're done with that, and you can change."

I do as instructed. I think I'm going to sit on a chair again and watch him cook as before while I ice my wrist, but I'm wrong. There is no sitting for me today. My ass is too sore and so I have to stand and lean against the counter instead. "You know, I could have just opened my cuff and rolled up my sleeve," I say. I've already caught him leering at me several times.

He's unapologetic. "But then what will I have to look at while I cook? It's only fair."

"You don't want help?"

"No. Your job is to ice that."

"Got it. No cooking for Finnegan with a sprained wrist." I enjoy watching him after that. I think he likes cooking. The salad he's making looks fancy with strawberries, walnuts and some kind of soft cheese. It's not 'rice,' but a pilaf and the steaks are fat with fresh herbs and spices.

The door to Xavier's place rings and he nods at me to answer, so he can continue his cooking.

"Whoa, we interrupting?" Grayson says when he sees shirtless me.

I roll my eyes. "You know you're not."

Grayson dives at my naked torso, squeezing it tight. Ani

steps in the door, pulling my travel suitcase behind him. "I packed everything you asked for, and more. Here, put this in Xavier's fridge, your lunch for tomorrow."

I'm so touched he thought of me for lunch tomorrow. I take the small lunch bag. "Thank you, Ani."

"Of course, baby." He fixes my hair, like he does, and I admire his hair like I do, still wanting to bury myself in it one night.

Remorse tugs me; I'm not going *home* tonight. As much as I do want to be here with Xavier, I think of all the things I'll miss with everyone. The inside jokes that seem to start on a continuous basis, the laughs we have at meals. Even at our first official House family meeting of this school year last night, there was fun amidst the rules; the rules that only brought us that much tighter together. Will announced that we would, from now on, be travelling to school as a family. Once we get there, we can disperse, but being on time is dependent on when we all leave. When complaints arose, he reminded everyone that he's at just as much at risk of punishment as the house head, more so if he can't get his house out on time. It's an exercise for both Tops and brats.

He also went over the other new rule, which was made because of Grayson and I: no brats left home alone for the next two months and he will revisit that rule then if everyone does what they're supposed to, which is telling him when they go out. I thought for sure Grayson and I would be the most hated in the house, but while yeah, there were a few jabs, it was mostly light-hearted teasing.

I asked Bray about that after. "Because, Finn, it's only a matter of time before another one of us does something to elicit a new rule and we hope the other brats will be as understanding."

Huh. Well then. Brats do have *some* honor.

I'm going to miss the morning chaos. Because there's always chaos and there's going to be more while we get used to the new rule. It's nice to have something like that to miss.

Grayson strolls into the kitchen like he owns the place. "I have a bone to pick with you, sir," he says, far too impudent for a boy who was only just strapped. "You can't just take Finn like this. I forbid it."

"Do you, Mr. Worthington?" he says, in his deep voice, wiping off his hands, letting Grayson know what he thinks of that by way of a cool gaze.

"Yes."

"He will be returned to you tomorrow. That's the best you'll get from this negotiation."

Instead of arguing back, Grayson clings to me.

"We should be going anyway," Ani says. "Hello, Headmaster Harkness, sir."

"Mr. Beauchamp. Thank you for bringing Finn's things. It's appreciated."

"You're welcome, and now I will take this one away. Say goodnight, Grayson."

"This isn't fair," he whines to Ani.

"C'mon. Finn's not movin' in. He'll be home tomorrow night."

Grayson gives me a suffocating hug. "You sleep with me tomorrow."

"I'll sleep with you tomorrow. Jeez," I say, and kiss him on top of his head.

When they're gone, Xavier has our plates ready. I notice my steak is pre-cut. I raise my brow at him. "I don't want you using that wrist. It probably got a lot of work today, it needs rest."

I take a look at the hard chairs at his dinner table, with no small amount of dread.

"I should make you sit on your sore arse, but here." He moves to grab a pillow and sets it down.

I smile. "Thank you, sir." Maybe he is softer with me.

After dinner, he runs me a bath and soaking my sore ass is divine. I put on the pajamas he's laid out for me and join him on the couch, where he's got my Tensor bandage and some arnica waiting for me. I also spy the aloe. "Come, let's get you taken care of so you can do your homework."

Xavier is diligent. He rubs the arnica into my wrist and up my hand some, and then he kisses it before wrapping the elastic bandage around it ensuring it's not too tight, but also tight enough. "All right, over my lap," he says, his eyes sparkling with mischief.

"You can't be serious."

"I'm very serious."

"No one's ever put aloe on me in that position."

"I'm not just anyone. C'mon, you'll enjoy it."

I lay myself over his thighs, a place that's becoming all too familiar and lift my hips when he instructs me, so he can pull my pajama pants down and rub the aloe in. "This looks divine, Finnegan," he comments, smoothing the aloe in slowly, taking his time to massage it deeply. "It happened again you know."

"What did?"

"Spanking drunk. There's something about spanking you that gets me there quickly."

I get warm all over. "My ass is never going to be white again, is it?"

"Not likely."

It's a comforting thought. He somehow refrains from spanking me while I'm over his lap and when he's done with the aloe, he pulls my pants back up. That is when I do get a hearty smack to my ass. "Hey!" Though to be honest, I'd be more surprised if I didn't get one.

"Homework. I want it all done. If you finish early enough, we can watch TV before bed."

There's little hope of that with the amount of homework I have. Thankfully, I begin my tutoring with Osh tomorrow. I'm already struggling, and that's one of those things I should probably tell Xavier. I don't though. If I still suck after tutoring, then I'll tell him.

He sets me up at the table and I wonder if I'm going to get a pillow again. I do and I'm fucking grateful. There's something oddly nice about sitting on an aching ass though. I'm complete.

Homework tonight is long, but not hard. It's an essay, which I'm decent at, and some reading. Xavier steals my laptop to read my essay, when I'm done with it. "This is good," he says. "You mind if I make a few corrections?"

"Isn't that cheating?"

"It is not. One should always get someone to read over an essay. I do the same. It's hard to see your own mistakes."

"Then by all means."

It's easy and quiet hanging out with Xavier. I thought I would be a nervous wreck, only because I'm always like that with new prospects. I'm really good at the one-night stand thing. Some might say I'm smooth and cool. Not so much in relationships.

But I want this one.

It's barely nine-fifteen when I start yawning. "Okay. Bedtime."

"Don't I have fifteen minutes?"

"You do, which is exactly the amount of time it will take to brush your teeth and do anything else you do before bed."

"It does not take me fifteen minutes to brush my teeth."

"Finnegan."

"All right, I'm going, I'm going." I shut my book and sling myself off the chair. I fish my toiletry bag from my travel suitcase and go through all my nightly abolitions thinking about how boring a night this really was. Nice, but homework is not what I would have preferred doing at Xavier's. Xavier joins me and holy shit, he's shirtless. I am not prepared for it. I have to pause my teeth-brushing to look at him in the mirror as he smiles that coy and beautiful smile of his. His eyes are almost shy, *almost*. His arms are folded as he watches me, and I change my mind. Getting to see Xavier in nothing but his black pajama bottoms makes this the best night ever. And I think, well I think he's admiring me too.

He totally is Finnegan.

When I'm done, he lifts me to sit on the counter which is thankfully cold for my poor ass, I still wince though. He knows and his eyes sparkle about it. I roll my eyes. "Fucking sadist," I say, without any malice.

He beams and continues on to brush his teeth. Who knew teeth-brushing could be so erotic? Well, it is, and I watch him in complete awe, barely able to stop myself reaching out to touch his skin. Then I remember, I *can* touch his skin. I can do that. Xavier, well he's mine right? I know I don't have as much confidence about that as I should, but I haven't been able to leave a mark on him and ...

... oh God, I really am a brat. Mark leaving is a total brat thing to do.

A bit of pride forms. Just a sliver, and I recall the loftiness in Bellamy's voice when declares himself a brat.

I shift sideways toward him, so I can reach out to touch his skin. He breathes in long and slow, like maybe this tickles him a bit, or maybe it's affecting him in other ways. I continue to run my fingers over him, tracing his abs and where the muscle sticks out to 'V' down his pelvis. "I'd be careful if I were you," he says, rinsing his mouth out setting his toothbrush in the holder.

My heart's beating so damn fast. "Why?"

"Because this might happen." He bends and places his shoulder against my torso, lifting me over it, gripping both my legs.

"Ah! Xavier!" But my shouting doesn't do any good and I'm mostly laughing anyway. He carries me to the bed and flops me down.

"Let that be a warning to you," he says, pulling back the blankets.

"Not much of a deterrent, let me tell you," I say.

He climbs into the bed with me and his hand slides down to his favorite place, my ass. I hiss when he squeezes, and my mouth opens in time to be captured in a kiss. It's a lot like the first time, but better. The electricity is there igniting a frenzy, one where I have to be close to him. His tongue is nearly down my throat and I respond in kind, our tongues tangling.

When I breathe, he breathes and we coalesce, becoming as close to one person as we can be. His hand moves down my leg, finding my knee and gripping it there, just under, then pulling it so my leg is over top of his, in that place where torso meets hip. His lips come off my mouth and kiss my neck and then suck at the juncture of my neck and collar bone.

It's one of my favorite places to be sucked, other than my cock. I shiver with the best tingles, while he suckles more, learning my body.

"You know, this might be considered 'fun' in some circles? Are you sure it's allowed?" I don't know where it comes from, it's fucking cheeky. I swear Xavier brings out the brat in me. I'm forever going to blame him.

He squeezes my ass for it, but he's amused. "You're right, this is too much fun. I'd better stop."

He so doesn't want to stop. Other than me really telling him no, which is not happening, I'm not sure he can stop. "I want you in me."

"As you wish, my darling."

That's all the sweetness that happens for a while. Once his cock is in me, slick with lube, he's pounding into me. We're both releasing all the pent-up sexual energy between us and it's glorious. He's so large, he consumes me, and I seem to be just the right size to fit against him. I'm in good shape too, from all the hockey I played up until this year, and one of the things Sam did make me do, was stretch, so I'm very bendy.

Xavier enjoys that, lifting one of my legs, pressing it up my torso and fucking deep inside me. We're sweaty and we slide and slip together, always together. If he thought I was responsive during a spanking, that's nothing compared to me during sex, and he's surprisingly noisy too.

I love all of his moans.

"Fuck, mmmmhhh, oh God, Brighton. Fuck, you're tantalizing."

I note the 'Brighton' to tease him about later.

We collapse on each other both still relishing in post-orgasm afterglow. I lay half on him, half on the bed, gripping his torso, toying with one of the marks I left on him, with the fingers of my wrapped hand, while he traces fingers over the Tensor bandage. "I didn't hurt this did I? I got kind of wild there for a bit."

"No. It's okay, really."

He runs fingers through my hair. "You do something to

me I've never felt before, Finnegan." I like hearing that. I hope I'm always this special to him. I ruin everything by yawning again. "Okay, it's time for sleep. Close your eyes."

"You're so bossy," I complain, but I'm barely awake as it is. Which is why I almost miss what he says, but I *just* catch it.

"I am bossy, but it's why you like me."

CHAPTER NINE

W e can't fit in the ducts, which once again proves that what you see in the movies is not real life. But we still have our massive blanket fort, which is totally awesome. After our short-lived vent adventure, we go back to snuggling in it, on the mattress, but then our stomachs growl and the smell of bacon wafting up from downstairs doesn't help. It's officially morning. Our family is below us, going about their day, not realizing where we are. *Yet.* It's still early.

"Let's try the window again," Grayson says, unwrapping himself from me. He moves over to tug and struggle with it again but nope, it's not budging. I head over to help him with my one good hand, but still no. It's like it welded itself shut.

"It's time to make noise," I say.

He nods.

We jump up and down, screaming at the top of our lungs and then we wait. We do this, ten or eleven times, our voices hoarse, but no one comes. That's when the real panic sets in.

"Oh God, what if we don't get out of here? We'll die and one day they'll find our lonely, rotted corpses. We'll try to haunt the place, but we'll be stuck doing it from here and we'll have to see ourselves, our skeleton teeth poking through decayed flesh. It's going to be so horrible," Gray says, clutching onto me for dear life.

Grayson believes in all that stuff. "Good Lord, Grayson. No. We'll get out of here. Promise. We just have to keep making noise. Maybe there's something in here that's loud enough. We'll keep looking, we'll get out."

But I don't really know if we will. I'm just as panicked, and I don't like the visual his description leaves in my mind.

"Osh, *please*. Don't make me write it out again." I'm not a mathematician; I'm a creative! I'm not sure there's any amount of times I can write out this math problem that will make it stick in my head.

"Again. Sixty times. That should do it."

"You're all sadists around here, that's the real problem."

"Excuse me?"

"Uh, nothing, sir."

"That's what I thought. You work, I'll make snacks."

I complain, but I adore Osh. Like Xavier and Will, Osh seems to bring out the brat in me. Actually, Osh might bring out the most brat in me. I'm developing unique relationships with each of the Tops in my life.

Osh is willing to let me play more, toe the line and let my brat roam free. Not Xavier. He brings the hammer down on me fast. He appreciates some banter, but I'm not allowed to step too far. I've noticed though, I don't want to with

Xavier. Not as much. I want to be—*oh God*—a good boy. Something I've recently had to admit to and process. Brat slips off the tongue easier these days, good boy still makes me flush with embarrassment even though I can't deny loving the hell out of the term and living for the moments someone calls me good boy.

As I live through more experiences with the domestic discipline stuff, I see how many onion layers there are to it. I didn't believe Xavier when he said I would need more than just him. How could that be? But Xavier does not prefer a bratty-brat. He likes a well-behaved boy. However, he knows I need that brat play sometimes, which is part of why he set up these tutoring sessions with Osh. Our energies clicked instantly, and I get to run off all my brat energy with him so I don't get into as much trouble with Xavier.

Which makes me all the more curious to meet Bellamy's Top. He has one, but I haven't met him yet. What is the kind of Top, who prefers one as bratty as Bellamy?

But Osh, he loves a brat, is amused by them. He plays back, which strengthens my theory about there being a little brat in every Top. Even still, I'm tempted to place Osh *just* after Will on my imaginary Top to brat spectrum chart. Not sure yet though, so I'll put him there in brackets with a question mark beside.

In addition to brats, Osh loves to cook as much as Xavier does. Ani does too, but they have different ways about it. Ani has a feminine quality to him, and it bleeds into the way he runs his kitchen. Osh and Xavier are more masculine, and they don't run a kitchen, they direct it. It's a lot more organized, but also less fun. I prefer cooking with Ani, and cringe when Osh or Xavier tell me I'm helping them.

I've enjoyed hanging out at Sigma Phi house every

Tuesday and Thursday after class. They have their own dynamics and I feel at home here too. It's not home-home, but it's an extension of.

Their kitchen has a long bar-top counter with five stools on the side opposite to where Osh likes to do most of his chopping and prepping. The stove is across the way against the wall and it's larger than ours. Ani's jealous of its six-burner top—he hasn't said so, but I can tell. They don't have as large of a table in their kitchen like we do. Just a small square table with four chairs on one side of the kitchen and a banquette seat built into the wall over near the door leading out to the deck that can seat up to five. They do have a nice dining room table in the next room over, which I'm told gets used often.

I do my homework wherever Osh tells me to set up and today it's at the bar-top. He sets a bowl of homemade soup beside me, which is my fucking favorite. "Let it cool, and then you may have a break to eat."

"It's about time, my hand is cramping," I say. Plus, I want to check my phone. I've felt it go off several times in my pocket, but that's a no go while doing homework unless I want it confiscated.

My wrist healed quickly with all the care it got, but it wasn't my right wrist anyway, which is the side I write with. I'm just complaining because I can. After I eat, he sits at the bar-top with me. "Now that you've written this out, it will be in your brain. The formulas will feel familiar to you and we can dissect where you're having an issue."

He is a good teacher, even if he's strict with his methods. He's also large and I love having his arm around me as we meticulously go over the problems together. "All right, enough for today. You are free," he says, when he's determined our time is up. There is no maximum amount of time, just a minimum. I have to receive at least two hours of tutoring, but I stay until he dismisses me.

"Sweet." I don't delay, packing up my book bag.

"Big plans for this weekend?"

"Just my first real date with Xavier on Saturday." That man is a stickler. Yes, I saw him at his place over the four weeks I was grounded, but he would not take me off campus. He did let my brother come and I got special permission to show him more of the campus, but we had to hang out at the house.

"Really, Finn? That much trouble in your first week?" Sammy said.

"I've been really good since then," I defended, but yeah, I didn't have much to run with. That was a lot for a first week. Well in for a penny, I was in for a pound, so I told him. "Also slept with the headmaster."

"Finnegan!"

"It's okay. We're a thing, I'm not like ..." I paused because how was I supposed to explain all of the dynamics that go on within the house, without it sounding like some kind of kinky sex cult? And maybe we kinda are, but it works for me. "We're together."

Sammy softened. "If you're happy, I'm happy. You're also approaching thirty and can make your own choices, it's just, did it have to be the headmaster?"

I shrugged. It didn't *have* to be the headmaster, it had to be Xavier who also happens to be the headmaster.

"C'mere." He pulled me into a hug I didn't pull out of immediately. "You're already different in a good way. Not that you were bad before, but you were miserable, and I worried. This place is making you shine, bringing out what I always saw in you. Keep following your heart, Finny."

I surprised my brother by initiating a second hug. He

was stunned when I gripped him tight, even going so far as to put my head on his shoulder. "Thanks for everything, Sammy."

I initiate a hug with Osh, like I did with my brother, even if it's a very different kind of hug—there are varying kinds as I've learned. That's a fact. My brother left before he could meet Osh, but I would have liked him to. Maybe next time.

Osh's muscles are large and toned, but there's a sponginess to them. He rocks me side-to-side, loving my hugs, crushing me with his return affection. "Do you know where he's taking you?" Osh asks.

"No idea and believe me when I say I've used up my pest quota for the week on that one. I will not tell you, Mr. Brighton," I say with my best Xavier impression. "But if you ask me one more time, I'll tell your bare-bottom something he'll be less than pleased to hear."

Osh laughs. "I guess I'll have to wait until Tuesday to hear all about it. See you Friday for discipline night."

Insane people like Osh look forward to discipline night. I kiss him goodbye and set off for home.

I open the door to a fight. Bellamy and Grayson are yelling at each other. No Tops in sight, just Bray reading a textbook in the armchair like nothing's happening and Chris scrolling through Netflix.

I am no Top, not even close, but I was right about one thing, I'm not as far toward the brat spectrum as Bellamy. Not really Grayson either, even if I have instants when I'm triggered about something. In addition to all of that, I'm *with* Xavier and some responsibility comes with that whether either Xavier or I would have chosen that or not. "Knock it off you two," I say.

"I will not, Finnegan," Grayson says, in the posh way he says things. "He's being an ass."

"Bell?"

"I wanted to watch my show, but Grayson claims it's his turn to watch, which it isn't."

"That doesn't mean tearing my show apart."

"I wasn't tearing it down, it's called a critique. Besides, it's not like you created the show, who cares what I say about it?"

Good Lord, how old are we? "Bray, you want to weigh in on this?"

"Already tried, Finn. All yours."

"Now Chris is picking the show. You can watch what he does or go do homework or something useful."

Both Bellamy and Grayson cross their arms at me. "Who died and made you Top?" Grayson says.

"No one. If you want to keep at it, by all means, I'm just trying to save you from yourselves. When Will comes home, neither of you will be watching TV for a week."

"He is pretty fed up with bickering this week," Grayson agrees. "All right Finnegan, you make sense. I will watch Christopher's show."

"And I'll watch my show on my phone with my head-phones," Bellamy says, snuggling up to Bray on the couch, who absently puts an arm around him and continues read-ing, acting like nothing happened.

Why didn't Bell just do that in the first place? I want to know this; everyone wants to know this! "Anyone know where Ani is?"

"Tom had to speak with him," Chris answers. "But ah, oh. He asked me to tell you to start dinner if you got home before him. There's a note in the kitchen."

He could have texted me, but Ani prefers notes, claiming that handwriting is more personal. There is indeed a note, but it tells me to commandeer at least two brats to help me. I didn't see Johnny Rae out there, so I text him to get his butt downstairs. I know the likelihood he's playing video games is high. *One more level,* I get back.

No. Now.

Jeez this house sometimes. I lean my head out the door. "Which one of you will help me?"

Nobody answers.

"Ani said two of you. I've got Johnny coming, I need one more." I give puppy eyes to Gray. I'm so not good at making people do stuff. Sure, I can talk a bit tough, and I've got logic on my side, but when it comes down to it, I'm not going to do more than throw a brat-fit myself.

"Ugh, fine," Grayson says.

I get the three of us started with Ani's instructions and thankfully he comes home when things really get going. "Okay you two, this is all good for about forty minutes, when you hear the timer go off, I need you back. Finn? Would you mind coming upstairs with me a minute?"

I frown and follow. He leads me to his room and pulls out the aloe. "Would you please apply some of this for me, Finny?"

"Of course."

He pulls his pants down and lays on the bed, I have to move his long braid to the side. "Wow, Ani. This is not discipline, this was punishment. What did you do?" I can tell things like that now, whether a spanking was discipline or punishment. It's hard on Ani, because disappointing Tom nearly breaks him.

His eyes glisten with unshed tears. "I took on too much,

more than I'm allowed to. But I can't help it sometimes, Finn."

I nod. That's a big rule between him and Tom. Ani takes on too much and then it leads to insomnia. His whole system gets out of balance. It's caused him health issues in the past. His tears are less about the punishment itself, and more about Tom's disappointment.

I lovingly rub aloe into him, like he so often does for me. "Aww, Ani. It's okay. I'm sure Tom forgives you."

"He does. Tom was wonderful. If he saw me still crying over it, he would think I needed more and maybe I do. I mostly feel better though. I think I'm just crying the rest out. Your care is helping too, sweetheart."

I smile. I love being there for him like he is for me.

"My mom's maiden name was Beauchamp," he says, the beginning of a story coming from nowhere like it can with him. Ani's a storyteller, he often tells stories to teach us something, or get something off his chest. "She's second-generation Métis, only she didn't know it until she chased after her ancestry. My grandmother kept it secret. She had to; her generation faced a lot of racism from both sides. The Métis didn't have a place they belonged except with each other, which is why I eventually took my mother's name, a form of solidarity. My mother, she doesn't let anything stop her. She married my father who was a good, strong Plains-Cree. He died horribly, I don't like to talk about it," he tells me. "I was fourteen when it happened."

I keep rubbing and move onto the sensitive thighs area—which I wince at, they look painful—and I recall the pain of losing a parent too soon.

"After he died, I felt responsible for Mama, even though she's so capable. In hindsight, I guess I knew how badly her heart was broken. I didn't want her to hurt any more than she had to, and I began doing everything I could, so there would be less for her to concern herself with. Most of all, I didn't want her to worry about me. It extended beyond Mama. I had to get good grades in school, perfect grades so she wouldn't worry. I had to get a good job so she wouldn't worry. I had to excel at that job so she wouldn't worry. My perfectionism had no bounds. All of it an idea I made up; my mother never expected anything like that from me.

"Sometimes, it creeps back. An old habit resurfacing and Tom has to take me to task. As you know, I came to this school to get help with my proclivity for taking on too much."

"Does it help?" I grit my teeth.

"Tremendously. You have no idea. You should have seen me when I first got here, Tom wouldn't let me do anything; I gained responsibilities as I went. I'm a bit funny in that I need the first spanking to get through the thing I need the spanking for, and then often another, to get rid of the guilt of doing the thing that resulted in me needing the spanking in the first place." He smiles at himself. "Then I'm good for a long while. I'll go see Tom again tomorrow, but you know? This is really helping. You're good at listening, Finn."

"Thanks. Though I wish I was as good at math as I was listening. Osh made me write out one problem sixty times."

Ani laughs. "You're also good at knowing when to make someone laugh."

I close up the jar of aloe; Ani pulls his pants up. I analyze him as he does and decide he needs another laugh. "All right darlin', bring it in for a hug," I say.

I get the laugh I wanted and Ani's glad to come in for a hug. "You turning into a mini-Will?"

"Not at all. Just wanted to see you smile your usual Ani smile."

"Thank you, honey. And Finn? I think you're settling into your role in our family. You were the missing piece, we needed someone like you. I'm so glad that you're here."

"Me too."

"C'mon, we'd better get down there before the timer rings. No way Johnny and Grayson are going to check in time and then we'll have burned buns."

Xavier takes me to the fanciest restaurant he can think of, frowns when I order their burger, but ends up stealing several of my fries, or 'frites' as the fancy place calls them, and tells me I'm adorable when I say we should blow this popsicle stand to get ice cream somewhere. We do. "Next time I will take you somewhere less formal," he tells me. "But you're special to me, Finn. I wanted to make a big deal."

"Big deal made. I did enjoy it, promise." I lean in to kiss the vanilla ice cream off his lips, which is fucking hilarious to me. Vanilla is the last thing Xavier is, yet it's his favorite ice cream flavor.

We head back to his place and I see he's got several implements laid out. I know exactly what they're for. Looks like I'm getting a spanking one way or the other, so I might as well enjoy myself. Time to be a cheeky brat. "*Yaaaaawn.* Well, looks like it's time for me to head home to bed. Thank you, the night's been lovely."

He slides the door to his apartment shut with purpose and locks it. His eyes glint, sparkling the bluest of blues and his teeth take the form of a shark spotting prey. "You're not going anywhere, except to my bed."

I cross my arms. "Make me."

"With pleasure." All he moves is his foot, but I see it and I take off. It's not a large apartment, there are only so many places to go. I head around to the other side of the counter. "If you break one glass back there, this will turn into a real spanking versus the fun one I had planned."

"There's nothing here to break. The person who lives here is an anal-retentive bastard; he puts his stuff away soon as he uses it."

"That's it."

I'm laughing, but not for long when he does eventually catch me and hauls me off over his shoulder to the bedroom, placing me succinctly over his knees and pulling my nice pants down; I pay dearly for the anal-retentive bastard comment. Then he pulls out his wooden paddle.

"What's this spanking for?" I ask.

"Did you think I needed a reason? If you need one, let's go with because you are utterly spankable." He smirks and then carries on.

I laugh though. It fucking hurts, but I laugh, go figure— it's a headspace thing. He then has fun with his tawse and a plastic hairbrush he wanted to 'try out,' and when he's done with me, he's all spanking drunk and I'm in that floaty, happy place spanking brings me. He sinks his cock into me and takes me to yet another place.

"So, what will you do with your newfound freedom?" he asks, when we're lying in bed together afterward.

"Nothing. I'm sworn off trouble. I'll sit at home every night doing my homework and behaving like a good boy."

"Good plan, even if I doubt that's what will happen."

"Ye of little faith."

"I just know a thing or two about you and brats in general."

"All right, you've got me. But I will endeavor to try."

"That's all I ask, just please refrain from things that get you hurt most of all. I can't bear it," he says picking up the wrist that was injured to kiss it.

"I can promise that much."

CHAPTER TEN

When I was a little boy, my dad would sit me on his knee, and we would read Peter Pan together. Or more like, he would read it to me and I would stare up at him in awe of the hard man become soft for a little boy. He didn't stay that way. As I grew, he became firm and I depended on it. Not because he made me that way, but because of the way I was wired inside. I knew early on I had this thing inside me, the thing that makes me need a spanking.

I think about these things, as I toy with Xavier's stapler. "Stop that," he says.

I place the stapler down, but I remain in front of him on the other side of his desk. He's seated, working from his laptop. "Do you think I have Daddy issues?"

"What?"

"Daddy issues. I mean, I know that's slang. It's more about attachment styles. I clearly have an anxious attachment style. My dad wasn't the most secure kind of parent, in some ways, but in others he was the most solid thing there was. When he was on, he was on, and when he wasn't,

212

he really wasn't. It was hard for me when he was distant. His attachment style was avoidant."

He looks up from his laptop. "How do you know all of that?"

"I've read a lot of books to see if I could figure out what was wrong with me."

He doesn't like that. "Do you still believe there's something wrong with you?"

"I'm not sure." I'm leaning across Xavier's desk now. I've taken to stopping by after school when I don't have tutoring with Osh to see if Xavier's free. He likes having me around even if it's in silence with him working at his laptop, and me reading one of my books for school. "What sort of grown adult needs to be spanked?"

He smirks. "I know many of them. If that's why you think there's something wrong with you, try again."

"Maybe there's something wrong with all of us and it stems from the relationship we had or didn't have with our parents."

"I know psychology speculates on this very thing, but I disagree with that hypothesis as an all-encompassing explanation. I've seen many boys over the years, and while it might be true for some, I don't think that's the majority. I think it's a simpler concept; it's the way we're made inside. The end." He's used his lecture-y professor voice, and while I haven't known him long, I know that signals something he's pondered and processed, probably for as long as he's had this school.

I sit down and open my book again, but I only pretend to read it. I'm thinking about what he's said. I was looking for something to be wrong with me for needing this, or something wrong to have happened, but maybe there isn't, and maybe it's just the way I'm made. Watching Xavier and the others is slowly allowing me to have pride in what I am.

And now that I think about it, there are people with the same issues I have, who have other methods of working through them, so that can't be why I'm like this. Maybe it is just the way I'm wired inside. Whatever the case, I like where I'm at.

Around Xavier, I can't help myself. I want to pester him. I want his attention, especially when he's not giving it to me. It's not long before I'm back to his desk, reaching out to play with his stapler again, he puts his hand over top of mine. "You're not going to get the good kind of attention that way. I will spank you. It will hurt. You might cry."

I smile. "I don't doubt that."

"You have no idea how much more tempting you are in your school uniform."

"You know, sir, if you wanted to take advantage of me in said uniform, I would be all right with that."

He closes his laptop, pushing it aside and crooks a finger at me. When I get close enough, he yanks me across the desk and into his lap. "My innocent, Mr. Brighton. I don't mean for sex—although I would never turn down that fantasy—I mean spanking. *Just* spanking. I love spanking schoolboys more than I have words to tell you. I love spanking you most of all."

I'm blushing, aren't I? Yeah, I'm blushing. The flames within me that continuously burn in Xavier's presence stoked. "Right. I guess that's no surprise with a whole school full of them."

He nods, his blue eyes dark as he pulls me in by my tie for a kiss. "But unfortunately, I really do have to get work done, otherwise you'd be over my knee already."

"All right. Maybe I should go pester, Osh."

"In a mood, are we?"

"A bit."

"If I were you, and this is just if I were you, I'd go home and make sure all my chores were done." I give him a questioning look. "William has been bemoaning to me, that Ani has been bemoaning to him, that people of the house are not doing their chores without reminders. He asked for my advice and I gave it."

I wince. Did I do all my chores for this week? If I have to ask myself, probably not. "And what advice did you give him, out of curiosity?"

"What do you think I said?" he asks, smirking away.

"Probably something like spank first, ask questions later." I'm up and off his lap, packing up my books with haste.

"Ah, you know me. But see how kind I am, warning you when I would much rather see your red arse after William's finished with it?"

"So kind, sir." It's hard not to roll my eyes. I grip around his neck and snuggle in before he kisses me one more time. "All right. I'm off."

"Very well, and Finnegan?"

"Hmmm?"

"Behave."

"Yes, sir."

Xavier wasn't kidding. When I get home, it's cleaning central. I might already be too late. Grayson is on his knees, scrubbing the bottom of a wall. "This is ridiculous," he says to me, not bothering with the formalities of hello, getting straight to the complaints. "I can afford to have this house cleaned professionally, there's no need for any of us to lift a finger."

His feathery hair is extra floppy today, as animated as

his face, which is glaring at the wall. "You're in trouble by the way," he says.

"What? Why?"

"Same reason all of us are. Not doing chores."

"But that's what I came home to do," I say, putting my bag down.

"Yeah? Well too fucking late." He looks around to make sure Will didn't hear him say that. "And we have your *boyfriend* to thank for the suggestions by the way."

"That I knew."

Will walks out from the kitchen with purpose. "Finnegan, there you are. Come with me please."

Finnegan. Ugh. Will reserves Finnegan for scolding purposes.

Grayson shrugs at me and keeps washing his wall, purposefully ignoring Will. I follow Will into the kitchen. Ani's there, cooking on his own today, while Bray and Bellamy scrub the floor on hands and knees. "Hi, baby," Ani says, far too innocently. He knows I'm a dead man walking.

"Hi, Ani."

Will spins me around to look at the chore chart. "Do you know what this is?"

"Yes, sir. I was just coming home to work on, uh," fuck, I don't know what my chores are. "All of this."

He takes me by the wrist and pulls me over to a chair, unbuttoning my school shorts. "No one should have to remind you, and chores around here don't get left to the eleventh hour. You know this."

In one fluid motion, my shorts and boxers are pulled down and I'm led over Will's lap, my bare thighs coming into contact with his hole-ridden jeans. He starts in spanking without much pomp and circumstance and he means business. "Ow, ouuuch! I'm sorry."

He continues to smack away at my bare behind, his heavy hand making firm contact. Will's hand always seems to cover the whole surface area, just like Xavier's does. It's a short spanking, but my ass stings when he stands me up. I rub it out. "Jeez, Will."

"Serves you right," he says. "Change and then get to work."

I twist my lips at him. Yeah, I deserved it, but still. I pull up my shorts. "Yes, sir."

When I've got one of my old white T's and a pair of my comfiest sweats on, I head to tidy the living room. That's where Grayson is, and we can chat.

I cringe at the disaster before me; looks like a cyclone hit it. The pale green couch is totally buried in junk, discarded plates everywhere and is that gum caked into the cracks of the coffee table? I was supposed to tidy the living room all week and I kept saying I'd do it later, but later never came. Guess this is a week's worth of everyone's crap.

Grayson is still on the same wall. "Something stuck on there?"

"Yes, and you don't want to know what, but I will be having words with Bellamy and Bray."

"I'll help you when I'm done with this disaster."

But it takes me a long while, and I'm still not done when he finally moves onto the second wall. Will comes to check on us, totally suspicious. "What's taking you so long, Graysie?" he asks. "You two talking or getting work done?"

"What's taking me so long is Bray and Bellamy's 'potions' experiment."

Will looks at the living room. I can tell he thinks I should be further along too. I spread my arms. "This place was horrendous, and someone was chewing gum and sticking it under the coffee table—took me an age to scrape it off."

"Lord help me. There are going to be firmer rules around here, let me tell you. Has Johnny Rae been through here?"

"No," Grayson tells him.

"If he's playing video games ..." Will heads up the stairs, we look to the other with wide eyes.

"He up there?" I ask.

Grayson shrugs. "Don't know. If he is, he asked for it, pushing Will when he's like this."

Sure enough, we hear the familiar sounds of someone—Johnny—having a chat with Will's hand. We look at each other and giggle. "Doesn't your hand get tired, William?" Grayson says when he returns, guiding a repentant looking Johnny by his neck. Johnny winks at us.

"I can handle, y'all," Will says.

By dinner, the house is the cleanest I've seen it in a while. Will still isn't happy with us. "I'm calling an impromptu House meeting," he says after dinner.

"Ah man," Chris says. "I've got homework to do."

"You'll have plenty of time. I just need your attention long enough to issue a warning; I'm tightening ship around here. I want a little bit of something done each day. If I have to police you, you will be spanked with my Lexan, no exceptions, no negotiations. Am I clear?"

He gets a firm round of yes sirs, from all of us, even Ani who never misses his chores and is the one who assigns them. It's Chris and Bray's turn to wash up, so Gray and I take off to the back porch to escape all Tops and their dictatorial moods. While we're out there, sitting on the porch swing, Xavier texts me.

I'm dying to know if William spanked you?

Ass!

You knew and you sent me to my doom.

He responds quickly. *Of course, I knew, and you deserved what you got. You need to start setting an example, Finnegan. So, did he?*

I should drag this out, but I can't. He's lowkey adorable thinking about my red ass. *He did, sir.*

Delightful. Come over when you're done with homework.

I smile. *See you later, Xavy.* I stare at that before I send it. I haven't called him by any nicknames yet. I take a breath and press send.

"Time for you to go see your boyfriend?" Gray says, crawling into my lap, the bearings on the porch swing creaking.

"Soon. A bit of homework left to do, and then I'll head out."

"Fine, but you sleep with me tonight."

I run fingers through his hair and kiss his forehead. A natural thing to do. "I'm not your fucking teddy bear, Grayson."

"You're in with Will and I tonight, Brighton. Fuck you."

"Will?"

"Yes, Will. You scared?"

"No, we've just never—"

"—he's been wanting to invite you into bed but feels like he should give you more time."

"Really?" He nods. "So what are you? Snuggle matchmaker?"

"Something like that."

"Okay, okay, fine." Truth be told, I wouldn't mind being wrapped up in the large cowboy's arms for a night.

When my homework's done, I change into a nicer white

'T' and some jeans Xavier won't spank me for and seek out Will. "Will? Sir? Xavier wants to see me."

He's on the couch going over something on a clipboard. "You want me to take you over, darlin'?"

"That's sweet, but I think I can manage."

"All right. Least I don't have to worry about you bein' home by curfew. Xavier will make sure. C'mere." He pulls me in to kiss my cheek. "Grayson tells me we're having a sleepover tonight. That okay with you? He's not pressuring you, is he?"

I laugh. "He is pressuring me, but it's more than okay. I've, uh, I've wanted to for a while."

"Okay then. I don't want you doin' something you don't want because you think you have to, but I'm looking forward to havin' you in my arms." I get hot all over. "See you later. Have fun."

I resolve to be better behaved for Will. He's so earnest. I always feel the worst after letting him down.

I take a campus golf cart over, but on the way, it makes a squealing sound. I pull over and take a look under the hood. The drive belt isn't sitting like it's supposed to, so I text Xavier that I'll be a few minutes late and take the time to peel it off the cam and reset it. It's probably time for a new one, but I don't have far to go, so this should get me to Xavier's.

It doesn't take me long, but I've got several messages from Xavier and a couple of missed calls by the time I check my phone and am on the road again.

What happened? Are you all right? Call me.

I let him know I'm on my way instead, since I'm close and continue on. When I get there, he's not pleased. His dark eyes look me over and squint at me. "Next time check your phone. I was about to come looking for you."

"Sorry, sir."

"What happened?"

"Golf cart broke down."

"Is that what's all over your shirt, and your face?"

I look down. Oh shit. I'm covered. "Yeah. Sorry about that too."

"Did you walk the rest of the way here? I could have retrieved you."

"Nope, drove the cart. Just a fan belt issue; I was able to fix it for now."

"You can fix cars?"

"Yeah. Dad showed me a lot and Sammy kept teaching me after he passed."

He crosses his arms. "I still have a lot to learn about you, Mr. Brighton. Come, I'll get you a clean cloth for your face, but lose the shirt. You won't need it for now anyway."

I follow him to the bedroom and spy the hairbrush immediately. In anyone else's apartment, a hairbrush on the bedside table is no cause for alarm. At Xavier's it only means one thing. "What is that?" I say even though I know exactly what that is, as I remove my dirty t-shirt.

He smirks. "You must have known you were getting a spanking coming over here, one way or the other. I was going to use the excuse that you are far too spankable, but now I have a real one. I'm sure once I'm done with you, you'll remember to tell me what's going on before you leave my mind to go wild with possibilities."

I laugh. "Was I dead in a ditch somewhere?"

"Don't give me ideas, brat." He smacks my ass. "Go wash your face." His demeanor tells me he's serious. Did he really worry that much? It's hard imagining anyone other than Sammy worrying about me, even though I'm starting to get the idea the House does. A lot.

221

I wash my face and hands thoroughly. When I come out to the bedroom, he's got his glasses on, which make him look like Clark Kent. He's also shirtless. His eyes look down his nose at me and I laugh. "What could be funny?" he says. "You are in a bit of trouble."

"I know, but I feel like I'm in a porn of some kind. You've really got the sexy headmaster vibe going on right now and like, you *are* a headmaster soooooo ..."

I know he's doing all he can to resist laughing and not ruin the 'you're in trouble' vibe he's trying to create. "You won't be laughing for long. Get over my knee."

I know the drill, *all spankings will be performed on a bare bottom, Mr. Brighton.* And if I was feeling cheekier, I would totally catch him on the fact he didn't instruct me to pull my jeans down, and hop over his lap as is, until he mentioned it. We can't make it too easy for Tops, but I pick up that I really did cause him to worry, so I give it to him. I undo my jeans and pull both them and my boxers down at the same time. He inspects it. "Mr. Colten barely warmed this up for me. I thought you said you were spanked?"

"I was! It hurt like the dickens when he did it. Not my fault I apparently have super healing factor, like Wolverine."

"Not to worry, I plan on doing a much better job."

And he does. With his hurt-y, plastic brush. "Ahhh! Ooouch! I'll let you know next time. I'll call you! Send you a freaking telegram!" I promise him the sun, moon and stars, so long as he'll throw that thing back to the fiery depths of hell, whence it came.

He sets it aside, but he doesn't let me up. "This is much better. This is the arse of a well-spanked boy who's going to do his chores and be wary of his overprotective Top who

222

will send the cavalry out after him, when he leaves cryptic little texts that worry the fuck out of him."

There's a swoop from my belly to my groin; delicious, non-sexual arousal. "Were you really that worried, sir?"

"I was," he says, rubbing his hand over my tender flesh. "And I'm beginning to realize that I don't do worry over you well." My jeans are only around one ankle at this point, from all the kicking. He takes them the rest of the way off, but he doesn't let me up. There's some amount of rustling while he fishes something out of his bedside drawer and then the *snick* of a cap before cool lube is poured between my cheeks.

"Spanking isn't super sexual for me," I realize as I say it out loud. "But it is to some degree for you."

"Correct. It's not always a sexual thing, and I can get arousal in a non-sexual way. But not right now. Right now, I'm hard as a rock and I plan on fucking you," he says, as he slides a finger into my ass. I spread my legs further.

"Mmmm, yeah, fuck. Th-tha-thaaaat," I moan as Xavier hits my prostate with his thick finger.

"You know, Finnegan, you're really good at reading people. Do you even realize? You're also good at figuring out why people do what they do."

I pillow my head into my hands, enjoying the combination of the sting on my ass and Xavier's long fingers hitting my prostate. "Everyone except myself," I say, and I'm kind of annoyed by that actually. I feel like I should be able to figure out myself to some degree, especially by now.

"That's always the way, my boy. You'll get there, I have every faith in you."

I let out a stifled cry as he adds a second finger; my cock hardens against his thighs. When he removes his fingers, I whine. His eyes glitter with mischief though. "On your hands and knees on the bed. I need to look at this while I drive my cock into you, it's too divine."

Can he ... can he like me that much? I want to believe it because I want it so bad and it fucking scares me. The more I fall for Xavier, the more I have to lose.

I do as instructed, getting on my hands and knees, trying to make myself as appetizing as possible. I know I have a nice ass—I have years of playing hockey to thank for that—and he gets on his knees behind me, sliding in using one smooth motion. He grabs my hips hard. Every one of his fingers presses into my skin as he slams his cock into me, pulling it out to push it back in.

Xavier always tells me I'm responsive, but so is he. "Dear God, Finnegan. How can one boy be so fucking amazing?" he says, between pants.

How do I make sure he wants me forever?

Sex with Xavier is as consuming as being near him is. I live to be owned, I live to be devoured, I'm all Xavier's right now, and I love the rawness in the way we fuck.

"You're mine, Finn," he says.

We both come, and then we collapse in a heap on the bed. Xavier pulls me into him so as much of my skin as possible is pressed against his. We're sweaty, we smell like sex, and with the added combination of the spanking beforehand, I'm content as fuck. "That was fucking incredible, my darling. God, I adore you."

I look up at him, best I can with him still crushing me to him. "What are we?" I say to him, unable to resist asking. Grayson keeps calling Xavier my boyfriend, and I don't correct him, but I don't really know if that's what we are. I don't need the label, but I do need the certainty.

"Whatever you want us to be. I'm all in with you."

"Grayson calls you my boyfriend."

"And? Are you happy with that moniker?"

Xavier feels like more than a boyfriend. We haven't been together long, but he does. He's the one for me. I don't want to say all of that and scare him off though. "I am."

"I call you my partner when I get hit on at events."

My eyes frown and form slits. "Who's hitting on you? You're mine."

He laughs. "Men and women at the boring events I have to attend; all of them want something from me."

"Yeah, like you fucking them." It's odd, I'm not really the jealous type, and I'm used to a poly-style relationship, but I do not like this. I know it's because there's part of me that doesn't feel good enough for Xavier. I'm sure there is someone more his caliber at the rich-person events he attends.

He presses my nose. "For what it's worth, I'm only into men, and as far as romantically is concerned, I'm only into you. I'll bring you sometime and you can stake your claim."

That is worth a lot. "So you tell them you have a partner?"

"I do. You feel like more than a boyfriend. I'm not sure what to call you, other than mine."

He's being vulnerable with me. I get brave and put my insecurities aside. "I feel the same way."

"All right then. You are mine and I am yours, and the outside world can label us however makes sense to them. As long as we know what we mean to each other, that's enough."

There are three more rounds of sex after that, with breaks to eat fruit and cheese while wrapped in his blankets on the couch, and all too soon I have to go back to the house. "You're the one who gave me the curfew in the first place, can't you make an exception?"

"Absolutely not. For starters, that's not fair to everyone else. Second, your curfew is for an important reason. It's about habits. I want you to have the good habit of being home at a reasonable hour, which, in turn will have you in bed at a reasonable hour."

I twist my lips. "All right. Okay."

"I will take you home. You can't drive the faulty golf cart."

"I'm sure I can find another on the way. They're all over the place."

"I love that you still think I make suggestions for the fun of it," he says, heading over to dress. He tosses a shirt at me. "Wear that. The other one's full of grease."

I salute him. "Aye, Captain."

He drives me back to the house, walking me all the way to the door and kissing me on the porch. "Behave, boyfriend of mine," he says, winking.

I'm over the moon when I walk in the door on time. Grayson is there. "It's about time," he complains, wrapping himself around me. "You smell like him. It's too soon for that, you're supposed to smell like us."

That catches my attention. I thought I was the only one who noticed weird shit like that, but I'm not. There are others like me in the world and I have found them.

We go through our nightly abolitions together, slipping into pajamas, brushing our teeth, washing our faces. "Awww, no one waited for me," Will complains, entering the communal washroom. There are three other washrooms in the house, but this one sees the most traffic and for some reason, all our toothbrushes are kept here.

"We brushed our teeth, we didn't leave you home without us," Gray says.

"I wanted to do all the stuff with y'all." Are Tops allowed to be adorable? Is that a thing? Because with his lip pouting like that, he is.

"Not to worry, we'll brush and braid your hair, William. Maybe even sing campfire songs." Grayson dodges the smack headed toward his ass, laughing. "Okay, okay. We're sorry."

I hand Will the toothpaste. "Yeah, we're sorry."

"Apology accepted," he says, taking the toothpaste from me. "But you two can wait for me."

Grayson rolls his eyes, hopping onto the counter, threading a leg between Will's thick ones. I don't have quite that level of comfort with the large cowboy and can only watch his wide lats flex, and his golden hair sway against his back as he gets ready. He's got grey cotton pajama pants on and nothing else. I can see the outline of his hard cock through the thin material.

Will has a large presence like Xavier does. He's firm. All air stops around him swirling there and forming currents that follow him where he goes, making him the force he is. I am calmed by it. Any nerves I had float away, join with his energy and are nullified there. They sift out as a gentle breeze.

"All right, hop on," he says, to Grayson, turning around, his back to Gray. Grayson clings to his neck and wraps his legs around his torso. Will reaches for my hand and I take it. "Bedtime boys."

The three of us are Xavier's, so we have a bedtime even though the rest of the house doesn't. This doesn't stop Will from sending people to bed if he thinks they need it. When Gray and I came up to brush our teeth, Ani was still on the pale green couch, reading, his apron finally off and hung on its hook in the kitchen.

I don't know what Bray and Bell were up to and frankly, it's best not to know most of the time. Chris and Johnny went off to Ani's room, telling Ani they were sleeping with him tonight. Ani didn't ask why, but said he'd see them in an hour or so.

It's creeping close to our bedtime, but we have time for some tomfoolery if that's where this is headed. Snuggling means snuggling around here. It's not code for anything, but that doesn't mean other things can't happen.

Nothing's happened between Will and I though. *Yet*. If I know anything about the tall cowboy, he's a southern gentleman. It likely won't tonight.

We get to Will's room and Will deposits Grayson on the bed. Will has the largest bed of us all, because so many come into his room for comfort. There are nights when he's had near everyone in with him. The mattress is twelve feet wide, there are fourteen pillows (regular pillows, not the fancy ones like in Ani's room) and two beige, king-sized duvet comforters overlaid at their ends in the middle of the bed.

Grayson and I climb under the covers as Will turns out the lights, leaving only the bedside ones on, some light from the moon shines in the window. Will climbs up the middle of the bed, his limbs weaving like a large cat, flopping between us like a tired rabbit. We settle him under the duvets with us, me on one side, Grayson on the other.

Even with the two of us on top of him, Will manages to be the mountainside we can't overtake. This is not my first snuggle-time with Will, but it is my first snuggle-time sleep-over, and it feels significant.

"So? Do I need to get this started?" Gray says. "I was

kinda hoping you would, William. You know I'm not good at that sort of thing. Threesomes are not my forte."

"We're not doin' that tonight, darlin'.'"

"We're not?"

"No. I know you two've already had nights like that together, but if Finny does want to do that with me, we'll have a night to ourselves first thank you very much, Grayson." Will kisses my head.

"Then why did you leave the light on? That's suggestive," Grayson complains. "Plus, you've got a hard-on the size of—"

"—okay, that's enough. The light's on because this is our first sleepover. I thought we could chat some before we close our eyes. You know? Have some of that fun you're always complainin' I never do."

I enjoy listening to the pair of them bicker; it's one of the sounds of home. I trace my fingers along Will's abs. "I'd like that, Will," I tell him. A night with him I mean. He knows.

"Okay, I'll plan it, sweetheart." He takes my hand, lacing his large one with mine. "But if you keep doin' that, I am gonna wind up inside of yah and I'll feel like a dog for days."

I raise an eyebrow in Grayson's direction, asking him to translate Will-speak. "He'll feel like he took advantage and didn't treat you as a gentleman should, as the precious raindrop you deserve to be treated as. If we're not gonna do it, can we just go to sleep? This sucks."

"Lordy be, Grayson."

I laugh at them. "What happened tonight while I was gone?" I ask.

They bicker over the telling of a story. Johnny and Chris made water balloons they used to ambush Bell and

Bray with, as a return for the great maple syrup debacle from last week. I was around for that one. Bell and Bray dipped Johnny and Chris's sheets into buckets of maple syrup, let them dry and then made up their beds with them. I knew something was going to happen sometime soon.

"It was awesome. Will actually let them retaliate until it got too close to the house."

"Normally I wouldn't have, but maple syrup sheets? That was rotten. Water balloons aren't harmful in the yard."

"Aww man. I missed a good time."

"Don't worry, they'll be a next time, Finnegan," Grayson assures me.

"Not till the summer," Will decrees. "I don't need, y'all gettin' hypothermia."

"And this is just what I mean about no fun. You need to lighten up, William. No one's going to get hypothermia."

"They won't, because I'm in charge and I won't allow it. All right you two, it's time for sleep."

We turn out the lights and close our eyes. I sink into deep contentedness against Will, wondering why I didn't do this sooner. I can see why everyone collects here through the night.

It doesn't take long for me to experience a taste of what it's like to be Will with his open-door sleeping policy. Johnny's the first. He climbs in on the other side of Grayson. "You okay, darlin'?" Will's sleepy voice says.

"Yeah, I just needed to come in here." Johnny had been in with Chris and Ani. I get it now though, sometimes you just need Will's massive energy.

Ani and Chris follow soon after. "Aww, we want in too," Ani says, sliding in on my side, spooning Chris.

"We're just missing—" Will begins.

He doesn't finish his sentence, Bray and Bellamy are

230

crashing inside the door having some kind of whisper argument.

"Just get in here you two and close the door," Will says. "If I don't have sleeping boys within the next four minutes, I'm handing out bedtime spankings."

Bray slides in on Chris's side, Bellamy on the other side of Johnny. We all fit snuggly, in harmony. It's not too much for the bed, or for us, it's baby bear: just right.

It took me a long while to get here, maybe longer than it should have, but it doesn't matter, I'm here now. I want it always to be just like this.

I sink further into my life here.

CHAPTER ELEVEN

I t's getting late and we can't hear much from below. They must be sick with worry over us, but we've been unsuccessful in gaining their attention. "I think we have to break the window, Gray."

"I did not think about that, but you're right. We do."

But then there are footsteps, beautiful footsteps in the hallway that lead to this door. We race out of the blanket fort and shout and bang on the door, stomping our feet, everything we can come up with to be heard. "I think I hear them," a familiar voice says.

"Will! Will!" we both yell.

It takes a moment for Will to unlock the door, but it gets unlocked and Grayson springs toward him.

The cool air from the hallway is a sharp contrast to the stuffy attic air, but I still can't get air. I slide down the door frame like a thick droplet of wax, trying to collect myself. *You're okay. You're all right. You're out.* It does nothing and I have to grip my chest, clawing. And tug my slick hair. My throat closes; the next breath pulls in too thick; the voices around me mute and muffle. I'm drowning.

I hear the world's best voice; it breaks through and pulls me above water. I catch the life raft.

"Finn? Oh my god, Finn."

Not Mr. Brighton, not Finnegan, *Finn.*

Xavier is there taking up all the space with his energy as he does, his long black jacket swaying stiffly, the green from his tie poking out. It's such a familiar sight, I cry. I look up at him when he's over the top of me unable to speak. I know how I must look, dirty from climbing the tree, greasy from drinking last night, and blood staining my shirt like tie dye from when I fell. I hold out my aching arm, showing him my cast, pleading for him to take me away from here.

Please pick up the pieces of me.

He lifts me from under my arms. I'm too big for him to carry down the stairs, even as strong as he is, but he can hold me for a moment as I cling to his torso, wrapping my legs around him. "You came," I whisper in his ear.

"Of course, I did. We've been looking for you both for hours." He sets me down. "Come. Let's get away from here —is that a blanket fort?"

"Yes."

"I—No, you know what? I don't want to know. Let's go."

Will and Grayson have already gone; Xavier brings me down to the kitchen where everyone is waiting to see how dead or alive we are. And when I say everyone, I mean *everyone.* Osh, Trevor, and Emmery from Sigma-Phi are here, along with a few others from their House, plus everyone from ours and some of their Tops. Ani's on me in a flash. "Oh baby. What happened to your hand?"

"It's broken."

I catch Xavier's eyes storming, like crashing waves. Torrents. He can barely handle me getting a paper cut, this is going to drive him crazy.

233

We get hugs from everyone who have to feel us to know we're alive. I also get disapproving looks from all of the Tops, with Osh in particular, telling me wordlessly with his eyes that we'll be having our own discussion. Technically, he's Emmery's Top, but we have our own relationship and I have accountability there too. Will takes Grayson away. "You will be coming with me, Mr. Brighton. Go pack a week's worth."

"A week? But sir—"

I stop my protest short when I see his look and shake of head, which is Xavier for, *Really not the time, Finnegan.*

I pack quickly. I am not good with this, so Ani helps me. I don't have to bring toiletries anymore, I have a set at Xavier's now, but I need books and clothes for school and lounging; I have sleep clothes there too. Even though I'm moving fast, I take too long, and I get a text.

Whatever you forget, we'll have someone bring. Time to go.

Right.

The drive to his apartment, in one of the campus golf carts, is quiet and the longest it's ever been. I know the way up, but I let him lead the way. I can feel the tension between us, and I hate it. I want to jump into the future, when this tension is gone, and I've been spanked, and he can forgive me, and I can burrow into his arms.

When we get inside and he walks away, an old pattern rises up, one in which I think he's going to abandon me even though I know Xavier would never do that, but it still lives in me and it comes up when I'm riled. I remind myself that it makes no sense for him to bring me all the way here just to ignore me. But as he moves across the floor to the bedroom, I lose my cool. "Xavier please. Just spank me or something. I can't handle this."

He rounds on me and I get the full effect of his anger. He doesn't shout though; Xavier almost never shouts. "I'm too angry to spank you now, that will have to wait. I understand it's hard for you when I'm upset with you, but think about how hard it's been for me to have you missing for hours." His eyes shine with unspent tears. "I couldn't even get in touch with you by cell phone, Finn."

Not Finnegan, not Mr. Brighton, *Finn*. It always hits different when Xavier uses Finn.

Watching your Top cry is about the most horrific thing a brat can experience. Tears come just looking at him. "I know, Xavy. I'm so fucking sorry I ..."

He yanks me to him, encircling me almost too tight and rests his chin on my head. I'm just the right height for him to do that, with him being so tall. "You're in so much trouble. You let your cell phone die, didn't you?"

"Not on purpose."

"No one does it on purpose, Finn. Hence why I bought you that special phone charger."

It's one that accordions out and then snaps in, so the wires don't damage. It fits in my bag so it can travel everywhere with me. "I didn't think we'd be out that late."

"You weren't supposed to be out at all."

I nod into his chest. There's been a bit of a Grayson and Finn ban on parties by ourselves since my first year. Okay, I see it. I understand why we can't be trusted. For the rest of first year, Will and Xavier wouldn't leave us home alone. We issued several complaints over the matter, all of which were denied by Tops who knew better, but finally, this year, they agreed we were ready. So far it had been good, until last night. "W-We thought we could handle it."

"Grayson got the news about his mother, and you've

been struggling with the new student. That's how we knew you couldn't handle it."

Gray was right. Xavier knew about Max.

"We're fine about those things." I recall us coming to that drunken conclusion sometime before I broke my hand, except it's all kinda fuzzy now, and maybe I'm not so fine about it anymore. I want to be though. I really want to be.

"Come, let's get you cleaned up, then we'll cuddle in bed and you can tell me all about it. I just need to be near you for tonight."

I sniffle. "Sounds good to me."

Laying in his arms is where I feel best and telling him everything doesn't seem as hard. We're in boxers since Xavier always says I'm too tempting when we're naked. The creamy silk of his black sheets brushes against us as we move. "I said I wouldn't do this again, but I freaked out and I didn't feel like I could talk to you about it."

"You can talk to me about anything, my darling."

"I know we're solid. You're the most solid thing in my life. It was stupid jealousy."

"Jealousy often doesn't make sense. I get jealous all the time."

"Yeah, but it doesn't affect me."

"Of course, it does. I'm sure you'd love to go shirtless at public pools."

"It's not on my list of dreams, no." Even if I like to toy with that one sometimes. Jealous Xavier is totally my jam.

"My point is, it's normal and we can talk about it. And

Finn? *You're* my priority. If it bothers you that much, I can assign Max to another professor at the school."

"I knew you'd say that, but that's exactly what I don't want. I'll work through it. I've just never had someone that I didn't want to lose before." Xavier turns my chin up, so I'll look him in the eyes. I don't like the look that's there, I know what it means. "No!"

"I haven't decided yet, but it is my decision to make. That's how we work, you know this. I will decide if keeping Max is what's best for *us*. You will accept my decision, Finnegan."

I don't like it, but yeah, I know how domestic discipline relationships work well enough by now. It's why I came to this school, it's what I've experienced working for me time and time again. I'm not about to back out now, just because we've hit a challenge. Xavier's never made a decision that hasn't benefited us both. I trust his lead. But I can't voice all this yet, so I just nod.

"What did the hospital say about your hand?"

"I need surgery, but there was nothing more they could do about it tonight. I broke the second and third metacarpals. I'll probably need more pain meds soon."

"I found them in your pocket, they're by the bed with a glass of water for when you need them. I hate that your hand is broken."

I knew that would be the thing driving him the most crazy. That and the disobedience aspect are up there for him. He really doesn't like it when I don't do what he says—it sets a Top's teeth on edge.

"How did you break your hand?"

"You think you want to know, but you really don't," I say, burying my head into him further, I can't look at him.

237

It's bad. Really bad and he's going to go into protection-overdrive.

"No, I do."

I sigh. "I fell off a ledge, bush broke my fall, eventually landed on my hand."

"*Finnegan.*"

"I told you, you wouldn't like it."

"Was alcohol a factor?"

"Yes."

"I didn't mandate it last time, but I think alcohol's out for you. Full stop."

He can't mean that, but I don't say anything about it now. It's not the time. Though it does affect me badly and I should probably not overindulge like that.

"You're lucky a bush broke your fall. It could have been much worse."

I know. I could have hit my head. He knows it too, but neither of us say it.

"We'll get through this," he says. "For now, it's time to sleep. We'll both feel better in the morning."

"What about school?"

"You'll live missing your classes for a day or three. That hand is going to be painful tomorrow and you'll need meds that will make it hard to think. You can go back when you're down to less-intensive medication. I've cancelled all of my appointments."

"You cancelled them all for me?"

He turns my chin up again. "When we couldn't find you, I nearly lost my mind. As much as you don't want to lose me, I don't want to lose you ten times as much," he says.

"Hey, why do you get to win that battle?"

"Because I do. Go to sleep now. I've got you."

I n the morning, Xavier's not beside me. The sharp aroma of coffee sinks into me. *He's in the kitchen.* I cozy down in the bed forgetting I have a broken hand. "Ow, fuck!" Even with the cast, pressing on it hurts. I look at the time and take more pain meds.

I pull on my t-shirt and pajama bottoms and stroll out to the kitchen. "Morning, baby," I say.

He stops what he's doing to kiss me and then interrogates me like he does. "How did you sleep? How is your hand? Did you take your pain meds?"

"Good, good, and yes, sir."

"Good boy."

Fuck that gets me in all the right places, though I remember that I was not a good boy last night. I set the table, one-handed, and he serves up the French toast and sausages, with fruit and more coffee. I think he's going to start in with the lecture I thoroughly deserve, but that's not the direction he goes at all.

"Move in with me."

"What?"

"I want you to move in with me."

"But, Xavy I—"

"—I don't expect you to move out of the House," he says. "In fact, I don't think that would be good at all. I'm not here a lot and you need them. I just mean, live here *too*, as in, you'll have your own key and stuff that's yours here. We can add décor that suits you, and you don't have to be invited to spend the night, you could come here when you need quiet or just when you feel like it. There's another benefit, you wouldn't have to leave here to be home by curfew, as long as you were at either place, it would count."

For Xavier, that's rambling. He's nervous. He's not the kind to get nervous often. I take his hand and put him out of his misery. "I'd love that. I'd love to live with you too."

He lets go a heaving breath. "Good. That's good. That's what we'll do."

We eat, and sip coffee and he looks at my hand too many times before I *have* to ask. "So, am I grounded for life?"

His lips form a wry smile. "Nearly. I can't spank you how you deserve to be spanked at the moment, so you're grounded until I can."

"But that could be weeks!"

His eyes form the dark torrents I know so well. "Shall I review the charges? The list is long."

"No need sir, but I would rather be spanked than grounded for that long."

"There is one kind of spanking I can give you in the meantime. One you need."

Xavier gives what he calls a 'thinking kind of spanking.' They still have a pain element, spanking needs it in order to work, but they aren't even close to what a punishment spanking is. Besides, spankings that are too nice are just a snooze. "Yes, sir."

His eyes narrow, his wheels turning. "How on Earth did you get up to the attic with only one hand?"

Fuck. I do not want to tell him that. Of course he'd think to ask. "It wasn't easy, and I fell into the window, sir." He flinches. "You're adding that to my tab."

It's not really a question, but he answers it anyway. "Absolutely. The time you sprained your wrist was bad, but you didn't do nearly the number of dangerous, life-threatening things you did this time around. Finn, you're not scared of me, are you?"

I laugh. "No. Only of your disappointment."

"We're going to talk about that too."

I circle my finger on the rim of my cup. "It sounds like we have a lot to talk about."

"We do. I'm dealing with you and Grayson separately this time. Missing curfew without a word—when you were at the hospital, you should have called someone—going to the party you were forbidden from attending, and not having your cell phone charged, are straight forward acts of disobedience and will be dealt with as such. Taking risks like climbing trees and not coming to me when you're struggling are more complicated. The first three are what you'll get the spanking for when we get your hand sorted, the other two we'll talk about now."

"Yes, sir."

"I am going to be disappointed with you sometimes, just as you'll be disappointed with me, but we'll get through it, no matter what. I promise. But you can't do this again, Finnegan. If you're in some kind of trouble, or have merely broken a few rules, find anyone of us, Will, Trevor or Osh if you can't come to me right away. You always feel better afterward, don't you?"

I set my coffee cup down on the table. "Yeah, I do."

"I've thought about Max, and I'm going to keep him for now. After thinking it over, it would be better for you to work through this one and see that you're still my one and only."

I know how unfair that is. I have sexual relations with Osh, Ani, Grayson and Will, while Xavier only has them with me and here I am obsessing over the way Xavier hugged Max. I think I might be more possessive of Xavier than he is of me, only not in the fun way. I have to work through this. "I'm mostly good these days, but something comes up randomly in my head, triggering thoughts of past failures, which lead to thoughts of 'not good enough.' I don't like bothering people with these thoughts, because usually they pass, and I don't want to put them on anyone."

"Or sound too needy?" He arches one of his large brows.

"Or sound too needy."

"I remember. This is old ground for us."

It is. Coming to him with concerns was the first thing we worked on. In the beginning, I had to go to him for even the smallest of things, or I would get a spanking. I got a lot of spankings during those weeks, but eventually going to him got easier. It resulted in feeling more myself, and it enabled me to take on more of a mediator role than one of full on bratness.

Extra-brat-like behavior isn't me, even if I am a brat, but during the first months, the first few weeks in particular, my brat wanted to run free seeing if people really would wrangle me in. They did and then some. The restrictions and consequences enabled me to relax. Knowing all I had to do was follow the lead of the highly capable Tops in my life was freeing. It left less for me to take on myself, so that the things I did take on were doable.

And I've grown increasingly confident. I've learned how to set boundaries for myself, because I matter. Through all of this, I'm learning what I like and what I don't like, which means I've made progress in the direction of school. The class schedules Xavier makes for me challenge me into finding out what I love, what I really hate, and what I'm capable of.

"What we've done in the past worked well, so we're going to return to some of it. Daily check-ins, especially about Max, and some of the little things too."

I nod. All of that might bother someone else and no doubt I'll complain from time to time, but for me? That stuff brings security. "Yes, sir."

He sighs a long breath, his eyes falling to my hand. He's having a rough time with it. He gets quiet when he worries, thinking about all the things that could have happened, like me dead in a ditch somewhere. I know to leave him be when he gets this way. It's hard though, because the silence kills me, but it's not on purpose. We all have our ways of processing. This is Xavier's. I have to pick up on his other cues in these times.

I think that aspect of him became clear to me most when I was injured in a hockey game last spring. I joined a league after getting all the required permissions—which let me tell you wasn't easy—and hockey tends to batter a person. It became clear after only a few games that hiding my injuries from view was best. Xavier knew they were there but looking at them was too hard for him. His jaw would get tight, he'd go quiet.

Inside he was in pain, constantly gripped by worry and concern, thinking, *'This time it was only his ribs, but what could happen next time?'*

Thing is, Xavier is good at handling any anxieties he might have, except when it has to do with the One Finnegan Brighton. So, when I came home from hockey, after a particularly brutal game with a swollen black eye that could not be hidden from view, he flipped out. He wasn't angry at me though, and it was a situation that wasn't convoluted by a rule I broke, like the situation now. Hanging out with him that week was not fun. He was quiet, distant and altogether unpleasant. He even refrained from spanking me for anything—because I totally tried to push him into it—which was not the holiday a brat dreams it is.

Spanking is the language we speak. Without it, life feels like it's forever missing something, and people like me don't feel whole. People like Xavier don't feel whole either. It's darkness.

But we all have our particulars and this one's Xavier's. We talked about it and he assured me he wasn't angry with me, he was angry with an imaginary source, because there wasn't one. It was a thing that happened that he had to find a way to live with.

When he gets like this, I've gotten better at the things he doesn't say. When he has to leave to do something else, to get his mind off of the worry, and to process, I don't take it personally. Instead I worry about him, which is also not what he wants, but there's nothing for it.

"It doesn't hurt," I assure him, even though I know it's not about that. "That hydromorphone stuff is the best, just makes me kinda sleepy."

He nods. "You should lie down. I'll set you up and then I'm going to go to the gym for a bit. You're not going to move from bed, except to use the loo."

"Yes, sir."

"Come," he says, crooking a finger at me. I go to him, climb into his lap and try to meld with him. "We're good, we're fine. I'm just having a hard time with the knowledge of how it happened and what you did after that. I want to bubble wrap you and lock you in a padded room."

It's Xavier's version of tenderness and it seeps into me, filling every crack and crevice with buoyant air, lifting me above water.

CHAPTER TWELVE

I t takes three days for me to get in for surgery and another five for me to switch out the heavier pain meds for lighter ones. My hand is in a cozy air cast and doesn't bother me much. What *is* bothering me, is the stuff unresolved between everyone and me. I'm owed a few spankings and I'm not good at asking for them like Ani is. Instead, I turn full on brat, and this is a problem.

I head over to Xavier's to study without distraction. The house is chaotic with Bellamy's video project, which Will allowed him to film at the house. "Sorry Finn, it's for school. Not much I can do about it except put a time limit on it," Will said, when I complained.

Some of my stuff lives at Xavier's now, or well, *our* place, I guess. He told me to think of it that way even though I don't pay anything toward the living expenses. "When you have a job, we can talk about it. I asked you to move in, knowing you wouldn't be able to financially contribute. I just want you here. Besides, everything I own is paid for. I know how it feels to want to contribute, but there are more ways to contribute than with money."

When I arrive, Xavier's in his home office. I wave, but he's busy, so I know not to go in. He waves back though, and I smile. I almost set up my books where I'm supposed to, at the kitchen table, but instead I choose the counter where the barstools are. Annoys the fuck out of Xavier because he can't cook with all my books there, but it's not a calamitous offence. Just one that gives enough hint of brat for him to use his scolding voice. I won't stop there, of course; I need this to go all the way.

As soon as Xavier sets eyes on me, I get his classic frown and his pensive, *Is he really doing this?* look. "Finn, I'm going to cook dinner. You know better."

That's not even level one Xavier. "Sorry. You know, I don't need to do this anyway. It's just the pre-reading and note taking crap Osh always goes on about. Not real home-work." I move to pack up my books and I can *feel* him squinting at me.

"You know better than that too. If Osh says to do it, then you do it. What's going on with you tonight?"

Okay, warmer. But he hasn't even moved toward me, or suggested 'help,' which is spanking in case no one's been paying attention. He's still unbuttoning the cuffs to his shirt, about to roll them up so he can cook. "Nothing. I'll just move to the table then."

"Thank you."

I wait until he's got his ingredients out and then I pull out my phone to text Grayson.

Hey man, what's going on over there? It's not long before Grayson's texting me back, complaining about Bellamy.

Come home right now, Brighton. I can't believe you abandoned me to this nightmare.

I laugh, that catches Xavier's attention. "I hope you're not texting instead of doing homework," he says.

"I wouldn't dream of it. I'm texting *and* doing homework."

"Give me that," he says, extending a hand for my phone. *You have reached level two, Finnegan.* I relinquish my phone without a protest. I might be smiling too big and he's suspicious, but he returns to cooking. "You know on second thought, maybe I'll head back to the house. You seem busy," I say.

"Forget it. If you want to go back to the house, you can finish your homework first. You're not leaving now just so you can go over there and put your books away. I know you, you'll procrastinate."

Whoa, that was a good shiver. I'm at third base. Now what to do for the home run?

I know. I get up to grab a drink from the fridge and then I take too long to get back to my work, setting my drink on the counter. That does it. Xavier seldom likes to tell me to do something more than once, definitely not four times. He spins me around and lays a crisp smack to my ass. "If I don't see you with your nose in that book, you're going over my knee and you can do homework with a sore bottom."

"You promise?" I say.

He pauses, mouth opens and then closes. I can see it come together for him on his face. "There are less suicidal ways of asking for a spanking, you know."

"Yeah, but only crazy people like Ani ask for spankings."

"I was having visions of my bamboo brush, just so you know. Think about that next time and asking may finally become appealing."

Oh yeah, ouch. That thing's a bitch the next day. "You may have finally found the inspiration I need. We'll have to see."

"Don't worry, brat. I am going to spank you. It's time. But I do have to be careful of that," he says, still not enjoying looking at the cast. "You just had surgery five days ago."

"I know, but I don't feel right, Xavy."

"Neither do I." He pulls me to him. "Your punishment will have to wait until that's healed, but I'm going to do the other spanking tonight, before bedtime, which I'll remind you is at nine-thirty."

I melt into him, into all the sternness. Tomorrow I'll care about early bedtimes, right now I just want more of that.

He tilts my face up by the chin and kisses me. "Until then, homework, young man." He sends me away with another smack.

"Ow. Yeah, yeah."

"Excuse me?"

I swallow. "Yes, sir."

At nine o'clock, he sends me to stare at a wall. I'm ready for bed, in a pair of black pajama pants, shirtless. "It's time for you to stand and think. How's your hand?"

"It's good. I promise."

He nods. "Hands by your sides then. Ten minutes."

When a brat is told to find a wall, he's often too self-righteous over being sent to said wall to consider thinking. I am no different, but tonight is and I think about what I want to let go of.

Because spanking is about more than penance although it is also about penance, in a concrete, tangible way. It's also how people like Xavier and I communicate. It's the place where we're both the most open we get, so we can surrender to the act and let go of what we need to.

I don't want to hold on to the belief that Xavier will decide he wants someone more than me. Xavier's never given me reason to think that. I also think about how much I hurt Xavier. I made his disappointment more important than him. I also made it more important than us and the contract we have together. And I don't mean the one I signed when I came to this school, though that one is important too, I mean the unwritten one. It's one made up of who we are inside and what we've promised to each other.

Xavier has every right to be disappointed when I disobey him. I'm breaking a promise, I'm saying I have little respect for what we have together and above all, that's not how we treat each other.

"All right my naughty boy, come here."

He's on the bed and I go to him. He pulls me between his legs. "I've had the chance to think on what I want to say to you. Staring at that hand every day, thinking over what could have happened to you ..." He pauses, closes his eyes, takes a breath. "For the moment, I'm not comfortable with you drinking, or going to parties without William, or Osh, or Trevor. I would consider Ani."

He said that before, but now it's official. I'm not as bothered about it as I thought I would be. "That's fair, sir."

"You have to come to me, Finn. That's a firm rule. Even if you can't get it out right away, that's fine, but at least I will know to keep a better eye on you. I can give you time. This rule is more than a simple rule like curfew, or getting your homework done without procrastinating. It's us, darling," he says, putting my hand over his heart. "I haven't been able to sleep when you're not here. I'm worried you're off doing something that'll get you killed this time."

Tears blink from my eyes. "I broke your trust."

He nods, solemnly. "Unfortunately."

That's hard to hear. "I'm sorry."

"I know. And I will get over it with time." He takes a deep breath. "I'm not good with the super brat stuff, Finnegan."

"I know, and I'm not a super brat, most of the time." My breath hitches, I'm trying not to cry, but I'm failing.

"No, you're not," he says, kissing my broken hand, gently. "You did this because you were scared of being rejected—rejecting me before I reject you. Does that sound about right?"

My voice cracks. "Yeah."

"It was also the most extravagant way to demonstrate that you don't care, I'm not sure if that was a message to me, or for yourself. Either way, caring too much terrifies you, overwhelmingly so."

I can't speak, it will only come out in sobs. The tears flow freely, soaking my face.

"This is going to make both of us feel better," he says, pulling down my pajama pants and boxers in one go and then guiding me over his knees.

Usually the point is to make a spankee the most off-balance they can feel, the loss of control helps with the surrender, but tonight Xavier has me lie with my body on the bed so I can take care of my hand. I can't put weight on it yet.

"Is your hand still okay, darling?"

"Yes, sir."

"I'm going to begin. Ten minutes," he says. "Tell me if your hand becomes an issue at all."

"Yes, sir."

I'm a seasoned spankee by this point, even if it's been a couple weeks. Xavier starts in heavy, his large hand covering a lot of surface area. I'm still a responsive kind of spankee, but it takes a little more to get me there than it used to. Xavier uses a rhythm that's slower than Osh, but faster than Will. I would say it still leans to the faster side of things, and it doesn't leave time for a rest. And with ten minutes on the clock, I want a rest, let me tell you.

Let it Go By Artsy Ape

It doesn't take long for the burn to build, which coincides with my squirming. Spanking brings odd things to mind, like that thing I said in fifth grade I wish I could take back, or the time I stole my brother's favorite shirt, wore it, ripped it and let him think he did it.

As the pain builds further, it's startling. I want to get out of target range, but I know I'm not supposed to, so I do what I can to stay and absorb the vexing sting as best I can.

Breathing helps. Xavier taught me that when I breathe through it, I can take more without trying to kick off a lap. *Smack! Smack! Smack! Smack!* It gets intense. He keeps his rhythm, never varying it, and I break. I can't keep still anymore. I move my legs restlessly, crossing and uncrossing them at the ankles, I kick them in tiny pulses, squirming from hips to torso and I subconsciously try to move away.

Xavier readjusts me like it's nothing. I cry out at my misery, which is all I can do. This is not a fun spanking. I put my head into my good arm and take what I'm given. There's always a point, the one I'm getting to, where it feels like he's going to spank straight through my cheeks, but that's never the case. *Smack! Smack! Smack! Smack!*

"I'm sorry. I'm—ow!—sorry, okay? Fucking Christ, Xavier." I'm lucky it's not Will spanking me. Xavier's not as concerned over curse words as he is.

"We're halfway."

Halfway? Only halfway?

He continues spanking.

I twist and I turn. He stops briefly to put his leg over mine, and the relief feels so good it makes the rest of the spanking that much worse.

Just when I think I can't take another swat, he stops and I let go all the tension that's built up, melting into the sheets. "How you doing, my Finnegan?"

Of course, like with all spankings, I go from, *I'm going to die*, to *really fucking amazing*, in a heartbeat. "I'm good, sir."

I hear the drawer open and I know what he's pulling out of there. I wince, but I don't complain. This isn't even half of what

I deserve. The implement is solid wood and in the shape of a ping-pong paddle. "This isn't quite a punishment spanking, but I do want you to learn a lesson. You have a responsibility to all of us, to keep yourself safe, Finn. Not just to me, but to everyone. I won't tolerate dangerous behavior. None of us will."

That breaks me. The pain in his voice is clear, I can picture all the austere faces in my spanking family, them sick with worry over me and Grayson. They absorbed me into the house from the first day, loving me dearly, doing everything to make sure I'm okay and taken care of. I can't handle letting them down like that. The tears fall, soaking into the bed. The huge knot in my stomach finally breaks free. I can let go. I can feel how much they all love me.

"You've got six with this and then we're done."

"Yes, sir." I know they'll be good ones, and when he pulls my pants down further, I know where they're going to go. In a fast motion, with quite a bit of his strength, he lays down the last six on the sensitive part of my thighs. It's enough to send me over the edge and I can allow myself to cry into my pillow.

Xavier sets the paddle down and rubs my back letting me cry it out. When it's just sniffles, he arranges us so he's snuggled around me. "I love you, ridiculous boy," he says into my ear.

I smile a watery smile. "I love you too. I'm sorry."

"None of that now. It's done. Do you feel better?"

"So much better. I feel safe."

"Good. I feel better too. Thank you for bringing yourself to my attention in creative ways."

Spanking isn't a sexual thing for me, but it is for Xavier. It's hard for him to resist my freshly spanked ass, and I expect him to undress us both and slide his cock into me.

He does settle us in our boxers, but he turns out the light and surrounds me with his body.

It takes me a heartbeat or so to figure out, but his breathing behind me is ragged and he sniffles. My chest clenches. "Xavier? You all right."

"I am."

"You're crying."

"Can't I cry after a spanking?"

I grab one of his large hands and press my lips to the knuckles.

It took me six months to figure out what Xavier's middle name was. He keeps it out of the records, all I had to go on was that it started with an 'H.' "Xavier. H. Harkness?" I said. "That's some name."

"I have my mother to thank for that. She liked to think herself mysterious."

"You take after her, mysterious is your calling card. I'm surprised we don't call you Headmaster Mystery."

I was lying on my belly, on his sofa reading one of my textbooks at his place. I don't know why I made the mistake of laying on my belly, that's open season for someone like Xavier. Tops can't resist, especially when brats are being cheeky.

He whacked my ass. *Hard.* I jumped to seated as quickly as I could, letting the sting run through me. Relishing in the heat of it. "C'mon. Tell me what it is."

"No."

"Why not?"

"Because."

"That's not an answer."

"It's the only one you're getting."

But in six months, I had long accepted my brat status. Embraced it even. I was willing to bargain with spanking chips, Xavier's favorite kind of chips, using my brattish charm. "Tell me and I'll let you spank me however you want, with whatever you want."

I wish I could go back in time and tell Past Finn how it *so* doesn't work like that. Though truthfully, I knew it back then too. It's basically how we flirt.

He narrowed his eyes into slits. "I don't make deals with brats. I will, however, allow you three guesses. Three. If you don't get it in three, I'm having a lovely caning session with your bare bottom." He was already smiling, delighted at the prospect, and in that moment, I knew it was happening one way or the other. "Each incorrect answer will merit its own kind of spanking depending on how far away you are from the answer."

I pouted as I realized how unfair his game was. "That's subjective. The judge of this game is severely compromised."

He smiled. "I know. I can't wait. Do we have an accord?"

I couldn't resist him though. There's something adorable about a Top, bursting with glee over how he'll spank you next. And for me, Xavier especially. I want to give him everything. "Oh God, fine. So long as you never ask if we 'have an accord' again."

"I make no such promises."

I laugh. "What do I win if I get it right?"

"Knowledge and a stern warning that if you tell anyone, ever, you'll pay dearly."

"That's a horrible prize." He was on the couch now, I put my book aside and climbed into his lap. I blinked pretty green Finn eyes at him, but he was not swayed. Much.

"I will allow you to use it when we're in private without consequence."

The way he was staring at me, the intensity in his breath—I wanted it. I wanted it because I knew it was an extraordinary gift, one he'd never given before. "I'm going to figure it out," I promised him.

"I wish you the very best of luck."

"No, you don't. You want to spank my ass."

He laughed. "I'll never deny that, but I do wish you luck, Mr. Brighton."

I enlisted Grayson's help. We scoured the internet for names beginning with 'H.' There were so many and I could only pick three. "I bet it's something ordinary like Harry," Bellamy said one day when Grayson and I were curled around each other on the pale-green sofa, sifting through a book of baby names we'd ordered online. The coffee table was littered with coffee cups and half-eaten plates of donuts. It was my turn to clean up the living room, but I hadn't done it yet. My project took precedence that week. Yes, I also met with Will's Lexan that same week for skipping chores.

"It would be Harold," Grayson said, his poshness shining through. "Not Harry. God. Xavier's mother has to have had more class than that."

"Could be Harrison too," Bellamy shot back. "That's fancy."

After much bickering and involvement from Bray and Johnny who joined our search (and threats of spanking from Will when we got too loud), we went with Hector. It seemed mysterious enough to us, and Hector was also the name of the Trojan prince, which made it very posh too. We were certain we had it.

The glee dancing in Xavier's eyes told me before he did that I was wrong, and of the spanking I was about to receive. He chose his favorite wooden paddle. He did not go easy. Said it would teach me not to be so curious. I should have complained but I didn't, bending over his lap to take my licks with pride. He enjoyed himself thoroughly. I laughed even though it fucking hurt, and then he fucked me against his white-marble kitchen counter.

When I got home, all eyes were on me. *Did we get it? Did we figure it out?* I turned around to show them my ass. They hissed collectively. "Jeez, Finn. You can take a spanking, eh?" Bray said.

"He can," Grayson answered for me, as proud as if he was talking about himself. "C'mon. I'll put aloe on that, and we'll start brainstorming our next attempt."

"Why do you get to?" Bray said. "You always get to."

"You two are not fighting over my ass." I looked around belatedly to make sure Will wasn't around to hear me swear. "C'mon. You can each have a cheek."

We belabored over names for a week and a half before I made my next attempt racing down to his office as soon as we settled on something. "Holden," I said proudly. We were *sure* this time.

When I entered Xavier's office, he'd just seen a boy—Tyler I think his name was—sent by his Head of House for too many missed homework assignments. Surely Xavier was too tired to spank me, even if we'd got the name wrong again? But the man never tires of spanking, ever. "Darling? Do me a favor and hand me that strap on the wall, would you?"

"Oh, c'mon! It's not Holden?" I stormed over and took

the strap—that was about to be used on my bare backside—from the wall, returning to him with it, smacking it onto his desk without grace.

"Decidedly not." His eyes sparkled with sprightliness.

He kissed me long and hard before bending me over his desk. He took great pleasure in painting my bare ass with stripes from his favorite strap. I couldn't remain still, kicking and howling. "God, I love your responses, Finnegan."

I called that strapping one of his tie-loosening strappings.

Xavier can strap all six of us—or well I suppose now all seven of us including Max—without breaking a sweat, without breaking stride. But there are times with me when he pauses not for my benefit, but his own. He says his heart beats too fast and his body gets too light, but at the same time, everything's too constricting. He has to loosen his tie and remove his vest to allow the buildup of energy asylum—because he's not allowing it to leave, just making room for it to settle over him so he can bask in it later.

When he was done strapping me—for the time being, he'll never be done strapping me, or spanking me—he yanked my school shorts off the rest of the way and sat my bare ass on his desk, turning my face up to his for a kiss.

"It's Heathcliff," he whispered.

And somehow that seemed monumental. That he *told* me.

"Dammit! I told Grayson that's what it was—from your mother's favorite book." She was a big *Wuthering Heights* fan. Grayson argued that it was too obvious and stressed the mysterious clue we'd been running off of.

He smiled against my lips. "You remembered. Finn?"

Not Finnegan, not Mr. Brighton, *Finn*. "Yeah?"

"I love you."

I took a hitched breath, I can't remember what I was going to say in return, he put a finger over my lips. "Wait. I need you to know that my whole heart is yours Finnegan. I am at your service for as long as you'll have me."

My heart wanted to burst. I've waited all my life to hear something like that from someone, but when it finally happened, I had no idea what to do with it. It was too perfect. I didn't want to taint it with whatever I could say because no other words could equal his. I didn't want to say something that would have him walking away thinking I didn't love him like he loved me.

So, I said nothing. I smiled and said nothing.

I pulled him to me by the back of his neck for more kissing. Sure enough, I was soon plastered, back to the wall, legs crossed at my ankles, gripping his torso at his low back, as he fucked into me.

"So we'll discuss the terms of your third spanking, the caning, after dinner tomorrow," he said afterward, a sly smirk on his face.

"Third spanking? Caning? You *told* me. Doesn't that null and void it?"

"Don't you know me by now, my darling? Even if you had gotten it right, I would have found some reason to spank you. I've been wanting to give you a proper caning for some time."

The last time he brought out the cane for me and Grayson was as a warning the week we decided blowing off curfew was a good idea. It was a protest, which lasted all of three days, before Xavier pulled out his cane, giving us each a taste and told us what we were in for if he learned we missed curfew for a fourth night. But I knew he itched to give me the full meal. It's much different, however, getting a caning for punishment versus getting one for fun.

Different headspace.

Xavier was too proud of the fact that he could find a way to spank me for anything, and too adorable to be put out with. Besides, he was right, I should have known—I was always getting three spankings, the true lesson being: don't get into spanking negotiations with him.

Two days later, I was on my way back from the library, heading toward the house. Between the southeast side of campus and the northeast side where the Houses are is a large expanse of meadow if you choose to walk it—you can also take a golf cart. My found family and I, we choose to walk it more often than not, except for Johnny Rae unless we make him. He loves driving the golf carts around.

I saw the tall, large form like a shadow at first against the bright sun, but then he began to take shape, the features I knew well chiseling in some places, rounding in others. His long jacket swung stiffly as it does. Light glinted off the black buttons, his messy hair at inflexible attention—which seems like an oxymoron, I know. But it's what Xavier's hair does, I *swear* it.

His blue eyes, the deep torrents, waves crashing within them; they struck me.

He saw me and smiled in a quiet way, and I was overcome with feeling for him. They say it's like falling off a cliff, or like your heart exploding, or even dizzying to the point of fainting. But for me, it was the most unreachable thing I finally touched, and I filled with profound connection. To Xavier and to myself.

I ran to him, expecting him to catch me. He did, my school blazer colliding with his wool jacket. My eyes were wet. "I love you."

"I know, Finnegan."

"No. You don't get it. I *love* you." Why is that word the most important, but also not enough?

He took my hand and placed it on his chest. "I assure you, I do get it."

I could feel him. I trusted. I had faith. It was bliss.

"Where were you headed?" he asked.

Were? "I'm on my way home."

"You *were* on your way home. Now, you have an important meeting with me."

He took my hand, and we began walking in the direction he had been heading. "Why does 'meeting' sound like spanking?"

"Probably because you're finally catching on."

"Xavier!"

"Well, how else does one celebrate? The love of my life just told me he loves me. I want to mark the occasion."

"I can think of several other ways if you want suggestions."

"No. I don't think so. There isn't another way. Not for us."

CHAPTER THIRTEEN

W hen my hand is better, weeks later, I receive the promised spanking for all of the broken rules. Xavier's much more exacting for broken rules than he is with any other thing.

I 've been in Xavier's office for more transgressions than I can recollect. Some real in the sense of what the rest of the world would consider real, others our own brand of real. Point is, we have practice at this now, and when I enter, I know what I'm supposed to do.

"Hello, sir." I bite my lip. Can't help it.

"Lip biting is prohibited at this time, Mr. Brighton." Well now I have to bite my lip harder to keep from smiling. He has to adjust his pants. Me in my school uniform, biting my lip is his weakness—Kryptonite for Superman. "The wall, please."

"Yes, sir."

I know the position well. Hell, I was just in the position

last night for sassing Ani about after dinner clean up. It never gets less embarrassing. I pull down my school shorts to just under my ass cheeks, baring them and face the red wall with my hands atop my head, legs spread as far as my shorts will allow for.

I used to deny I was a brat. Standing here facing a wall with my pants down, the truth washes over me—happens every time. I denied it because I thought it was a bad thing. I denied it because I'd never really experienced the brat in me. Ani was right, it's an energy thing and certain people bring it out. When they do it's right, it clicks, you're an active spark in their life and it continues to fuel yet more sparks of *this*.

And it's special, because it's something understood at a level beyond words or cognitive comprehension. A spark absent from all other connections in your life, one you're relieved to come home to.

Brat now means: *I fit with you.*

This position isn't an easy one to keep. Too soon my legs ache. A brat always tries to move his feet minutely enough to fly under the radar of their Top, but their Top always notices. "Finnegan, you know better."

His deep voice runs through me. I do my best to keep still. My arms get tired though and I want to put them down, just for a second. If only I could see him—maybe he's concentrating on some papers, or his laptop, maybe he's writing an email. He could be, but I don't know. I try to look, but I can only see as far as the two-story mini-library.

I return to staring at the red wall and think about every-thing, but it's been weeks and I've already thought about and talked it all through with everyone. I'm really just here to pay my comeuppance.

It's been hanging over my head. It's been hanging over Xavier's head.

"All right, Mr. Brighton. Come here please."

I know better than to pull up my shorts so I make my way over, with them around my ankles. It's a slow journey, but he waits, his demeanor calm. Watching. Enjoying. I stand before him.

He's leaned against his solid mahogany desk, his green tie perfectly knotted, his blue eyes the crashing torrents they always are, his biceps about to pop out of that shirt—he's been spending a lot of extra time at the gym, working out his feelings about all of this. He needs to give this punishment as much as I need to receive it. "You broke some rules, Mr. Brighton."

"Yes, sir."

"Which ones?"

I've been preparing for this. "Missed curfew, disobeying you, not keeping my cell phone charged and drinking irresponsibly."

I spy what's on his desk. I knew I was getting this, but seeing it has me clenching my cheeks. There are varying sizes of canes. Xavier uses a thin, whippy one with a crooked handle fashioned from rattan. I've met this one before, but not for such catastrophic grievances.

"That's a hefty list. We've already taken care of why you were so misbehaved ... unless there's anything else you need to tell me?"

I don't want to say it. I wish everything could be taken care of in one swoop. I wish my inner self-doubts would resolve themselves faster. But Ani said it best, "Oh baby, I've had issues with self-doubt for thirty-one years, why do you think you have to tie all the loose ends of yours in two?"

I smile at Xavier. "I'm not fully done with that, no, but I

am okay about it today. I've been okay with it all week. Tomorrow? I don't know, but I will talk to someone." In other words, I could need another spanking for it, but it would be a different kind than this one. I'm clear that today is about broken rules.

"Very well and Finnegan? I appreciate your honesty. It's noted."

"Oh good. Does that mean less time with that?" I say, motioning my eyes toward it.

"Not on your life."

Something settles within me, *that* feeling utterly intact and refueled.

"I also see someone started on this for me."

"Ani. Hairbrush."

"Oh? A sassy boy, were we?"

"Very."

That breaks the stern demeanor he's trying to cultivate. He laughs. "Do I want to know?"

"Probably, but at this juncture, it's better for my ass you don't."

He nods. "Very well. Remove your blazer Mr. Brighton. Place it on the leather chair." As I do that, he lifts the chair from beside the desk on his palm. It spins in a practiced motion, landing in the same spot it does, the carpet worn where the chair legs settle. He sits in the chair and pulls me forward by my wrist. "It's time to get serious, Mr. Brighton. Even weeks later, I am not pleased over your disregard for the rules. *My* rules."

My cheeks heat. That never goes away either, especially not when combined with the, *'you've been a naughty boy,'* lecture. It works well on me. "I'm sorry, sir."

"You're going to be sorrier. You know I don't tolerate disobedience, or disrespect. This is your consequence." He guides me over his lap, tugging my shorts down further, but not off.

The oddest thing, something I still haven't figured out: how having your shorts on, only pulled down, feels more naked than all the way off. Grayson and I have analyzed this many times. We have theories, but we can never be sure.

The nerves in my stomach are there. My ass knows it's going to hurt and that I have to take it. I hate it when I've disobeyed him, displeased him. I do prefer to be his good boy. That's me and Xavier, our energy together. As much as I am a brat, it's only meant to be the fun kind, not the over-the-top, selfish kind who has no respect for the rules I choose to keep with him.

He positions me so I'm off balance, my fingers tent, the tips press into the ground. When his hand connects with my bare ass, I close my eyes, breathing into the sharp slaps. I always try for stoic, though I don't know why. It never ends there. So gritting my jaw, I hold back the cries I want to release.

Xavier's hand has had more practice at this than can be imagined. Grayson and I were goofing around one day, and we wanted to see if we could give a spanking, since Tops make it look so easy. We both ended up bruising our hands. We did very little to the other's ass.

"It's an art and a science," Xavier said, when I complained about my hand. He had a good laugh.

His hand doesn't bruise though. It has endurance, and it smacks true on my poor backside. "Ah! Jesus, Xavy." My ass is hot and tender.

I get a harder smack for that. "I believe sir, is the word you're looking for."

"Ow. Yes, sir." Stoicism goes out the window with my pride. I cross a leg over my other, rubbing shin over calf.

The burn builds, I'm wiggling too much, I'm moving too much.

"This is exactly what naughty, disobedient boys get, don't they?" he says.

"Yes, sir," I whine. I'm already flushed, but I flush some more. The sting brings tears, but I don't cry. I struggle over his lap in misery. I twist my torso. My breath comes in heavy pants, sweat forming in sticky droplets, dripping from my forehead.

I finally get a break after I don't know how long. "I know why you disobeyed me, but it doesn't excuse you from the consequences. There are always consequences, aren't there, young man?"

"There are, sir." I grimace, knowing him, knowing he's going to start again.

He does and it's worse. He alternates cheeks, without much time between, it's just searing pain. "I won't tolerate such behavior. You're going to have a very sore bottom for the next week."

"Oww, yes, ow! Yes, sir." More panting. More grunting, more whining. I can't hold still. I move enough that he has to readjust me several times. The smacks are loud and so are my cries. It's without a doubt the most intense spanking he's ever given me.

At long last, he's patting my bum. I collapse over his lap. "Come, Mr. Brighton. We're not done yet."

Oh God. Right.

I think about telling him how I've learned my lesson, how my spanking card's been fully punched today, but even I know I earned this. I won't brat about it. It's not like I'm going to escape the cane by complaining. He knows how much I can take.

267

Xavier helps me stand and removes my shorts the rest of the way. "Over the desk, legs wide."

I do my best, but I'm shaky. He offers assistance.

"How are you doing?" he asks, when I'm in place, my torso flat against the wood.

"Sore, but good, sir." As we journey down the spanking path, knots loosen, anxiety settles. The guilt I struggled with over disobeying him floating away to obscurity.

"You'll take twenty with my cane as penalty for your behavior. And then it's over."

"Yes, sir."

The cane whistles through the air and lands with precision across both cheeks in a snappy, well-practiced motion. Cane strokes are devilish. At first you feel nothing and it's deceiving because you relax, your guard is down. But then the burn ignites, lighting a flame across your ass in the shape of a line. "Ahhhh!" I bang my fist against the desk, only just remembering protocol. "One. Thank you, sir."

"Thank you, Mr. Brighton. Only nineteen more to go."

I groan at my misery.

I get through six more. He pulls the cane back with his strong arm and it *swooshes* through the air, smacking against both cheeks in a new line each time. The delayed smart each time settles, never leaving, then another stripe joins.

This cane leaves raised lines that start white and end up red, which Xavier feels makes for a pretty design.

Getting through twenty is hard. I break form several times and Xavier should catch me out on it, but he lets it go and I remember his huge soft spot for me. My back arches, my toes curl, I grunt and make other indescribable noises.

I don't forget to count each one. "T-Twenty. Th-Thank you, sir."

When it's over, my ass throbs and everything is limp

spaghetti. I take a moment to breathe letting the ache wash over and through me. I'm spent, but I'm also whole again.

Xavier lifts me, and carries me through the door, to the room where we go for discipline night. He lays me on the bed, curling around me. We lay like that for a good while. I'm in a floaty state of bliss after a spanking like that. Xavier runs fingers through my hair, traces my skin, and can't resist touching his handiwork. "This is gorgeous, my darling. I'm almost glad you gave me an excuse to do it, almost. But I would rather you be safe than anything else in the world."

"I'm surprised you haven't made up a reason. It's been a while," I say, foolishly.

A wide smile spreads across his face. "I think I shall. That was too tantalizing to make myself wait for too long before I get to do it again."

I laugh, giddy from endorphins. For him, I'll take many more cane stripes. I love how much happiness it brings him —not that I'll tell him that. "Did it make you, you know...?"

"Spanking drunk? Yes. I'm likely floaty as you are."

"Good, but gotta tell you, I'm not going to be lining up for a punishment like that again. I have learned my lesson."

"I hope so. I'll never deny how much I enjoy spanking you, but I meant every ounce of scolding I gave. You won't do this again, Finnegan."

That dive happens, the one a brat gets when he's disappointed his Top, like a rock sinking to the bottom of a lake. "I won't, sir."

"All right, let's take you to the House. If I keep you too long, I'll be in for a lecture from Grayson, which will lead to a sore arse for him."

"And since when do you turn down spanking anyone?"

"Since one mischievous boy made me dizzy from spanking."

I look at him like I've never seen him before as he helps me off the bed. "Are you saying you actually need a break from spanking? Who are you?"

He laughs. "Not exactly. My hand is always at the ready if need be, but I'd like to keep this particular feeling as long as it will last for me. It's from *you*. No one else makes me feel like this."

Thankfully, Xavier walks me home. I don't think I could sit in a golf cart just now. I don't think I'm gonna sit on an anything just now. He kisses me on the porch. "I don't have to tell you to make sure someone takes care of this?" he says, patting my ass.

"You know seven people are gonna be on me as soon as I get in the door. No worry of that." Some of said somebodies are probably watching through the living room window.

"*Finnegan.*"

"Yes, sir. It will be taken care of by someone."

"Thank you. And this means you're free now, but maybe baby steps? Stay up late tonight, but maybe stick around here?"

I have been grounded for weeks. But I have no plans. "I'm not going anywhere with my ass like this, except maybe the tub."

He squeezes me to him. His chin rests atop my head, and he breathes me in. "I know I have to give you to them tonight, but come home to me tomorrow."

He's still having a hard time sleeping, which guts me. I did this. I did this to us. "I can stay here for dinner, come home to you after."

"No. You need them too. I respect that. And they need you. Tomorrow, Finn."

Not Mr. Brighton, not Finnegan, *Finn.*

"Okay. Love you, Heathcliff."

He smiles and kisses me. "Love you more, naughty brat."

I head into the house where Grayson is waiting for me by the door, glaring, hand on his hip. That lasts all of a second. He throws himself around me. "Finnegan, you lived!"

"Of course, I lived. Xavier wasn't trying to kill me."

"But it was the cane."

It was the cane. Not something he pulls out often, although I did break a million rules in the worst way I could have.

"You wanna see?" I'm kinda proud of the spanking I took. Glad as fuck that it's over, but proud.

"One thousand percent."

There was a time I would have made Grayson come upstairs to see. Now though, I pull down my school shorts thinking about how much Xavier loves giving a good naughty schoolboy spanking, especially when it's his own naughty schoolboy, and lift my shirt and blazer. "Whoa! He gave you more than he did me. These are nice."

"They don't feel nice."

"Yeah, I bet not."

I also don't doubt he went harder on me. He usually does for no other reason than I'm with him. He expects more from me. "I'm glad it's done, so we can move on. It was starting to hang over both our heads."

He continues to admire, running his hand along the warm skin as I shiver. This was a hard spanking to take purely because of the intensity. It wasn't emotional and I

271

didn't cry. Broken rules are just broken rules even if they do weigh on me when I break them, until we resolve it this way.

Bellamy and Bray abandon their schoolbooks, racing over from the homework table, to see what all the fuss is about. "Holy shit, Brighton," Bray says. "Look at that."

Harsher spankings, like this one, don't happen often in this house. You have to be a real fucking brat to earn one or do what Gray and I did. "Okay, okay you guys," Ani says, coming from the kitchen, a dishtowel thrown over his shoulder, his hairbrush never far poking out of his apron. "Finn, pull up your shorts unless someone's putting aloe on that, and you two. Bray, I need your help in here. Bellamy, back to work or you're coming in here to finish."

"C'mon. I'll do it," Gray says.

We head up to Will's room, to use his large bed. I catapult onto it, undoing my pants again and shimmying them down. "You're not sitting on this tonight," Grayson says.

"No."

"God it's pretty though. Have you seen it?"

"Not yet. Can still feel every place the cane hit. I'm staying far away from that thing for a good long time." I let myself relish in the care with the cool aloe and Grayson's careful attention, and I would have fallen asleep, but Will barges in. To be fair, this is his room.

"Oh, Finny, you're back. How you doin' darlin'? —*Ouch!*" He must spy my ass.

"Note to self, do not freak the hell out of Xavier and break a bunch of rules along the way," I say.

He laughs. "This mean I'm gonna have two boys in my bed tonight?" I can hear the sounds of him changing behind me and I picture the way his large torso V's down to a narrow waist, with another 'V' toward his pelvis.

Sometimes, Grayson and I follow him around, cuddling nearby, while he makes household repairs. He's often shirtless and glistening with sweat which serves to highlight the curves of his muscles, especially his broad shoulders. His biceps flex and extend as he tightens bolts and lifts heavy objects. No, we don't always help him, unless he needs extra hands. He likes us watching him.

Will is also a good post-spanking teddy bear and I do plan on casting myself to his body tonight.

"Yeah, huh," I reply in a lazy fashion.

I know when it's his hand on my ass—my ass is familiar enough with his hand to know these things. "Gosh this is delectable. I'm surprised Xavier didn't keep you."

"He had one of his events. It's going to go too late for me to attend."

"Oh, the hardship," Grayson says. He knows I hate those events and prefer not going, but sometimes I do for moral support—Xavier's not a huge fan either.

"All right, at least you two in my bed, probably more by the end of the night. I'm off to shower. Finish up here and then downstairs."

"Yes, sir," we both say.

After an intense spanking, like the one I had, endorphins are high, and a drop is more likely. Will likes to keep an extra eye.

"We're both free now," Grayson says. "What adventure will we fly off to next?"

"No, no, no. No flying for this bird. Are you not seeing my ass?"

"Too soon? All right, Brighton." Gray lays a kiss on a sore ass cheek, which is sweet for Gray. "C'mon. Will's gotta do his Top thing and watch over you. If we don't get the TV before Bellamy and Bray do, we'll be watching their pick and if I've got to sit through another show about Vikings, I'm going to stick a horn in their—"

"—*Grayson.*" I roll to my side, slide my boxers up so the elastic doesn't catch my tender ass and take my school shorts the rest of the way off. I borrow a pair of Will's grey sweats, too big for me, but nice for my ass. I grab his hand.

"Well? How many times do I have to come home to mead experiments gone wrong before Will bans that show? It's a bad influence."

Downstairs, the TVs free—for once—and Grayson lets go my hand to barrel toward it, in case Bellamy thinks he's going to pause doing his homework to fight over the TV with him. Dear Lord. Not that it's an unlikely possibility, but usually people behave after warnings. Unless they've got something else going on.

"What do you want to watch, Brighton?"

"Whatever your heart desires." He'll just complain till I pick what he likes anyway. "I'll get snacks."

I think I'm fine, until the sight of Ani's loose hair moving as if it's got its own natural breeze, while he spirits around the kitchen, clenches my heart. I want to bury my head in his dark locks.

He spins around, his hair flaring with him like a black fan. "There you are. What took you so long? You're on lettuce washing duty."

My mouth drops. "But, but Grayson and I were gonna watch TV." So not a reason for anything around here.

"Not anymore." His apron swooshes as he sets the salad spinner by the sink for me. "It's a nice standing job, since I doubt you'll be sitting any time soon."

My lip wavers, *because it's in the way Ani knows.* I should be grumbling about my lost TV time on principle. Instead, I see this for what it really is: comfort. I collide with his torso, squeezing for all I'm worth, burying my head in his gossamer hair like I wanted to. He encircles me. "As if anybody's letting you out of sight for long today after that spanking." He kisses my head. "Didn't Will tell you to get down here?"

"Yeah, but I'm fine in there with Grayson."

He gives me a look that says, *Is this your first day?* "After a spanking as intense as what you got? You're staying in sight. *My* sight. Now get to work."

I let go to head to my lettuce duties—Grayson will figure out I've been commandeered. It happens frequently around here.

Bray's near the sink too, lips rested in a serene smile slicing cucumber, dicing bell peppers, having watched the whole exchange between me and Ani. He leans into me. "I'm glad you're here, Finny."

I rest my head on his shoulder, letting the gentle warmth of him flourish against my skin.

CHAPTER FOURTEEN

A week later, I'm in bed alone—it's a rare occurrence these days, but it does happen—my mind loud and whirring. I choke sobs into my pillow until my throat is raw, while pathetic thoughts war for territory. Trying to shut them up is exhausting.

I do this for too long. The night ages.

Go, to him Finn.

My bare feet hit cool, laminate wood and carry me over a familiar path down the hall and to the right, without conscious thought. I stand in front of his door, at war with myself: I'll be fine, it will pass. Don't wake him for something so trivial. He needs sleep.

You said that last night, Finnegan.

I remember what I promised Xavier. I also remember I'll be yawning all morning like I did this morning, and no one's going to buy my excuse about drinking too much water before bed a second day in a row. I wish I could do this *only* because I promised Xavier I would, but that's not how I work and it's the latter that gives me the extra push I need.

Ani's hairbrush on your bare ass at the breakfast table is not a fun wake up. That clicks for me. It reminds me: I'm supposed to do this. They want me to bother them.

I draw a frayed breath that chafes my raw throat and open the door.

"Um, Will?" I say, trying to hide that I'm crying.

We've formed a special relationship over the two years I've been with the House. Yeah, he's the teddy bear Grayson and I share, but he's more than that. He's a wall, a net, a best friend, a lover, a disciplinarian.

He's Will.

Will.

The gentle, but firm cowboy is the only person I can imagine going to when the emotions driving me to distraction are still ill-formed impressions. Ones I don't know how to talk about.

He rubs his eyes and opens his comforter for me. "C'mere, darlin'. You okay?"

I bound onto the bed. "No Grayson tonight?" Grayson rarely sleeps alone.

"He's with Ani."

I nod into his chest and now that I'm here, I let go and cry some more. He encourages me to cry until I'm done. "You ready to talk about it?"

"No, but I'm under orders."

"Xavier didn't mean you don't get privacy."

"No, but he was pretty clear he didn't want me chewing on stuff and that I should come to one of you if I was doing that. I am."

"I appreciate that, and I know he will too." He kisses the top of my head. "Jus' get it out best you can. Even if it's messy, we'll clean it up like always, okay?"

I give it my best shot. "It's Max. Dumb thoughts. He's so

good I feel inadequate. I keep thinking, why would Xavier stay with me when he could have a worry-free brat like him?"

Will laughs, but not in a mean way. "Sweetheart, ain't you been paying attention? Xavier *likes* your kind of brat. He'd be bored as hell with Max."

"You think?"

"I know."

"But he hates the super brat stuff. Loathes it." It's been a week, and I haven't forgotten the cane stripes.

"He does, but you're not like that, not the majority of the time. You have your moments, but you're no Bellamy."

"That's good to know."

"It is, but darlin'? You need to know beyond that. Even if you did suddenly turn super brat, he'd make it work. He loves you."

"He does, I know he does. Why am I doubting?"

"I think you've hit another layer. It's time to go deeper."

"I don't know where to start."

"Everything's a habit—it's even how the brain works—so create the habit of looking for how he loves you, rather than how he doesn't."

"I-I can do that."

He nods. "Love is a journey of faith. You have to believe in it without tangible proof or promise. It's scary for most of us, and that much more for you."

Yes. That's exactly it. People can do and say things that could mean love, but it's all subjective. There is no official list to say that x, y, z equals love and now you know. You're left to trust that x, y, z means they do.

"It is scary. I'm better about it than I was, but it lives there on nights like tonight." I squeeze him. "Thanks though, this was helpful. I can go back to bed and let you sleep."

"No chance of that happenin'. You stay right here with me. Just close your eyes. I got you."

I love being in the big cowboy's arms and I sleep safe and secure.

Tops must think looking at walls is a pastime we brats enjoy. Well I'm here to say we do not. Osh got fed up with me though, enough to send me to the wall. I wasn't being agreeable, I don't feel like doing anymore math for today, dammit. Unfortunately for me, I'm going to be writing lines and lines for him on a sore bottom. This isn't my first rodeo, getting in trouble with Osh.

He's far more lenient than Xavier, but cross him too many times and he's done.

He's so done with me.

While I'm looking at the wall, Max comes in. I hate that he'll see me here, my 'naughty-bottom' on display for all who walk by the kitchen to see and know I've been misbehaving. I'm also going to have to tell Xavier. Today fucking sucks.

A chair slides out from the kitchen table, which must be Max. I know it's not Osh, because he's cooking as per usual. I can't see him, but I know he's got a red and white dishcloth that says, *I love cooking!* on it with a Canadian maple leaf above the font, slung over his large shoulder. His long hair is up, revealing his undercut, shaved close to the scalp. I can picture the bulky way his muscled form moves as he's talking. "What happened, Max-a-Million?" Osh says.

Max is quiet. Does he know how I feel about him? "S'okay, Max. You know Finn's one of us. You can say it."

"I can't find my rabbit. I've looked everywhere."

He has a rabbit?

"Did you check by the door? You often leave him by the door."

They can't mean a real rabbit; you wouldn't leave a real rabbit by the door. Maybe it's code for something?

"He's not, Osh. He isn't anywhere." His voice wavers with vulnerability.

Wait, that's it. That's what draws people to him. It's natural to be drawn to protect him—which is like a bat signal to a Top—he's the kind of boy you want to see abound with joy. Even I want to race out and find whatever 'rabbit' is and I rank low on the Top spectrum along my imaginary spectrum chart. I sit somewhere just before Grayson, but close enough to him, I see why he thought we were the same in my first year.

"Poor baby. We'll find him before bedtime. Promise."

Wait. Is Rabbit a stuffie?

Meanwhile, my legs are getting tired. The arms holding my hand on my head are getting tired. I want to be out of this corner. I don't get relief that easily though. I have at least another quarter of a century here, while Osh serves up a small after school meal to Max.

At long last, Osh comes over to deal with me, and I would sigh in relief, but I know he's not done with me yet.

"Put your hands on the wall, Finnegan. Bottom out."

I do as told. I want out. "Yes, sir."

"When I say do something, especially when I'm asking nicely, I don't want sass all day long, and I don't want arguing with everything I say. It's disrespectful, am I understood?"

280

"Yes, sir." Fuck, this is going to hurt. Why oh why can't I just behave myself? He lays down a decent number of whacks with his bite-y, devil spoon and I'm apologizing, man am I apologizing. After, I'm a world better though: calm, floaty, easy.

"You can write out these math problems thirty times each," he says, helping me pull my boxers and pants back up.

"Yes, sir. I'm sorry, Osh," I say, wanting my damn after-spanking hug.

He smiles wide and encircles me in his large arms. "You're trouble sometimes, Mr. Finn, but I love you." He smoothens my hair out and kisses my crown. "Now, be a good boy."

I sit on my ass, which no longer likes this chair and I see that Max's mouth is gaping. He's frozen in place. "You okay, pal?"

"Yeah, wow. That was amazing."

He's awed? "You think?" I say, checking to see where Osh is. If he catches me being too chatty when I'm supposed to be doing work for him, and most especially when I'm still on thin ice, I'll be bending over again. He's busy at the stove, so long as I keep quiet, I should be okay.

Said the brat, very brattishly.

Yeah, yeah. Shut up brain.

"I do. I'm working at it. I'm not so good at the hard spankings. You've probably noticed at Friday night discipline."

No. I hadn't, because I've been too busy seeing the other things I wanted to see. I shake my head.

"Xavier says I might not be a brat that can handle a harder spanking, but Finn you're amazing. I want to be like you."

281

Huh. Wow. Well then.

I've spent all this time thinking he was special. Meanwhile, he's been thinking I'm special. Maybe I've had it all wrong? And if I've had this much wrong, what else am I seeing through clouded lenses? *Go deeper*, Will had said. *Time to level up, Finn*. I check for Osh again, still busy, but he'll have an ear out for me. I talk quietly. "So uh, you lost Rabbit...?"

He catches on that I'm being careful not to get caught and he smiles wide, having fun. Suddenly, we're brat comrades in arms. "Mr. Rabbit," he says, just as hushed.

I nod. We both look to Osh together this time, to make sure he's still got his back to us and won't catch us fraternizing.

"*Finn*," Osh says. We both jump. "I hope you're not chatting instead of getting your work done. You know better." Somehow, he knows to scold, without having to turn around.

Damn Tops and their brat sixth sense.

Max and I wince at the same time and have to cover our mouths to keep from laughing out loud. "I'm doing my work, sir."

I write a note for Max this time.

If that were Xavier, I'd be back in the corner already.

His eyes laugh. They're hazel and they match his dark hair nicely. I start on my work, or it's never going to get done and I'm going to be late going home to the apartment. Max sits with me, in solidarity and there's a fun energy sizzling between us. I shake out my hand when it gets a cramp and when I'm finally done, Osh comes over to check my work and help me with anything I need help with.

"Okay, brat. You're done for today." He puts his arms around me from behind and squeezes me tight. "If Xavier didn't already stake his claim on you, I would have. Love you, kid."

I relish in his adoration of me and it occurs to me how many extra special relationships I ended up with in our House and our extended House family. Now that I'm paying a new kind of attention, I notice Max awestruck again watching me and Osh interact.

You had no reason to be jealous, Finn. You have so much now, you got scared.

Yeah, yeah, I did.

"Love you so much, Osh. But you sure you could have handled both me and Emmery?"

"Do you need more of the wooden spoon to show you how strict I am?"

"Noooo, sir. My bad. You would have been just fine."

He laughs. "Will you come at the weekend? Stay over?"

I can't resist his big eyes. "I will, providing I get the necessary permissions." I wink. I will because it's Osh.

"Okay. I'll look forward to it, *amai otokonoko.*"

That's sweet boy in Japanese. "See ya around, Max," I say, before I head out.

"See ya, Finn."

But I only make it partway down the lane when I spy a patch of pale blue, in the mud by a tree. When I pick it up, I know it's Mr. Rabbit. He's caked with mud, because of the rain, but I can still see he's got a pink nose, even if the rest of him's pale blue. He's a floppy sort of thing with a body that resembles a bean bag, and saggy arms and legs that hang off him. He's kinda adorable, mud notwithstanding.

I head back to the house. Max is full on crying in Osh's arms. "We'll find him. He'll turn up somewhere." Osh sees me. "Forget something, Finn?"

"Found something," I say.

When I present Mr. Rabbit, Max lights up. He squeezes the stuffed rabbit to him, getting himself full of mud, causing Osh to wince. "Oh, thank you, Finn, you found him."

"I did. You must have dropped him."

He nods, but he can't meet my eyes. "Uh, you don't mind that I have a stuffed animal I carry around with me? I-I don't know why I'm like this."

A phrase we know, Finn.

"I don't mind at all, and anyone who does can answer to me."

He perks up. "That means a lot, Finn. Say, do you think I'd be able to come to Alpha House sometime? Maybe for a sleepover?"

"Whoa there Max-a-Million. We have to talk to Trevor about sleepovers. Let's start with a movie night."

"Gray and I will make it happen," I tell Max, lowering my voice to a whisper, knowing full-well Osh can still hear me.

"That's it, you. Shoo, before I grab up my spoon again."

I head on back to my new second home with Xavier. I'm still getting used to calling it home, but it's getting easier. When I walk in, Xavier's nowhere in sight, but then I hear him from the office. I stop and listen to that voice. I let it beat through me, reverberating into my soul.

I change out of my school uniform and into something less formal, one of my classic white T's and a nice pair of jeans. Since Xavier's still on the phone, I wait on the couch and turn on the TV. I'm halfway through a rerun of *Supernatural*, when Xavier comes in. "Your homework done?" he checks, before exchanging pleasantries like hello.

He's not being an asshole; it's the way he is. He views it as taking care of me first—despite my whining, which I only do when I haven't got it done—and then he can relax and do things like ask me how I am.

To be fair, I *will* procrastinate. I've made an art out of procrastinating.

"Yes, sir. Done."

He puts a knee to the side of my left leg and the other to the side of my right leg, bracing me there, on the couch. I let my head fall back, submitting to whatever he's planning. He sucks on my neck kissing up my chin and to my lips. My cock springs to life. "You feel guilty, my darling. What did you do?"

Dammit. He's too good and he knows me too well. He's gonna see my ass anyway if this continues to go where I want it to, but that doesn't mean I have to give in right away. "Who me? I'm a perfect angel."

Xavier laughs a hearty laugh. "And I'm Santa Claus. Out with it."

"I was a fucking brat for Osh today."

"Working something out, were we?" he says, sliding a hand into my hair at the base of my skull, tilting my head up so he can kiss me some more.

"A bit. I was in a churlish mood. Osh pulled out that damn wooden spoon." I tug on his tie, working out the knot. When it slips undone, I begin on his shirt.

"Whoa. Churlish indeed." We both know Osh had to be pretty annoyed with me to pull that out. "I look forward to the view."

Xavier takes me slowly tonight, spending time undressing me, inspecting Osh's handiwork with dedicated interest, adding his own handprints when he, of course, deems it not enough for brattiness. When he's in me it all makes sense. Every single bit of it from the rules to the scolding and the spanking, his cock in my ass just an added layer to the whole.

Later, when we're naked on the couch together, under a thin blanket I tell him. "Last night I was upset, but I went to Will and we talked."

"And? How are you now?" He moves the hair from my eyes.

"You were right, it helped. And today when I was over, Max was there. I chose to go deeper like Will advised. I was able to view him from a whole other perspective and, well, I don't think this ends well for you."

"Oh, really?"

"We're now friends, in a bit of a brattish way. I think he wants me to help him to learn how to take a spanking better."

Xavier smiles a smile that doesn't mean anything good for me, and his eyes delight with mischief. "How wonderful of you to volunteer. We'll book a lesson straight away. He can watch as I spank you in a variety of ways. I've got several new implements to try out, and of course we'll have to use the old and faithful. Important to master the basics, after all."

I groan. I never win wars of wit with Xavier, so why do I try? But I'm smiling on the inside. This is my happiest place in the world, Xavier and I involved in some kind of spanking banter, with me knowing how true and real it is. Because now that I've unwittingly volunteered, he will have his lesson, and it will be fulfilling in some kind of way. Always is, even if he'll find a way to make it count.

That's half the fun of it, Finnegan.

It is.

"I love you, Xavy."

His smile widens. I don't initiate things like that often. I want to do that more. "What was that for?"

"You're just my favorite."

"I love you too. C'mon ridiculous boy. Let's go to bed."

He pulls me off the couch and I lead where he follows. "To bed? Or over your knee because everything I do seems to result in me being there."

"That's at least half the reason you love me."

Lord help me, but it really is. I do end up over his knee and he spanks me before he puts me to bed, and I'm smiling all over.

Spanking is the language we speak. Some might not get it, but we do. We do on a level that goes beyond the cerebral, into the realm of energy far below the surface of consciousness. It's how we communicate, how we understand each other and how we love.

THE END

GLOSSARY OF IMPLEMENTS

Frat Paddle

A wide, wooden implement. Packs a thwack! You do not want this used on your bare bottom. It's heavy and it hurts.

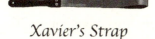

The Cane

Thin, whippy instrument. Usually used by Xavier for harsher punishments. It's exacting and leaves line-shaped welts.

Xavier's Strap

A long, leather strap attached to a firm leather grip. Often used on Friday discipline night, but it is a favorite of Xavier's, so the men of this school can expect to see it often.

Wooden Spoon

The infamous wooden spoon, favorite of both Ani and Osh. It's stingy and hurt-y. Best to avoid sassing them!

Hair Brush

Hair brushes. Innocuous in most homes, but are often employed on campus for discipline. One in particular lives in Ani's apron. Will be used on sassy boys, swiftly.

Meetings with these can be avoided by behaving.

Art by
Artsy Ape

ACKNOWLEDGMENTS

My Ducky Friend. Our friendship began over our love of spanking, domestic discipline fiction and Dean Winchester. You listen to me whine when I struggle to get the right words, oh so patiently, and tell me I will figure it out. You have been one of my strongest supporters for seven years as well as an ally in many a kink campaign. Thank you for your love, and encouragement. Thank you for polishing this book to its current, shining glory.

Artsy Ape. Thank you for lovingly creating the inner art for this book. Your enthusiasm for this story brought magic to it that it wouldn't have without you. I am grateful we met through our shared love of Charlie Weasley (among other things).

Sparkley Sparkle. Thank you for creating the Mocki-verses theory and making me laugh and all your fanart for my stories. You are a true fan and a friend. You keep me going on a lot of days.

KJ. Thank you for cheerleading me through this; making me laugh, the chats, your love and for being my friend across the distance. My books are so much more because of your magical suggestions.

To all my betas. All authors should be so lucky as to have an army like you. Thank you for making my book better.

Readers. I would be nothing without you and I mean that. Your fairy clapping nurtures my muse. I thank you for that with all my heart. I'm the luckiest author on earth, with the best readers on earth—no one can tell me different!

And to my husband. My love. This stuff makes you giggle like a little boy, but you listen to me talk about it anyway. Thank you for your love and support.

A WORD FROM THE AUTHOR

Dear Reader,

Thank you for reading *Xavier's School of Discipline*. Your support gives this book life. I can't wait to bring you more in this series. The topic I write about can be a delicate one and so I want to give it the care it deserves, with all the feels ones like us (who enjoy these things) want to feel. Books on this topic can still have heart, family and maximum entertainment. I endeavour to bring many stories like this one to the community.

Self-published authors like myself depend on reviews so that we will show up in the Amazon Marketplace. If you enjoyed this book, would you please consider heading over there and writing a review for me? It can be a short one!

Meanwhile, I will be in my writing cave, writing more for you.

All my love,

Mock (S. Legend)

Join Mockingbird Publications for new release alerts, book excerpts, free stories and more!

Follow on Instagram

Follow on Bookbub
Follow on Amazon
Follow on Goodreads
Other books by Mock (S. Legend):
Tristan Series

ABOUT THE AUTHOR

Some of you know her as Mock, others as S. Legend, or Miss S. She welcomes all names but will often go by Mock, a name given to her by her readers.

Mock is an ambitious creative, weaving the most precious aspects of her soul into stories. She is an architect, building fascinating worlds, designed from inquiry, rooted in worldly wonderings. It's an intuitive process where she is the scribe, the translator, the conduit.

It helped that storytelling was the language spoken at home. One simply didn't say, "We have an ant infestation," in Mock's family it was, "I was on my way to the living room, when a peculiar ant crossed my path. I looked to my right, a suspicious line of them marched toward the pantry. In that moment I knew; my kitchen was under siege." The natural flow of conversation always took this form.

And so.

When Mock wrote her first novel, she didn't plan it chapter by chapter, there was no outline, no "plotting" to speak of. But she didn't "pants" it either, she didn't make it up as she went along. She knew how the story felt, where it curved in places and hollowed in others; she knew the destination it rushed toward. Instead of orchestrating, she let the world inspire her, and held space for the words to come, trusting the characters knew what they were doing. All she had to do was tell a story, as she always had done; like breathing.

This is her peace, her healing and solace: Gifts better shared.

Mock's works are the comfort you seek when you need to come home. Her unique writing style will take you, wayfaring reader, to unexpected destinations.

She always says, "I'm not in the business of making up stories, I couldn't if I tired. I'm lucky enough to get picked to share someone else's story when I ask a question to the universe. Someone answers; I write it down."